At Rope's End

by

June Summers

At Rope's End

Cover Art by *The Wild Rose Press, Inc.*

The Wild Rose Press, Inc.
PO Box 708
Adams Basin, NY 14410-0708
Visit us at www.thewildrosepress.com

Publishing History
First Edition, 2023
Trade Paperback ISBN 978-1-5092-4869-8
Digital ISBN 978-1-5092-4870-4

Published in the United States of America

Then he started walking deeper into the shed. Everything seemed to be in order.

Wait! Something was back in the far left corner where the light didn't reach too well. Sonny hastened his steps.

"Oh, my God!" he yelled out loud. Dominic Amato, the older son of Tony and Theresa, lay on the concrete floor in a fetal position. Was he sleeping? Sonny stepped over to him. He shook his shoulder. "Dominic, are you okay? Dominic?"

Dominic didn't respond or move on his own in any way.

Sonny reached for his arm to take his pulse. As he turned it toward him, a needle slipped from Dominic's forearm. "Oh, no!" Sonny yelled. He still grabbed the boy's wrist to check his pulse. It was weak, but at least he had one. His face was extremely pale, and his lips were bluish-purple. His body was clammy to the touch.

Sonny gently shook the boy's shoulder. "Dominic, wake up. Wake up, Dominic."

There was no response. Sonny pinched his shoulder and called out his name again. But Dominic remained unconscious.

Immediately, Sonny dialed 9-1-1.

"9-1-1. What is your emergency?"

"I think a boy has overdosed. He has a pulse, but it's weak. So is his breathing."

Dedication

As always, to Wendy, who still gives me strength.

Chapter One

It just wasn't right. Once a guy made up his mind to kill himself, there shouldn't be a problem with it. Maybe it's hard to understand, but you should have a right to do what you needed to do with your own body, your own life. Right? It's your body. If you wanted to off yourself, then nothing, or no one, should get in your way. That's just how it should be. Yet the crazy story about Victor Anton Dankovic proved that what you wanted and thought you needed wasn't always the way things worked out.

Everybody called him Sonny. When he was born, his father was so proud to finally have a son after his wife had two miscarriages and the birth of a girl that he never introduced the boy by saying, "This is Victor." No, he would say, "This is my son. See my son. I have a son." It was to the point where some of the family's friends and relatives didn't know the boy's real name. Truth was Sonny had even forgotten it until he started school, and his teacher forced him to print *Victor* on his papers instead of *Sonny*. It was a bit confusing to a little five-year-old kid.

Sonny worked as the superintendent of the 1010 Colleda Avenue Apartments located at the corner of Oak Street and Colleda Avenue on the east side of Youngstown, Ohio. The tenants in the building called it the 10-10, definitely easier to say than the long, drawn-out 1010 Colleda Avenue Apartments. The location of the 10-10 wasn't in the classiest part of town, and the building itself wasn't the most trendy of establishments either. No new paint jobs with each new tenant; no updated carpet every five years; appliances replaced only when old ones completely stopped working with rancid meat in the refrigerator's freezer or potatoes partially cooked on a stove whose burner died in the middle of a meal preparation. When appliance replacements were finally made, Esther Feingold, the owner, would only buy refurbished appliances from the secondhand store on Market Street that were possibly a bit better than the ones thrown away. She might not always have been the most generous landlady, but she had so much to deal with since her husband died and left her in charge of all their properties and finances.

Maybe the 10-10 wasn't in the best neighborhood, or it wasn't the finest edifice in Youngstown, but those who resided there were satisfied with their living quarters. Besides, most of them couldn't afford much better accommodations. Several of them had lived there for many years, and they were happy with the services Sonny provided them. He kept the 10-10 clear of dirt, clutter, bugs, and rodents. The tenants could always call on him to help with any emergency repairs they required, no matter what time of day or night. Actually, the emergency didn't have to be of a repair nature, and it really didn't have to be an emergency at all. He often ran errands for some of the tenants—grocery shopping, package drop-offs at the post office, picking up prescriptions, or providing transportation to their medical appointments, to name a few. He was even known to lend money to one or two of them when they were really strapped for cash.

In the evening when he wasn't working, Sonny preferred to relax and partake of his beer or weed—sometimes more than just a little. He tried to keep his vices a secret, but it really didn't matter. All the folks in the building already knew about his habits. No hard stuff for him, like crack or heroin. He wasn't that kind of a guy. Just the weed—for medicinal purposes, of course.

According to Sonny, the tenants in his building were good, friendly people who caused no trouble, like complaining about every little thing or expecting concierge treatment included in his service. They knew their facility had its issues. They also knew because of his management, they couldn't find a better place to live for the rent they could afford.

Sonny got along with all the tenants. Well, he had one exception, that smartass dude in number 3-0-3, Rusty Morris. Not that Rusty was a bad-looking guy. There was that weird red hair of his, which was long, straggly, and five different shades of red. And he was such a show-off, walking around as if he were hot stuff and his poop didn't stink. Wearing the type of clothes a rich man wore. The thing was, if he did have money, he wouldn't be living in a place like the 10-10. Without a doubt, he'd be living in some exclusive neighborhood in Poland or Canfield.

Please don't misunderstand. All those things about Rusty weren't Sonny's issue with the dude. Who cared what he looked like or what he wore? Not Sonny. He also wasn't too concerned with Rusty's obnoxious attitude. The dude always complained about everything. His rent was too high; his shower didn't have enough water pressure; the fridge didn't keep his beer cold enough. Things like that. Hey, nobody forced Rusty to live there. Right? Sonny didn't have to love the guy, so he ignored all those constant complaints and his crappy attitude. They went in one ear and out the other. He never planned to be best buddies with the guy.

But here was the worst thing about Rusty Morris that Sonny couldn't ignore—the man beat up his girlfriend on a regular basis. Addie Thompson, the hot chick who lived with him, was a real looker with long, blonde hair, gorgeous smile, perfect, perky nose, blue eyes that sparkled like stars, and a body that wouldn't quit. She didn't flash her goods around like some hotties did. And she didn't complain about anything, even when everybody knew Rusty hurt her so many times.

"None o' my business," Sonny would say. "What goes on in that apartment doesn't concern me. I ain't no cop or social worker. I just get paid to do my job. That's all. And that don't include messin' in Rusty and Addie's private stuff."

Sonny made no bones about not liking Rusty, but his perception of him wasn't why he finally made Rusty's business *his* business. The part of Sonny's story when he first tried to kill himself actually started with Rusty and Addie.

****

Rusty Morris and Addie Thompson had only moved into the 10-10 about a year before Sonny's first attempt at suicide. In the beginning, Sonny had no problem with them. At that time, Rusty was even rather friendly with everybody in the building. Not that he'd invite them in for a bottle of beer or a cup of coffee or maybe watch the Browns on television. But he'd talk to others if he passed them in the hall or out on the parking lot. Who even knew why Rusty's disdainful attitude eventually began to show its ugly face? He constantly sported a surly scowl and refused to speak to anyone, even when they spoke to him first.

Sonny always tried to do his job and mind his own business, but he could take just so much. The other tenants in the building disapproved and constantly complained about Rusty. Mostly about the noise coming from his apartment. Not so much about the music or loud conversations they heard. Undoubtedly, those types of disturbances were frequently resounding from his place. No, the tenants ignored most of the loud drumbeats and guitar riffs. As it happened in apartment buildings, the walls weren't always as thick as the tenants wanted them to be. At times, they were all guilty of some type of loud disruptions. What they did oppose was the sounds of Rusty's drunken rages or Addie's gut-wrenching cries and screams when he'd beat her. Sometimes Sonny saw her with a black eye or a big bruise on her cheek. "Oh, Addie, what happened to your pretty face?"

"Oh, it's nothing, Sonny. Just a little bruise. I bumped into the bedroom door. That's all."

She always had the same excuse. Sonny didn't believe her. "I don't know, Addie. Are you sure that's what happened? You've been bumpin' into a lot a doors lately."

"Of course, I'm sure. I ought to know." She sounded snippy and upset and continued up the stairs as if everything were fine.

He knew she was lying by the look in her eyes. It

was as if she was pleading with him to do something to help her, and yet, she was afraid that he actually might try to intervene in some way. But Sonny's hands were tied. Every time he asked her, she'd say, "Nothing is wrong, Sonny. Honest, I'm fine."

Finally, after many complaints from the other tenants on the third floor, Sonny took action to curtail whatever went on in 3-0-3 that was causing such disturbances. He knocked on the door to talk to Rusty. "Hey, Rusty, I don't know what's goin' on in there, but can you keep it down? It's after midnight, and the other folks are tryin' to sleep. They got to go to work in the mornin'."

Rusty opened the door and glared at Sonny. "Dude, why don't you mind your own freakin' business? I pay my rent. What I do in this shithole is no concern of yours or anybody else. Now get the hell outta my face and leave us alone."

Sonny didn't want to get into a big argument with him, so he simply walked away. However, he turned as he reached the stairs. "Just keep it down, man."

Under the circumstances, Sonny felt he was powerless to take any action at that time. If Addie wasn't complaining, what could he do? Like he said, she was very pretty, but if Rusty kept beating on her, she'd have so many scars she wouldn't be pretty anymore. He'd speak to old lady Feingold and leave it in her hands.

In spite of what Rusty did to Addie, no matter how she felt or looked, she still went to work at the Turner Medical Clinic in Boardman every day. Rusty's day often began in a much different manner. He only went to his job when he wanted to, which was if he didn't have a hangover or when he wasn't coming down from some drug high. Sonny couldn't complain. As far as he knew, as Rusty had told him, they paid their rent every month. Although, if they paid or not wasn't any of Sonny's business either. That was Feingold's problem, not his.

Let's be perfectly clear about this from the get-go. Rusty wasn't the reason Sonny wanted to kill himself and leave the world behind. No way was that creep even worth his time of day. But here's what happened that started a very bizarre chain of events:

It was a Sunday morning in September when Sonny visited his sick mother in the Austintown nursing home where she was living. She'd been a resident there for a few years, and she wasn't getting any better. While Sonny sat in the room in a chair beside her bed, his mother went on and on about Saint Vincenca. Sonny was tired of hearing the same old memory of hers over and over again, but he couldn't tell his dear old mother to shut up just because he'd listened to that story a hundred times already. He couldn't do that to his mother. She was a sick, old lady, and he respected and loved her with all his heart. He simply nodded his head and endured the tale one more time, knowing it wouldn't be the last he'd hear it. "Yes, Mama, yes. Uh-huh."

He didn't tell his mother his plan to commit suicide in the near future. She would never understand why he had to end his life, even if she knew what was going on in his head. He definitely felt terrible about doing this to her, but he thought he had no choice. Marta, his sister, would take care of their mother once he was gone. At least, he hoped she would. With any luck, his mother would understand that he was not doing this because of her. Not at all.

On his way back to the 10-10 from seeing his mom, Sonny decided that night would be the night he'd kill himself. Very early Monday morning at about one o'clock, he sat on his single living room chair, staring at the silent, blank television screen in front of him, trying to build up the courage to do what he had to do. It wasn't every day a man took the fatal step to kill himself and end up being food for the earthworms. Right? The thought of his pending action caused him to hyperventilate, and he felt his heart rapidly pounding in his chest. "Oh, man, I have to calm down. This is gonna take more nerve than I expected."

He got off the chair and entered the kitchen. Reaching into his refrigerator to get his water bottle, his hand shook so much he had to use both hands to remove it from the shelf. He unscrewed the cap, was about to take a drink when suddenly he thought of an issue. "I can't drink no water. I can't drink nuthin'. I don't want to piss my pants after I'm dead and end up in a smelly puddle of piss. How'd that look? I have too much pride than to do that."

He replaced the bottle of water and returned to the living room chair. For at least ten minutes, he sat there, breathing deeply with his eyes closed, and his head resting back on the chair. When he thought he was ready to prepare for his deadly feat, he bounced out of the chair and strode into his bedroom, mumbling to himself, "This is it! This is it!"

Before old man Feingold, the owner of the 10-10, had died, he gave Sonny a Glock 19 to protect the premises in case of any burglaries or other illegal incidents. The pistol hid beneath Sonny's underwear in his top bureau drawer. He opened the drawer, pushed the underwear aside, and grasped the cold, metal gun in his hands. Holding the pistol in his right hand, he pointed it toward the floor. While closing his eyes, he tilted his head toward the ceiling. "This is it!" he said one more time.

Next, he stepped over to the tiny nightstand on the side of his bed. Opening the single drawer, he reached around the pencils, coins, notes, and other bits and pieces to the back and withdrew the gun's magazine containing fifteen nine-millimeter bullets. With slick and sweaty hands, he clicked the magazine into the handle of the pistol. It was ready for its deadly mission.

Again, pointing the gun toward the floor, he circled around and entered his small bathroom a few steps away. He placed the gun on the edge of the bathtub and knelt down, maneuvered his butt onto the cold, cement floor, and leaned with his back against the chipped, grimy bathtub.

In Sonny's mind, this was the best way for him to check off this planet. Shooting himself in the head would be quick and deadly. He was ready. Once he shimmied down to the frigid floor and supported his back against the tub, he lifted the Glock from the tub's edge and immediately pressed it to the side of his head. The cold metal from the barrel felt like an ice cube on his skin and as hard as a steel pipe digging into the membrane of his tender right temple. He shivered as the uncomfortable pressure of the circle at the end of the gun barrel sunk into his flesh. His nerves were on overload. After all, he'd never tried to shoot himself before. No wonder he was having a difficult time calming himself enough to complete this formidable task.

He was dressed in gray sweats and a grungy, black T-shirt because he didn't want to be found dead in his skivvies or with his junk flapping around. How would that look to the people in the 10-10 who respected him? Sure, he'd be dead. He wouldn't even know about it, but just the same, it was that pride thing.

In that strange position on the cement floor, the sweat rolled from his body like the moisture dripping down an ice cold can of beer. His entire body shook to the rhythm of an off-balanced washing machine. With the Glock furrowed into his temple, he placed his finger on the trigger of the gun, but he had to grip his right hand with his left hand to steady its trembling motion. Otherwise, he'd accidently remove the gun from his temple target when firing and shoot up into Cappy's Bar above his basement apartment, killing someone at the bar about to take a swig of their whiskey or down a swallow of fresh cold beer.

With sweat sheeting down his face and drenching his back and entire T-shirt, he finally got his sticky hand still enough to do what he had to do. He wiggled his index finger about to firmly pull back the trigger so he could get this sordid task over and done and move on to oblivion. He counted down, "three… two… o—"

Suddenly, he heard a loud pounding and yelling at his apartment door.

Chapter Two

When entering his bathroom to kill himself, Sonny had closed the door. Therefore, he couldn't clearly make out who was pounding on his apartment door or what the hell they were shouting about. It was obvious he didn't want anybody seeing what he was about to do, but he had no choice. He removed the gun barrel away from his head.

Reluctantly—but secretly grateful—grabbing onto the tub, he heaved himself off the cement floor, laid the Glock in the bathtub, and closed the musty, gray shower curtain. He hurried out of the bathroom and closed the door behind him, yelling as he hastened toward the sound of the pounding, "I'm comin'. Hold your damn horses."

When he opened the apartment door, José Cortez from 3-0-2 stood in front of him, prancing from one foot to the other and shaking as much as Sonny's hand had shaken when he was holding the gun trying to blow his brains out. José's dark ebony eyes bulged out of his saddle-brown face as he yelled in his slightly accented Hispanic voice, "Sonny, Sonny, you gotta come quick. I think the guy in 3-0-3 is killin' his girlfriend."

For a single moment, Sonny had to clear his head to understand what José was saying. His mind was still back in the bathroom with the gun in his hand. Undoubtedly, he was upset, being stopped from completing his plan after finally getting up the courage and the nerve to face his final curtain. But what the hell? This wasn't right. Rusty Morris. Sonny had about enough of that dude. He needed to put a stop to that creep's beating on poor Addie Thompson for her sake and that of the other tenants in the building.

He quickly blurted, "Gimme a minute."

As he rushed back toward his bathroom, he yelled to José, "Call 9-1-1 and unlock the main door! I'll get right up to his apartment."

He crashed open the bathroom door and reached in the tub to grab the Glock, stuffing it in the waistband of his pants. Before exiting the apartment, he seized his master keys from the hook near his front door. Still in his sweats and no shoes, he took the steps two at a time up to the third level. As he approached 3-0-3, Rusty and Addie's apartment, he heard the loud and abusive sounds of Rusty cursing and swearing. Addie's constant cries and moans signified she was in great distress. The tenants from the other apartments peeked out their doorways as Sonny pounded on 3-0-3's door. "Rusty, this is Sonny. Lemme in right now."

For a moment, Rusty stopped cursing, but Addie's anguished pleas continued. Rusty's menacing voice yelled back at Sonny, "Get the hell outta here, Sonny. This ain't none of your business."

Sonny responded in an authoritative voice, "The hell it ain't my business, Rusty! You're causin' a disturbance in the whole buildin'. What're you doin' to Addie? You ain't hurtin' her, are ya?" He knew damn well Rusty was inflicting some kind of pain on Abbie, but he figured it was more important to try to be nice at first and calmly appease him.

"I ain't hurtin' the bitch. We're just havin' a little disagreement. That's all. So get the hell outta here."

Sonny knew better than to believe him. "No, Rusty. I ain't goin' nowhere. It sounds like you're tryin' to do bodily harm to the girl. I'm gonna come in now."

Rusty's voice was loud and commanding. "No. No. You'd better stay where you are, Sonny. I'm warnin' you."

Sonny didn't heed the warning. There was no time to do any more negotiating with Rusty. Sonny took his master key from his sweatpants' pocket and quickly unlocked the apartment door. As he briskly shoved it open, he removed the Glock and pointed it outward. Right away, his eyes saw what was happening. Addie half lay on the couch with her legs dangling to the floor and her head pressed against a beige pillow, holding a very bloody cloth against her mid-section. Bruises and welts on her face were growing in size and color. Rusty hovered over Addie, but when he saw Sonny, he lunged toward him. In his hand, the blade of a butcher knife pointed outward as he dived quickly at Sonny.

Sonny, seeing the gleaming blade coming in his direction, bellowed, "Stop!" But Rusty refused to falter or halt. Sonny had no choice. He had no intention of killing the guy, but he also didn't plan to get stabbed in the gut like Addie. He needed to get the situation under control. While Rusty loomed toward him with the sharp knife, without hesitation, Sonny pulled the Glock's trigger. The bullet instantly penetrated Rusty's left leg a nanosecond after the flash from the gun's barrel. He dropped to the floor, the knife flying from his hand and sliding across the slick linoleum. He yelled, "Damn! You shot me!"

Sonny hurriedly kicked the knife farther out of the way before Rusty had a chance to realize it wasn't in his hand any longer. "Damn right, I shot you. Did you think I was gonna let you stab me like you did Addie?"

Rusty grabbed his leg.

Sonny shouted to José, who was standing in the doorway, mouth agape, "José! Hurry! Gimme your belt."

José hastened into the apartment, removed his leather belt from his waist, and tossed it to Sonny. As Sonny began affixing the belt around Rusty's leg to stop the bleeding, he bellowed to José, "Check on Addie. Make sure she's okay."

Immediately, Sonny fixed a tourniquet around Rusty's thigh while José went into the bathroom, returning with a couple of towels to stop Rusty's and Addie's bleeding.

As Sonny finished with the tourniquet, sirens wailed in the distance. He rushed over to Addie, who had stopped crying but appeared to be in shock. Her left eye had turned purple, and her left cheek puffed up like pink cotton candy. Cuts and scrapes covered her arms. "Are you okay, Addie?" Dumb question. Sonny knew she wasn't okay, but the words just came out of his mouth. "Lemme see your side."

Addie slowly pulled off the bloody cloth from her skin. Instantly, Sonny suggested, "Better put it back on. That's a pretty deep cut." Her skin was ashen and clammy, and she looked like she was about to pass out.

"Why don't you lie down on the couch until the paramedics get here?" He lifted her legs and helped her stretch out while the sirens howled closer. He pressed an additional towel against her wound to try to clot the blood more efficiently.

Most of the tenants in the building anxiously stood outside 3-0-3. Although he looked as if he had just seen a ghost, José remained in the apartment, in case Sonny needed him for something else. It was difficult to tell whose face was paler, José's or Addie's. Sonny asked him, "Are you okay, dude? You look like you're gonna hit the floor."

José shook his head while adjusting his body weight from one leg to the other. "Uh... No, I'm okay, man. I just never saw that much blood before. It kinda gets to me."

The police department was on Boardman Street in downtown Youngstown. The fire department was on Martin Luther King Boulevard also near downtown. It took the teams of police and paramedics about ten minutes to get to the 10-10. They arrived at the building while Sonny was comforting Addie on the couch. The tenants quickly shuffled out of the way when they heard the emergency personnel tromping up the flights of staircases, sounding like a stampede of wild horses. Upon entering the 3-0-3, the paramedics rushed to care for Addie and Rusty, attending to their wounds, administering fluids, and then transporting them both on stretchers to two awaiting ambulances.

The police spent several minutes questioning Sonny, José, and the tenants congregated in the hallway outside the 3-0-3. A cop named Clancy approached Sonny, "Sir, what is your name?"

"Victor Dankovic, but everybody calls me Sonny."

Sonny still had the Glock dangling from his right hand. Officer Clancy demanded, "Sonny, I need to take your weapon until after this incident has been investigated."

"Sure, no problem."

The officer opened up a plastic bag, and Sonny dropped the gun into it.

Officer Clancy then took out a small spiral tablet and a ballpoint pen from his shirt pocket. "Okay, Sonny, can you tell me what happened here?"

Sonny cleared his throat. "Well, I'm the super of the buildin', and José came down to my apartment tellin' me about the fight goin' on in 3-0-3."

"Uh, who's José?"

"Oh, sorry, officer. He's that dude standin' over there who looks like a ghost ready to pass out."

The officer grinned at José, and then looked back at Sonny, who continued relaying his version of the sequence of events that occurred after he used his master key to enter Rusty and Addie's apartment. When he finished his account, the officer turned to both Sonny and José. "Could the two of you come down to police headquarters and give us your official statements of what happened here?"

The police escorted the two men down the stairs and placed them in separate cruisers for the trip to the station. When they arrived downtown, the officers took them to separate interrogation rooms. Sonny sat opposite the detective in the small room. He was calm; he knew he had done the right thing in shooting Rusty. He knew it was what he had to do to control the situation. Surely, all the witnesses would vouch for him. It was evident he hadn't tried to kill Rusty, just stop him from doing any further harm to Addie or anyone else, including himself. If he hadn't gone in that apartment, he was convinced Rusty would've killed

Addie, or she would've bled out from the stab wounds to her side.

Sonny answered all the questions the detective asked him. When he asked about the Glock, Sonny stated, "It's legal, and I got a concealed carry permit," which he removed from his wallet to show to the detective.

After their interviews, a policeman drove Sonny and José back to the 10-10 in the same patrol car. They didn't talk much on the ride back, but when they reached the apartment building and were out of the vehicle, José placed his hand on Sonny's shoulder. "Thanks, man. Thanks for takin' care of that situation. I've been worried about that woman ever since they moved in here."

"Yeah, me, too. But this stuff is just part of my job, José. Thanks for your help too, dude."

"No, man. I don't know of any other super who'd put his own life at risk in a situation like that. You're a special dude, Sonny."

José went back to his apartment on the third floor, and Sonny walked down to his in the basement. He didn't return to the bathroom to finish the job of killing himself that early morning. Actually, he couldn't have shot himself that morning. The police still had his Glock. Of course, he could've thought of another method of self-destruction, but he was way too tired and in no mood to think about other alternatives at that time. He needed to sleep on it for a while.

Rusty Morris was in the hospital for a couple of days. Then he was sent to jail pending his trial for attempted murder. Addie's knife wound to her side was rather serious. She stayed in the hospital for about a week. The knife blade had nicked her kidney and her intestines.

While Addie was resting in the hospital, the other tenants got together and sent her a large bouquet of colorful, fresh-cut flowers. After the police were finished with the crime scene in the apartment, the ladies in the building cleaned it up, blood and all, so it would be presentable when she came home. She didn't need another reminder of what Rusty did to her. How Addie planned to handle the rent, now that Rusty wouldn't be around, was Addie and old lady Feingold's problem. It wasn't Sonny's concern.

Chapter Three

Victor Anton Dankovic. Yes, everybody called him Sonny. Third-generation Croatian. Dark chestnut-brown, wavy hair with eyes like the desert sand, a big guy about six-three and thirty-five years old. He was losing weight but hadn't gotten on the scale lately to see what he weighed. What did it matter? He wasn't going to be around much longer. Leon, his *tata*—the Croatian word for dad—died about twelve years ago. As mentioned, his mama, Blanca, was in the nursing home in Austintown. His sister Marta, who was two years older than Sonny, lived in Canton with her husband, Aaron Wilson, and two children, Jenna and Carter, but they hadn't been very close for the last few years. Sonny wasn't exactly sure why. Guess they didn't have much in common anymore. Marta called him once in a while, mostly just to talk about their mother.

Sonny visited his mother every Sunday, even though she didn't always recognize him. Sometimes Blanca thought he was Leon, her dead husband. One thing was certain—almost every time Sonny did visit her, she remembered to tell him over and over again about how on the day he was born, she had this vision of Saint Vincenca kissing Sonny on the cheek.

When Sonny was a teenager, his mother told him the whole story about his very difficult birth. The doctor thought both mother and child wouldn't survive childbirth. However, according to Blanca, she saw Saint Vincenca save them when she kissed Sonny and blessed the new mother. Saint Vincenca is the patron saint of Blato, a city on the island of Korcula in Croatia, where his *deda*—grandfather—and *baka*—grandmother—were born. Sonny always thought it was a bunch of hogwash, but he listened to his mother every time she told him the story as if he had never heard it before. She was his mother. He had to respect her.

However, there was a very weird thing about this Saint Vincenca story that even Sonny was surprised to learn. April twenty-eight was Saint Vincenca's feast day, and it was also Sonny Dankovic's birthday. What a hoot! Made him sometimes wonder if there might be some truth to his mother's crazy tale. No, not possible. Just a story. Right?

Sonny wasn't married. Never had been. Was going to get married once, but the damn bitch ran off with his best buddy. He wasn't his buddy anymore, and she sure as hell wasn't his girlfriend anymore, either. Sometimes he went on those dating apps and met a couple of babes, but nothing ever got serious. A few good one-nighters, but that was about it. Most of those chicks were just after a guy to spend money on them and take care of them for the rest of their lives. That wasn't Sonny. He had a hard enough time taking care of himself.

According to Sonny, one thing was certain. If Sweetie, the name he called the beauty in 3-0-4, would ever give him the time of day, man, he'd jump on that chance. Ha! You know what he meant, right? Double meaning here, guys.

Why was Sonny's story being told in the first place? Wasn't he just some good-for-nothing guy wasting his life away working in some dumpy apartment building inhabited by a bunch of losers and located on the somewhat seamy side of town? Probably that was why he wanted to off himself. Wrong again. Another thing Sonny's mother always told him, "Don't judge a book by its cover." His story won't show that he became a famous movie star making so much money that he threw $100,000 parties every weekend. Or maybe that he robbed some bank and killed the guard, and now he sat on death row in the state pen. Nope. Nothing like that at all. Guess the words will tell it all.

As for the tenants of the 10-10 building, Sonny never considered them losers. They were all good people, willing to help out each other any time they were needed in any type of situation.

****

What was it really like working as the super of the 10-10? Sonny did a little plumbing; cleaning up hallways and stairs; some painting; changing light bulbs; putting up ceiling fans; and replacing worn-out appliances. Things like that. Basically, anything to keep the place running smooth as silk. He usually didn't do any big construction or renovation projects like tearing down walls or remodeling a whole bathroom or kitchen. Hell, ever since old man Feingold died, none of that had happened anyhow. Besides, Sonny didn't get enough bucks for those kinds of jobs. He was okay with that. The dough he made kept him in cigarettes, booze, weed, and pizza, all of which he knew he could do without. Oh, well, since he was going to kill himself, it really didn't matter what he did to his body, did it?

His apartment, number 10, was in the basement next to the huge gas furnace that supplied heat to all of the units—most of the time. His place was smaller than the other units. It had a galley kitchen only big enough for his sink, stove, small refrigerator, and a very tiny, scarred wooden table at one end. His living room had a stained couch, one lumpy chair, a couple of small, worn side tables, and his ten-year-old television on a rusty metal stand. His postage-stamp bedroom held a single bed—more like a very uncomfortable cot with no headboard or footboard— a wobbly, plastic nightstand, and a bureau, its drawers held together with duct tape and glue. The closet in the room was barely large enough to hold his meager wardrobe. The entrance hallway closet was slightly larger, but the space was taken up by heavy winter gear and storage containers filled with personal items.

Of course, he had a bathroom of which you are already aware. It too was far too minuscule for his size and bulk, but he managed.

On the other side of the cellar was the tenants' laundry room with three big washers and two industrial-size dryers. When Sonny first started working at the 10-10 about seventeen years ago, the tenants constantly argued over the use of the laundry facility. Seemed like everybody needed to wash their damn clothes on the same day at the same time. He used to get complaints every day about so-and-so hogging the machines. Luckily, the problem was solved when Luther and LaWanda Jackson moved into apartment 2-0-2 with their two kids, Jamal and Gardenia. Since they had younger children, LaWanda needed to wash clothes more often than some of the other tenants. But somebody was always using the machines when she needed them. To solve their dilemma, LaWanda had

Sonny call a meeting of all the tenants to discuss the matter of the laundry room.

They attended an evening get-together in the Jackson's apartment with LaWanda serving everybody coffee and a piece of her amazing sweet potato pie. Over coffee and pie, they came up with a schedule that gave each tenant their own weekly time slot to use the laundry facilities. Sonny got the timetable printed, and everybody received a copy. It was also posted right above the washers. If tenants had to deviate from their assigned spot for some reason and no opening was available, they had to trade with somebody who was willing to switch their time. When a new tenant moved into the 10-10, they took over the slot of the old tenant in their unit, or they worked it out with somebody else. It seemed to work okay. Whatever, Sonny hadn't heard any squabbling about it. It was no longer his business. He would just update the schedule when necessary and pass out new copies to the tenants.

Sonny's tool room was also in the basement. His tools were old and worn, but he wouldn't spend his own money on new ones. If old lady Feingold wouldn't buy them for him, he'd do without. Why should he pay for them himself? She received the big bucks from her tenants' rent, not him. He did admit that once in a while he'd shell out his own money to buy a new screwdriver or pliers if he really needed them. He also had to admit that he didn't always get around to telling Mrs. Feingold what he needed.

Yeah, Esther Feingold, she was the owner of the 10-10. Her husband Harvey Feingold died about five years ago. Some kind of stroke. Left the wife with a bunch of money and a lot of property. But she didn't take care of them as well as old man Feingold did. Sonny thought she might have been overwhelmed with all that was involved with the upkeep of all her properties. Whatever, not his business.

Chapter Four

The episode with Rusty and Addie was Sonny's first strikeout in killing himself. It wasn't his fault he didn't accomplish the deed. What choice did he have? It was absolutely necessary for him to stop Rusty from killing Addie. She didn't want to die, and Sonny actually didn't want Rusty to go to prison for life for her murder. He needed to be punished for hurting her, but neither of them should have had his or her entire life ended or ruined.

As it turned out, Sonny's next attempt to go to his eternal slumber happened about a month after the Rusty-Addie debacle. It took him that long to work up his nerve again. It wasn't every day that a guy could get into the right frame of mind to go belly-up. But he knew it was time for him to once again try to cash in his chips. Yep. To kill himself. Like the old saying goes, "If at first you don't succeed, try, try again." His second attempt would do it. He was sure of it.

A cool, blustery Halloween night descended on the east side of Youngstown that year. Despite the wind and cold, kids trick-or-treating inundated Colleda Avenue and the surrounding neighborhood, wearing store-bought Ninja costumes or homemade Dracula outfits. Princesses, fairies, football players, and cartoon characters all paraded the streets of town. Kids of all sizes. Babies in strollers dressed like bunnies or lambs with their moms pushing behind them. Teenagers with black makeup under their eyes, wearing oversized, graphic T-shirts and wielding pillowcases for their bounty, some looped over their shoulders, and some being dragged and sweeping the sidewalks of all the dried, fallen leaves. For the most part, drivers drove slowly down the avenue. If any were in too much of a hurry and travelling too fast, parents on the sidewalks with their young ones yelled to deaf ears, "Slow down, jerk. Can't you see the children?" It was a night anticipated by every child of any age. Free candy was definitely a powerful incentive.

As for Sonny, his mood was nothing like that of the trick-or-treaters. He was pretty bummed out that night. He saw his mother the Sunday before, and she didn't even know him. To his surprise, she failed to talk about Saint Vincenca; she didn't even mention her name. She simply sat on her rocker and gazed into space. Sonny hated seeing her like that. Sitting in her chair and staring out the window with a melancholy frown on her face and moisture in her eyes, sometimes trickling down through the crannies in her cheeks. He could only imagine what went through her fragmented mind. She used to be so happy and so lively. Always telling dirty jokes at her ladies' pinochle card club. Always playing games with Sonny and Marta and allowing the kids from the entire neighborhood to play in their backyard, dislodging any grass that attempted to grow. When they needed a break from their games and sports, she'd serve freshly baked cookies and homemade lemonade. She was the best mother ever. But now, Sonny sometimes didn't know if she was even there anymore.

Please, do not misunderstand. That was not the

reason he wanted to kill himself. However, it really didn't help the situation any. And the news he had personally received the week before made him more determined to find a way to face his final curtain, however possible. And soon. Time was running out.

Trick-or-treating at the 10-10 was a big deal. The front entrance was left unlocked so the kids from the neighborhood could enter the building with their scary, silly, or funny costumes, carrying plastic bags from the grocery stores, pillowcases, or buckets to collect their goodies. All the tenants opened their apartment doors, sat on their folding chairs outside their doorways, and passed out candy, trinkets, or homemade baked goods. The kids visited all the floors because they knew they'd always get some kind of treat from every tenant in the 10-10.

Sonny set up his chair outside the cellar door with his dishpan full of the small chocolate candy bars sold in big bags at all the stores. He gave each kid two bars. If a costume was very scary or exceptionally cute, he might even give that child three pieces of candy.

He enjoyed watching the kids as they stopped at his door and as they scampered up and down the stairs to the other levels. However, when darkness fell and the trick-or-treaters no longer came around for their treats, he became sad and despondent. Thoughts of his mother and his pending future invaded his mind. It was time again to do that hari-kari thing he tried once before and failed. Yes, commit suicide. However, he didn't plan to stab himself in the belly like those Japanese samurai dudes sometimes did or the way that jerk, Rusty, stabbed his girlfriend, Addie. He also ruled out using his Glock this time, even though the police had returned it to him a couple of weeks after he shot Rusty. After the last attempt with the gun, he knew he'd probably freeze while trying to pull the trigger. So stomach stabbing and shooting himself were both not in the cards for his end-of-life method. He needed a better plan.

Sonny liked his beer. There's nothing like an ice-cold beer on a hot summer day to quench a man's thirst. Or sitting in front of the television and watching the Browns slaughter the Steelers. Now that's what he called a good time. So he did drink beer, even though he wasn't supposed to drink any type of alcohol. But the hard stuff? Not his cup of tea. Yet he thought maybe if he drank enough whiskey, he might have a happy and easy death. One time on the late news on TV, he saw a clip about those college kids trying to get into fraternities and sororities by doing stupid things like scrubbing a parking lot with a toothbrush, streaking across their campus butt naked, or defacing a monument on the college campus. He heard this one kid actually died because his fellow frat brothers kept pouring booze down his throat. Sonny didn't think that sounded too bad of a way to end it all. Right? He'd probably pass out long before he'd die, so he wouldn't even know he was dying. That type of suicide sounded like a perfect solution to help him croak. He decided that would be his method of self-annihilation.

Before the liquor store closed, Sonny went out to the parking lot and got in his 2010 dark-blue pickup truck—although now the paint was faded, and the body was dented. He planned to hurry to the nearest liquor store and buy a bunch of bottles of cheap whiskey. No sense wasting his money on the good stuff for the purpose he had in mind. He started up the truck, but before he pulled out onto Oak Street, he thought of a huge problem with his plan. If he passed out, how would he get enough booze in his system to actually kill him? No way could he ask anybody to pour it down his throat, like what happened to that college kid on the news. Who would ever agree to do something like that for him? Can you imagine him knocking on Arnie Hathaway's door and saying, "Hey, Arnie, I can use your help to kill myself. All you gotta do is pour booze down my throat after I pass out. Do ya think you could do that for me?"

Arnie would jump at the chance to help out. Right? I don't think so. He was too nice of a guy to agree to something like that. Then, again, too bad Rusty Morris was in the clinker. He'd be more than willing to help Sonny kill himself after what Sonny had done to him.

Discouraged, Sonny turned the truck around and parked it in the lot on the side of the building again. He went back to his basement apartment to think of another plan. Although he knew he shouldn't, he grabbed a beer from the fridge and ambled into the living room, sitting on his worn recliner to try to come up with some other idea not so stupid. He took a few sips of the beer as he stared at the ceiling.

Suddenly, a light went off in his head. Maybe he wasn't so stupid after all. How about booze and *pills*? Taking them at the same time, lots of each. Don't they do something to your body? Stop your heart? Slow down your breathing until your lungs no longer force air in and out? Maybe booze and pills would be enough to cause him to breathe his last breath. What if he took his high blood pressure pills, his sleeping pills, and his water pills with the whiskey? Yeah, maybe that would work. Maybe it would be a pleasant death. He might just fall into a deep, calming sleep and never wake up. Wouldn't that be perfect? No pain. No suffering.

With his new plan in mind, he hurried out to his truck and drove to the liquor store. He bought six bottles of the cheapest whiskey he could find and took them back to his apartment. Taking them out of the heavy bags, he lined all six bottles in a row on the kitchen table. After staring at the weird reality of his method of destruction for several seconds, he darted into the bathroom and retrieved all three containers of pills from the medicine cabinet above the sink. Walking back to the kitchen, he set them on the table next to the whiskey bottles. From the kitchen cabinet next to the sink, he took out a big, tall glass and put it next to the pills. He grabbed the first bottle of whiskey; he unscrewed the tight cap; and he poured the foul-smelling liquid to the top of the tall glass, making it so full that the whiskey dribbled down the side. Next, he opened all three pill jars, spilling about ten tablets each onto the table. He remarked aloud, "This should be easy-peasy. I got this." He was even feeling a little giddy.

Once the whiskey and pills, his weapon of choice, was ready, he sat down on one of his two rickety, wooden kitchen chairs and took a couple of deep breaths. He repeated, "Okay, this is gonna be easy." Sure. It wasn't like shooting himself in the head or stabbing himself in the stomach. It might even be enjoyable. The sensation of gradually feeling your muscles relax, not having a care in the world, everything getting hazier and hazier, and drifting off to an eternal sleep. Sounded great. Right? Who was he kidding? He was still as nervous as hell.

With his hand shaking, he raised the whiskey glass to his trembling lips and tasted a small sip. He coughed and sputtered, spilling some of the whiskey out of the glass onto his T-shirt and the floor. "Gawd! This shit is awful. It tastes and feels like drain cleaner. How the hell am I gonna drink all this?"

He coughed a few more times, cleared his throat, and calmed his breathing. Then he took another deep breath and lifted the glass to his lips, preparing to take a huge gulp this time to really get started with his mission.

Just as the mouthful of whiskey entered his open mouth, his cellphone rang. Coughing and choking from the strength, taste, and size of the gulp of whiskey, and the interruptive ring of his phone, he rushed to the sink and spat out what liquid still remained in his throat before saying, "Damn! Who the hell could that be now?"

Chapter Five

When his suicide attempt was interrupted by the ringing of his cell phone, Sonny swiftly placed the big glass of whiskey back on the table, spilling more of it onto the loose pills scattered near the whiskey bottles. He quickly removed the cellphone from his sweatpants' pocket. Looking at the name of the caller, he noticed it was Mrs. Mercer from 2-0-3. Hmm. She never called Sonny that late in the evening. She was usually in bed by nine o'clock. This could be important. Perhaps something happened with the trick- or-treaters.

Clearing his throat of the remaining residue of whiskey, he sat back on the chair and with a hoarse voice answered the phone. "Hey, Mrs. Mercer, what can I do for you?"

Edith Mercer lived in 2-0-3 behind Arnie Hathaway in 2-0-1. She repeatedly told Sonny he should call her Edie. Sonny obliged her for the most part if he remembered, but he felt strange about it. His mother always told him to be respectful to his elders. He didn't think calling old people by their first names was very respectful, especially ladies. For some reason, he had no trouble calling Arnold Hathaway, "Arnie." He wasn't sure why.

Mrs. Mercer was in a wheelchair, even before Sonny became the super of the 10-10. She had polio when she was a kid. As she grew older, she developed rheumatoid arthritis in her joints so she couldn't walk at all. Years ago, a carpenter remodeled her kitchen and bathroom to make her doorways, cabinets, sinks, and appliances more accessible to her and enabling her to be more independent. She still did her own cooking and, for the most part, took care of herself. Edie told Sonny she had paid the carpenter for the remodel. The Feingolds wouldn't dole out money for that big of a project, especially on a rental property. But since Edie paid for the construction, they allowed her to have it done. She had been a long-time resident of the 10-10 and planned to stay there for many years to come.

When Edie cooked, Sonny rarely smelled any of the odors coming from her apartment. However, when that odor did reach his nostrils, he was always happy she didn't give him any of her culinary creations. He wouldn't admit it to her or anyone else, but the aroma of that food reeked like some animal crawled inside the walls of the 10-10 and died.

Sometimes Edie paid Sonny to shop for her groceries at the market, giving him a list of the products she needed. He was hesitant about taking her money, but she insisted. Sometimes he did heavy cleaning for her, also. Again, she paid him but not as much as she'd have to pay a cleaning service. Whatever she paid was fine with him. He knew she couldn't afford much. After all, she lived in the 10-10.

****

As soon as Sonny answered the call that interrupted his attempt to overdose on the pills and booze, Mrs. Mercer was on the phone with a problem. "Oh, Sonny, I've fallen out of my wheelchair, and I think I might've broken something. Can you please come and help me?"

Sonny stood so quickly his chair tipped over, and his body bumped the table, knocking over the glass of booze. "Shit!" He didn't say that into the phone to Mrs. Mercer. To her, he said, "I'll be right up, Mrs. Mercer."

Leaving the bottles of whiskey and the pills spread out on the kitchen table with a spilled, sticky mess expanding on both the table and the floor, he kicked the fallen chair out of his way and quickly went to the sink to rinse out the remaining whiskey from his mouth. Before rushing out his apartment door, he grabbed his keys from their hook. Climbing the stairs to the first floor, he stopped briefly to unlock the outside doors in case he had to call 9-1-1. Then he climbed the next staircase to the second level while still talking to Mrs. Mercer. "I'm on my way up, Mrs. Mercer. I'll use my master key to get it."

"Oh, thank you, thank you. Sonny. What would I do without you?"

He arrived at 2-0-3 and promptly unlocked the door. He glanced around the living room. No Mrs. Mercer. From the kitchen he heard, "I'm in here, Sonny."

As he entered the kitchen, she lay on the floor with her wheelchair halfway on top of her. Her eyes were glassy with fright, and her face grimaced with severe pain. Bright red blood saturated her white hair. The first thing he did was to lift the wheelchair off her body. "Can you tell me where it hurts?"

"It's my hip and my leg." Tears streamed down her cheeks, mixing with the blood. "My head, too."

Sonny looked down at her. "I don't wanna' move you in case somethin' is broken. I'm gonna call 9-1-1."

He dialed the number and relayed to the dispatcher, "This is Sonny Dankovic at the 1010 Colleda Apartments. The tenant in 2-0-3 fell out of her wheelchair. I think maybe she broke her hip or her leg or somethin'. Can you send an ambulance right away, please?"

After he hung up the phone, he rushed into the living room where he found a good-sized pillow. Seizing it, he took it back to the kitchen and put it under Mrs. Mercer's head. "Here, Edie. This will make you a little more comfortable. It shouldn't be much longer until help arrives."

Then he tried to comfort her while they waited for the paramedics to arrive. He didn't want to move her and risk causing more damage. Kneeling down beside her, he took hold of her hand and reminded her, "The ambulance will be here in just a few minutes." He patted her on her shoulder and tried to keep her talking so her mind would stay off her pain. "How did this happen, Mrs. Mercer, uh, I mean Edie?"

With tears still flooding her eyes, she sobbed, "Oh, I was being stupid. I thought I could reach a bowl on the second shelf, but I didn't have my wheelchair close enough or locked in position. As I reached for it, the chair got stuck on the table leg and tipped. Since I was leaning so far forward, I also tipped just as I grabbed the bowl, which fell and hit me on my head."

Sonny saw the broken pieces of the ceramic bowl on the floor. "Well, you sure did a number on yourself, didn't you?"

He gave her a sympathetic look. "Do you want me to call anybody to meet you at the hospital?"

She sadly shook her head. "No. There's no one to

call. My daughter lives in Texas, and she's got her own problems. I'll give her a call when I know what damage I've done."

"Are you sure? I can at least tell her you fell."

"No, no, I'll call her later. I don't want to bother her with my problems right now."

It was none of Sonny's business, but it seemed to him a daughter should know if her mother was hurt. But what did he know? He had no children. Besides, he didn't know what kind of relationship Mrs. Mercer had with her daughter. Family situations could be tricky. He knew that because of his own situation with his mother.

Instead of notifying Mrs. Mercer's daughter, he got up and took a handful of paper towels from their holder near the stove. He ran them under the cold water and used them to wipe some of the blood from Mrs. Mercer's face and head. He noticed he was making things worse by turning her white hair to a soft shade of pink.

While they waited, Sonny picked up the pieces from the broken bowl and threw them in the waste basket. He didn't want the paramedics to trip or cut themselves on the glass when they arrived.

When Sonny had come up to help Mrs. Mercer, he had left her apartment door open so the paramedics could get in quickly. Hearing the commotion in their apartments, some of the other tenants began to gather in the hallway, wondering what had happened and looking worried and concerned. LaWanda Jackson from 2-0-2 tentatively stepped into the apartment. She saw Sonny and Mrs. Mercer on the kitchen floor. She peeked her head through the doorway. "Sonny, what happened? Is Edie all right?"

Sonny peered up at LaWanda. "I don't know. I think she broke somethin'. The paramedics are on their way. I don't wanna move her and make things worse."

LaWanda put her hand over her mouth. When she removed it, she asked, "Is there anything I can do to help?"

"I don't think so right now. Maybe later, okay? The paramedics should be here any minute now."

"Sure. Just let me know." LaWanda quietly went back and joined the other tenants waiting to see what was happening.

Finally, sirens resounded from outside the building. Soon Sonny heard footsteps trouncing up the stairs. The paramedics rushed into the open door of Mrs. Mercer's apartment. They dashed into the kitchen and briskly took charge, caring for her immediate needs, inspecting the damage to her body, and giving her fluids and medications.

Sonny had moved far out of their way. He couldn't help noticing that each one of them was very strong, even the female paramedic. Perhaps if Sonny didn't have his problem to deal with, he could be a paramedic. But he couldn't because—well, that problem. Anyhow, he was going to be dead soon. No sense thinking about the impossible future that would no longer exist for him.

He was about to ask if he could ride in the ambulance with Mrs. Mercer, but then he remembered he'd need to return to the 10-10. Instead, he asked where they were taking her so he could follow them.

"She'll be taken to Saint E's downtown," the female paramedic replied as she helped lift Mrs. Mercer onto the gurney.

While the emergency crew strapped Mrs. Mercer snugly onto the gurney, Sonny hurried out of the apartment to go down to the basement for his wallet and truck keys. Before he could get by the other tenants in the hallway, Arnie Hathaway from 2-0-1 stopped him. "What happened, Sonny? Is Edie all right?"

Sonny tried to respond quickly so he could get to his apartment before the paramedics were ready to leave. "Don't know, Arnie. I'm gonna follow them to the hospital. I'll let you know when I find out more, okay?" He stopped suddenly. "Oh, hey, Arnie, will you be sure Edie's apartment is locked after they leave for the hospital?"

"Will do," agreed Arnie Hathaway.

The ambulance took Mrs. Mercer to Saint Elizabeth Hospital on Belmont Avenue. When they arrived, Sonny rushed to follow them into the emergency entrance. He caught up to them at the double doors leading into the emergency cubicle area. As they wheeled her through the doors, he assured her, "Tell them I'll be out here waitin' to hear what's goin' on." She nodded her head, but he could tell she was still in a lot of pain.

Sonny gave his and Mrs. Mercer's names to the attendant at the desk and asked to be notified as soon as there was word on her prognosis. He sat on one of the upholstered gray chairs in the waiting area and leafed through a sports magazine that he grabbed from a rack on the wall, not really paying attention to any of the articles as he looked at them. He waited for about an hour or more, getting antsy and more concerned as the time passed.

Waiting in the emergency area of a hospital was

definitely not where Sonny had expected to be at that time of night. The room wasn't very crowded. No one appeared to be in dire pain, only concerned friends or relatives waiting for updates on their loved ones' conditions. They often got out of their seats and paced the floor. Some went for coffee or snacks to help the time go faster until a nurse or a doctor came out to talk to them.

As for Sonny, he sat for a while with his magazine. Then he bought a cup of coffee from the machine, but it tasted like dirt. He ended up throwing most of it away and sat back down to stare into space like his mother often did.

About midnight, a woman dressed in green scrubs with a mask hanging from her neck came out from the heavy metal door of the area where they had taken Mrs. Mercer. The room had gradually emptied of most of the other people waiting there. Only two others beside Sonny remained, and they had only arrived about a half hour ago. He jumped up from his chair, hoping the woman wanted to talk to him.

She looked over his way. "Are you the family of Edith Mercer, sir?"

"Uh, no ma'am. I'm just a friend. Mrs. Mercer don't have no family around here. I'm the one that called the ambulance when she fell."

"Oh, uh, okay."

The woman appeared as if she wanted to say something else, but she kept silent for a few seconds. Sonny took the initiative. "How is Mrs. Mercer doin'? Is she gonna be okay?"

Apparently, the woman decided to talk to Sonny. "Well, she has a serious break on her femur bone and a crack on the right side of her pelvis. I'm afraid she's going to stay at the hospital for a few days. She'll also be required to go to a rehab facility for about a week or two. When she returns home, she'll still need assistance for a while. She told us she has a daughter in Texas. We're trying to get in touch with her to apprise her of Mrs. Mercer's condition, but thus far, we've been unsuccessful. Do you know of anyone else who could help her out? Otherwise, she'll need to stay in rehab for a longer period of time. She isn't sure how much her insurance will cover her convalescence."

Sonny thought for a couple of seconds. "Uh, I don't know nobody right off hand, but I'll look into it and see what I can do. You know she can't walk, anyhow. She's been in a wheelchair for a long, long time."

"Yes, she said she's been confined to a wheelchair for many years, but she said she was able to be fairly independent in her apartment. However, she will be bedridden for a couple of weeks, and because of the pelvic crack, she won't even be able to use her wheelchair. She'll definitely need some help after rehab."

"You say she'll be here for a coupla days?"

"Yes, I'd say at least three. She also has a severe bump on her head that has to heal. Then rehab."

"Okay, lemme give you my phone number. You can let me know when she'll go to rehab. When she's ready to leave there, I'll make sure somebody picks her up and takes care of her at her apartment as long as she needs it."

Sonny removed his wallet from his pocket, took out one of his business cards, and reached in his pocket again for a pen. He wrote his cell number on the back of the card and handed it to the woman. "Here's my name and number. Gimme a call when she's gonna go to rehab." He hesitated. "Uh, what's your name, ma'am?"

She smiled at him. "I'm Doctor Amanda Drake. I'll give your number to my staff. They'll contact you in a few days." She looked at the card Sonny gave her. "Thanks for your concern, Mr. Dankovic. I'm sure Mrs. Mercer is glad she has someone like you looking out for her welfare."

Sonny left the hospital and went back to his apartment, dreading the mess he left behind in his kitchen.

Chapter Six

It's time for a bit of reconnaissance on the 10-10 building's layout and inhabitants. Names and apartment numbers had been tossed at you with no idea who was where or where was where.

In the 10-10 building, Cappy's Bar and Grill was the northern corner business facing Colleda Avenue with large windows both on the Oak Street side and the Colleda Avenue side. On most Friday nights, Cappy held a fish fry, serving luscious, battered fish, French fries, and coleslaw. Sonny and several of the tenants ate there almost every week. Cappy gave tenants a special rate on the dinners.

The southern corner of the building was occupied by Alonso's Barber Shop. When Sonny got a couple of extra bucks, he'd pay Alonso to cut his hair. Alonso would express his annoyance with Sonny. "Why the hell can't you wash your hair before you come for a cut? I don't have no time for this."

Sonny would simply respond, "Who cares, dude? It's my rug."

"Well, I have to use my clean shears and razor on your greasy mop."

They'd probably have this discussion every time Sonny went for a haircut, which wasn't often enough. Sometimes he'd go months without one. By then, his hair would be touching his shoulders.

Between the two business establishments was the entrance to all the residential apartments. A parking lot for the tenants was located next to the barber shop. The parking area for Cappy's and Alonso's was in the back of the building. Patrons of the two businesses entered that parking lot directly from Oak Street. The back entrance to all the apartments was also on the rear of the building between Cappy's kitchen and the 10-10's storage area.

Tenants had keys to both entrances into the apartment building. When entering the door facing Colleda Avenue, a bank of mailboxes was located on the left side of a small hallway. Buzzers were positioned below each mailbox to connect to the apartment number listed on the mailbox. Walking a few steps farther was another door that remained locked to the public. Opening these doors led into another hallway where a staircase appeared that went up to the second and third levels of the building. A door to a staircase leading to the basement was next to the exposed staircase. Sonny's apartment, number ten, was down that staircase in the basement.

Esther Feingold, the landlady, didn't pay Sonny to do any work for the bar or the barber shop. Cappy's wife, Stella, cleaned both of them. Cappy and Alonso had some kind of deal where Alonso's brother would do any big plumbing jobs, and Cappy's uncle would do the electrical chores. Once in a while, Sonny did small jobs for both of them, like cleaning out a drain or replacing fans, and they'd pay him a few bucks. But he rarely did any big jobs for them, although, one spring he tiled Alonso's barber shop floor and made a few extra dollars.

Sonny had been the super of the 10-10 for almost seventeen years. While growing up, his father taught him many of the skills needed for such a vocation. He quit high school in his junior year, knowing he wasn't going to advance to the twelfth grade, and got a job doing custodial work in a couple of the grade schools in the city. When he was eighteen, he applied for the position of superintendent of the 10-10. Harvey Feingold interviewed him and saw he had a lot of the raw talent needed for the job. To Sonny's surprise, Feingold took a chance and offered the job to him. And he had worked there ever since. Even after Harvey Feingold passed away, his wife Esther kept Sonny on as the super. He often thought he should go back and get his GED, but what would be the sense of it now that he would be dead soon?

The building had eight "suites", four on the second level and four on the third. Fancy name, right? Each suite had two bedrooms and one bathroom. They had a decent-sized living room and an ample kitchen. "Suites." That's what old lady Feingold called them. 2-0-1, 2-0-2, 2-0-3, and 2-0-4 were directly above the main level businesses. The floor above these had 3-0-1, 3-0-2, 3-0-3, and 3-0-4. A storage space in the basement was included with every apartment. Not big enough for a room of furniture, but enough for a bunch of boxes and other personal effects. Sonny didn't know what they kept in them. He'd say, "It's none of my business. If it ain't illegal, like drugs or stuff they stole, I don't give a damn what's in those places."

Like Sonny said, normally, he didn't care. However, one summer, a rancid odor eventually released itself from the storage unit that belonged to the woman who lived in 3-0-3 before that jerk, Rusty Morris, and his girlfriend, Addie Thompson moved into it. Sonny had a key to these units, but he didn't like to go in them without the tenant's permission. He decided he'd ask the woman in 3-0-3 to open it for him to check out what was causing the offensive smell. As he walked up the stairs to 3-0-3, he heard music coming from her unit. He had to knock several times and very loudly before the woman, Florence Randall, finally came to open it. Sonny asked, "Hey, Flo, can I axe you somethin'?"

Sonny could tell Flo was either drunk or high, and it was only ten in the morning. "Uh, sure Sonny, anything. Anything you want. You want a beer or a shot? Maybe you wanna get high? Come on in. I need some company."

He quickly responded before she dragged him into her apartment, "No, no, nothin' like that. It's just that there's this bad smell comin' from your storage unit, and it's gettin' worse every day."

She braced herself against the doorway and stood very still for a moment. She looked at Sonny as if he had two heads. Then her eyes popped wide open, and her hands flew to cover her gaping mouth. "Oh my Gawd! Oh my Gawd! I forgot. Stupid me. I forgot." She started to cry and ran back into her apartment. "Lemme get my key. Oh, no!"

Sonny had no idea what to think. He waited until she came back and staggered out the door. She started tripping down the stairs toward the basement. He followed close behind her, hoping she wasn't going to lose her balance. In the basement, Flo fumbled to find the right key as she teetered to her unit. She struggled to unlock the door. Sonny took the key from her. "Here, lemme open it for you."

As soon as the door sprung open, the odor was so strong, they both were forced to reel backwards. Sonny clasped his T-shirt and pulled it over his nose and mouth. Flo almost fell to the floor before she started screaming, "Nooo! Nooo! Mitzi! Oh, Mitzi!"

Directly inside the doorway was the decaying carcass of a small, emaciated kitten.

Later, Sonny learned that in one of her drunken stupors, Flo had found the kitten foraging in a garbage can for food. She brought her home, and knowing no animals were allowed, put her in the storage unit. Flo had the presence of mind to give it a dish of water and some tuna that evening. She had planned to feed it and give it water on a regular basis, but that never happened. After the first night, she didn't even remember the cat was in her storage unit until Sonny told her about the odor. Poor little Mitzi, she never had a chance.

When Sonny buried the kitten in the small yard next to the parking lot, Gardenia Jackson, the little girl in 2-0-2, convinced her mother to have a little funeral service for Mitzi. Amazingly, almost all the tenants attended the service. Arnie Hathaway said a nice prayer at the gravesite, and Vito Amato played "Amazing Grace" on his clarinet. Sonny had placed the little corpse in a cereal box and a grocery bag, and Gardenia picked some wildflowers that she placed on the little grave with a cross made from two sticks held together by bread ties. Sonny made a sign out of a small piece of plywood and painted "Mitzi" on it before attaching it to the makeshift cross.

Flo didn't attend the funeral. She was too strung out to even get down the stairs.

It wasn't too long after they buried the kitten that Florence Randall's drinking and drug problem got the best of her. She was taken to a rehab center and had to lose her lease on the apartment. Sonny later learned the rehab didn't work. She was found in the same alley where she'd found Mitzi, dead of a drug overdose.

****

Time to get to know the people who lived in the eight apartments of the 10-10 building:

Mr. Arnold Hathaway—2-0-1.

The Jackson Family: Luther, LaWanda, Jamal, and Gardenia—2-0-2.

Mrs. Edith Mercer—2-0-3.

Albert and Linda Abbott—2-0-4.

The Amato Family: Tony, Theresa, Dominic, and Vito—3-0-1.

José Cortez, Sophia Espinoza, and baby Mateo—3-0-2.

Rusty Morris and Addie Thompson—3-0-3—until until his jail sentence, then Addie lived alone for a while.

Sherry Sweet—3-0-4.

Some of the occupants had lived in the building forever. Take old Mr. Arnold Hathaway. His apartment was over Alonso's Barber Shop. He was a good old guy. Took a walk every day up Oak Street and back. Oak Street Food Mart was two blocks away from the 10-10. Arnie would sometimes come back carrying a couple bags of groceries. Once in a while, he'd ask Sonny, "Hey, Sonny, you need any cigarettes or a candy bar. I'm making a trip to the food mart."

Sonny would give him some money. "Yeah, Arnie. Pick me up a pack of cigarettes and one of those big chocolate bars."

Arnie didn't have a car. He once told Sonny, "I can't drive anymore because of this glaucoma thing in my eyes. Nobody would want me on the road, anyhow. I can't see worth a damn anymore."

Arnie Hathaway also had a bad heart, and his doctor told him to exercise every day. Consequently, that happened to be one of the reasons he walked so much. But Sonny was concerned about him going up and down the steps. No elevator was in the building. Wouldn't that be a hoot if there was one in a place like the 10-10? Sonny was afraid Arnie might fall on the stairs one of these days. More than once he warned Arnie, "You be careful now, Arnie. You know, you ain't no spring chicken no more."

Arnie told Sonny, "No need to worry, my friend. I'm very careful and I use both handrails all the time."

But you never know, do you?

Anyhow, if Sonny didn't see him out walking or sitting on the cement slab at the side of the building just chilling in his folding chair, then he'd knock on his door to make sure he was okay.

Arnie was married once, but his wife Sylvia died of some strange disease a few years after Sonny took over as super. He couldn't remember the name of it, something rare. He thought he should ask Arnie again what it was. Maybe not. Now that he had those fatal plans for himself, what difference did it make?

Sonny thought Sylvia was a very nice lady. When she was younger, she was a schoolteacher and always tried to get Sonny to use correct grammar. She'd often say, "You're a tough case, young man, but I'm not giving up on you." For a while, he was doing better, but then she died, and he went back to his old habits. He wished someone else was around who'd help him out in that area. But, here again, it really didn't matter anymore.

When Sylvia was alive, she'd bake quite often. Sometimes she'd give Sonny some of what she made. Like her homemade chocolate chip cookies. Yum-yum, his favorite. Excuse the expression, but they were "to die for."

Albert and Linda Abbott in 2-0-4 were in their forties. Al wasn't a very big guy, maybe about five-six, but his nightly beers were expanding his belly. Linda could've lost a couple of pounds, too, but that wasn't any of Sonny's business. He just liked to make observations. That's all. It could have been because as of late, he had been losing weight himself.

The Abbotts' daughter, Lisa, attended college in Columbus. She came home every few months and on holidays. As a kid, she was a little sweetheart. She'd bounce around the 10-10 as if the entire building belonged to her, and everybody invited her into their unit to play or to have a cookie or a piece of cake. The Abbotts were okay with her visiting others in their units, for they trusted all the tenants. Mrs. Mercer said little Lisa helped to keep her young. The two of them would often work jigsaw puzzles together on a card table Sonny helped Edie set up in the middle of her living room. A little secret—don't mention this to Mrs. Mercer—Lisa never ate the chocolate chip cookies Edie baked. She'd wrap them in a paper napkin and put them in her pocket. When she left Mrs. Mercer's apartment, she politely said, "I'll eat them after supper. Mommy will be mad at me if I eat them now, and it spoils my dinner."

However, Lisa threw them away as soon as she got back to her own apartment. "Mommy, I can't like her cookies. They taste like nasty." Very diplomatic for a child. No one ever breathed a word of this to Mrs. Mercer.

Al worked at Temus Auto Body Shop on the north side of Youngstown. Linda helped out at Cappy's Bar whenever she was needed. Most of the time, the Abbotts were a quiet couple. Once in a while, Al tied one on after work on Friday nights, but he wasn't obnoxious and didn't disturb anyone too much. He just stayed in his apartment, playing his eighties music a little loudly, and Sonny or one of the second-floor tenants asked him to turn the music down. He'd always oblige them without any flack about it.

Residing in 2-0-2 was the Jackson family. When LaWanda made her fried chicken, the lip-smacking smell came through Sonny's cellar air vents. He wanted to poke holes through the two ceilings separating their apartments, latch on to a few pieces of that chicken cooking on her stove, and pull them down to him. Wouldn't that be a hoot? Sometimes if she had leftovers, she'd give them to him. He often said to her, "LaWanda, if Luther ever leaves you, I'm gonna be the first to propose to you. One thing, though, you gotta do all the cookin', especially your fried chicken and sweet potato pie."

Luther Jackson worked at the Forrester Aluminum Container manufacturing plant in Youngstown. He was the supervisor on his shift. He was a large but gentle family man, always looking out for his wife and children. He bought his son Jamal a new bike to ride back and forth to school. Jamal kept his bike outside their apartment chained to a heavy metal post Luther had made for that purpose. It took up space in the hallway, but Jamal kept it as close to the wall as possible. Leaving it outside was not an option, even locked with a chain. Some sleazy character in the area would surely steal it and hock it for dope, cigarettes, or booze.

The Jackson daughter, little Gardenia, was such a cutie-pie with her big Afro hair that was so large it looked like it might topple her over someday. She refused to get it cut, so LaWanda had to work with it every day to keep it manageable. The longer it grew, the bigger the Afro grew.

Gardenia also had these mega brown eyes that looked like two buckeyes staring at you. Sonny wasn't sure of her age, only that she was too young for school. Sometimes she played outside by herself, but LaWanda was worried about her. She constantly looked out the window to keep an eye on her. Sonny was a little fearful, too. The neighborhood wasn't the safest place in town. A little girl on her own could be a target for who knew what kind of wacko.

The Amato family lived on the third level in 3-0-1. Tony and Theresa had two teenage boys, Dominic and Vito. Tony was a long-haul truck driver for a major home improvement store and was on the road for a couple of days every week. Theresa was a beautician at Prestige Hair Salon in Boardman. Her own hair always looked like it had been professionally styled every day. Not a strand was ever out of place. No wonder all her customers adored her. They probably were of the opinion that when she did their hair, they looked as good as she did. Whatever the case, she had an active schedule every workday.

Vito was their younger son. Sometimes he hung out with Sonny when none of his friends were available, or he had nothing else to do. Sonny tried to teach him some of the things he knew, like fixing cars, plumbing chores, and electrical projects, so he'd know how to do those things for himself when he was older. Vito especially liked it when Sonny worked on his pickup truck. The kid was a fast learner and caught on to things easily. Sonny had a high opinion of Vito; he was a good kid.

Dominic, their older son, was about to graduate from high school. Undoubtedly, he was very different from Vito. He didn't talk much, and he was gone from home most of the time. Sonny would say "hi" to him when he'd see him in or around the building, but Dominic wouldn't respond to him or even look at him. He acted as if Sonny hadn't even spoken. Sonny was concerned about his attitude, but hey, none of his business. Right?

Another troubling problem with Dominic was that the kid hung out with some bad news dudes. Sonny caught them hanging out behind the utility shed in the parking lot several times. He knew they were smoking weed, but he also suspected they were up to something far worse. However, Sonny wasn't Dominic's father, so why should he care? Again, none of his business. But maybe he should have a talk with Tony. With him being gone so much and with Theresa working full time, maybe somebody should give them a heads-up.

José Cortez lived in 3-0-2 with his girlfriend, Sophia Espinoza, and their new baby, Mateo. About eleven o'clock at night a week before the baby was due, Sophia started having contractions. José was at work at the convenience store on Route 422 and had to find a replacement before he could leave the store. Sophia called Sonny while he was relaxing with a cup of coffee. "Sonny, are you very busy right now?"

Sonny put down his coffee on the side table and sat upright. "I'm just havin' a cup a joe right now. What's up, Sophia?"

"Oh, I hate to bother you, but can I ask you for a very special favor?"

Sonny thought Sophia sounded a little worried and stressed. "Sure, what do ya need?"

"Well, uh, I think I'm going into labor."

"Holy shit!" Sonny jumped out of his chair, almost knocking over his coffee. "Oh, uh, I'll be right up." He darted to his apartment door, took a light jacket from his closet, grabbed his keys and wallet, and rushed up to Sophia's apartment.

Sophia already had her door open when Sonny arrived. "Thank you so much, Sonny. I didn't know what I was going to do. The baby isn't due until next week, but I think he wants to come early. Wouldn't you know it? Starting next week, José took off work, and right now, he's the only one at the store. He can't leave, you know. He told me to see if you could take me to the hospital while he tries to get somebody to fill in for him."

"Hey, no problem. Let's go. If that baby wants to come, we'd better get you to that hospital right away."

Sophia hurried into the bedroom and seized the

pre-packed bag filled with her personal essentials and the necessary baby things for his homecoming. When she came back out and locked up her apartment, Sonny retrieved the duffle bag from her and helped her down the stairs while she held onto the railing and her swollen belly, moaning with each step she took. In the parking lot, he had to lift her into the front seat of his pickup truck, the rise being higher than she could manage in her condition.

The ride to the hospital was rather wild. "Sonny, slow down! You don't want me to have this baby in your truck, do you?"

"Oh, hell no, ma'am." He let up on the gas pedal. He surely didn't want to deliver a kid in his truck. Actually, he wouldn't want to deliver a kid anywhere. He knew zilch about a woman's plumbing, aside from the pleasure it could bring a man.

They made it to the hospital safely and in plenty of time. Sonny waited around until José arrived about a half hour before Mateo was born. When José found out Sonny brought Sophia to the hospital, he was very grateful Sonny had been available. Jokingly, he said, "You know, Sonny, for a handyman you come in handy for all sorts of things besides handyman stuff." They both chuckled. "Seriously, though, thanks so much. I don't know what we would've done without you."

As for Sonny, he was also thankful they had made it to the hospital for the birth of Mateo because the little guy had some kind of serious health issues. In no way would Sonny have been able to handle that type of situation. A couple of times since Mateo's birth, the paramedics had been called because the little man had problems. Poor thing. He was so scrawny. Sonny hoped he'd grow out of it someday

Apartment 3-0-3 formerly was occupied by that asshole, Rusty Morris, with his girlfriend, Addie Thompson, until Rusty was arrested for beating Addie. Sonny had to testify at his trial. The judge sentenced Rusty to five to ten years in prison. Addie would be safe for a while. So far, she was doing okay. She was trying to get a female to move in with her to help pay the rent since Rusty was out of the picture. Some of the prospective roomies were pretty hot. Then again, some of them coming to see the place were dogs. Sonny hoped she'd choose a good-looking one to give him something fine to ogle.

3-0-4 was the apartment of the sweetest thing Sonny had ever seen, Sherry Sweet. He had the worst crush on that woman. She was really a hot number. His entire body would sweat just thinking about her. She was a tall blonde with boobs that wouldn't quit. Sonny would love to toss those puppies around a little bit. Maybe more than a little bit. He didn't think she was flirting with him when she asked him to fix her sink or the burner on her stove, but maybe she was. Her voice was always like butter, throaty and real sexy smooth. It was confusing. He couldn't tell if she was giving him the come-on or just being nice. Maybe she talked like that to everybody. But when she talked to him, she made a certain part of his anatomy roar up like a bucking horse. You know what he meant, right?

That introduction took care of what encompassed the 10-10 from bottom to top except for the attic. Not much up there but old furniture and some of Feingold's boxes. Nobody went up there. Only Sonny and Feingold had the keys.

Sonny wasn't involved with collecting any of the tenant's rent payments. They paid their rent every month and put it in a locked box outside Sonny's basement office. There was also a different box next to it for notes, suggestions, and requests for Sonny. Old lady Feingold picked up all the rent envelopes on the fifth of each month. If somebody didn't pay, Sonny was not aware of it. If they paid their rent or not was none of his business.

The notes in Sonny's box usually consisted of requests to fix something for a tenant. Sonny often wished someday he'd find a card or a note from Sherry Sweet in the box, inviting him up to her place for a social visit. Wishful thinking, right?

More often than not, the renters called Sonny when they needed something repaired rather than putting those requests in the box, especially in cases of emergency. Feingold actually gave him a cellphone so they could contact him when they needed something. Good thing because he was not going to buy a phone with his own money.

Chapter Seven

Sonny returned home from the hospital after making sure Mrs. Mercer was settled in her room and given pain medication. Several of the tenants gathered on the cement pad near the parking lot, wondering what had happened and how she was doing. As he got out of his truck, he was barraged with questions.

Arnie Hathaway asked, "Sonny, what happened to Edie? Is she okay? We are all worried about her."

Sonny stopped to acknowledge the group. He shook his head and frowned. "Well, she ain't really okay. She fell out of her wheelchair and broke her leg pretty bad and cracked her pelvis. She's gonna be in the hospital for a coupla days. The doctor said she's gotta go to rehab for a while afterwards, and then she's gonna need help at home 'cause she has to stay in bed for a while longer. She ain't allowed to put any weight on her leg for a long time. With that crack in her hip, she won't even be able to sit in her wheelchair for a while, either."

"Oh, that's too bad," said Theresa Amato. "Who's gonna take care of her then?"

Sonny shrugged his shoulders and shook his head again. "I dunno. She has a daughter in Texas, but she didn't even want me to call her. So I dunno what's goin' on there. I guess I could call the daughter and see what she thinks."

Sophia Espinoza had also been concerned about Edie. She carried a sleeping Mateo with her when she joined the group. "I wish I could help, but Mateo has just been so cranky lately. I wouldn't want to try taking care of Mrs. Mercer with a baby crying all the time. She'd never get any rest and get better."

Sonny glanced around at everybody. "Well, guys, if you can think of anybody who can help, will ya let me know? In the meantime, I'll try to get in touch with Mrs. Mercer's daughter to see if she can help."

He started walking toward the door leading into the apartment portion of the building. Most everybody followed him. He opened the door into the entranceway, then walked over to the door to the cellar. "Goodnight, guys," he said as he opened the cellar door. Everyone said their goodbyes and climbed the stairs to their own units.

When in his own apartment, Sonny walked into his small kitchen. To his dismay, the bottles of cheap whiskey and the pile of pills he had planned to use to kill himself stared back at him from the table. He breathed a heavy sigh. "Hell, I can't throw in the towel now. I got to find somebody to help out old Mrs. Mercer."

And how would he do that? He could at least try to contact her daughter, even though he didn't know her name, let alone her telephone number. He couldn't call the hospital and disturb Mrs. Mercer with the question. She was in a lot a pain, and they probably had her sedated, hoping she'd sleep and start healing. Besides, she didn't seem to be too open to him calling the daughter when she first was injured. Therefore, he figured the only way he could get any type of information on the daughter was to canvas Mrs. Mercer's apartment. Surely, she'd have some data about her somewhere in there. After all, it was her daughter, for Pete's sake.

However, there was a problem. He didn't want to just start snooping around her place like a criminal. Did he have a choice? How else could he get in touch with the daughter? Perhaps somebody else should go in the apartment with him. What if something ended up missing or broken? He would want to have a witness to verify he wasn't stealing or destroying anything. He was simply entering her apartment looking for her daughter's name and phone number. But who could he get?

He checked his pocket to make sure he still had the master key and left his apartment to trek to the second floor. Since Arnie Hathaway's place was on the same floor as Edie Mercer's, Sonny decided to knock on his door.

"Who is it?" came Arnie's voice from the other side of the door.

"Arnie, it's just Sonny. I hope you aren't in bed yet. I need to axe you for a favor."

It took the older man several seconds to get to the door. He already had on his flannel robe and leather slippers. "What is it, Sonny? You want to come in for a cup of tea?" Sometimes he and Sonny would get together in the evening to watch television. Arnie always had hot water on his stove for tea.

"No, no, sir. Here's the thing. It's about Mrs. Mercer. I gotta call her daughter to tell her what happened, but I dunno her name or her telephone number. I don't suppose you know anything about her, do you?"

Arnie held the door open while he tentatively shook his head. "No, I don't recall Edie saying much about her daughter. Seems to me her name started with a B, like Brenda, Bonnie, or, uh, Bertha. Oh, no, wouldn't be Bertha. Nobody names a kid that nowadays. Sorry, I can't help you out there."

"Well, here's what I was thinkin'. I was gonna go in her apartment to see if I could find somethin' about her daughter, but I don't want nobody to think I'm sneakin' in there to steal somethin' or just to be nosey. Do ya think maybe you could come in there with me?"

Arnie put his hand on Sonny's shoulder. "Sure, son, I don't think anyone would ever accuse you of stealing anything, but I'll come with you just the same."

Arnie grabbed his keys, closed, and locked his door, putting his keys temporarily in his robe pocket. The two of them went down the hall to Mrs. Mercer's place in 2-0-3. Sonny used his master key to open the door and entered with Mr. Hathaway right behind him.

"Hey, Sonny, can you turn on some lights? I can't see a thing in here."

It was dark inside the apartment. Mr. Hathaway had turned out the lights when he had made sure the door was locked after the paramedics left with Mrs. Mercer on the stretcher. And Arnie's vision wasn't the greatest anymore. He had glaucoma, which was gradually getting worse.

"Sure, Arnie. "I forgot about your eyes bein' bad. Sorry."

The lights from the parking lot shone through the living room window to some degree. Mrs. Mercer had a table in front of the window. A lamp sat on an off-white lace doily in the middle of the table. A framed photo of a young Mrs. Mercer, a tall, handsome man, and a smiling, blonde girl around ten years old rested next to the lamp and faced into the living room. Sonny turned on the lamp switch.

"Ah, that's better. I can see now so I won't break my leg like Edie did."

Sonny added as he looked around the room, "Or break any of Mrs. Mercer's stuff and then blame it on me. Ha!"

"Oh, no, I'd never do that, Sonny. You know that."

"I know, I know. I was just pullin' your leg, Arnie."

The furniture in the room appeared shabby and old, but neat and clean. The same type of off-white doilies draped on the backs of the dark-merlot-colored heavy couch and chair.

Sonny stood in the middle of the room, casting his gaze around. "I don't know where to start lookin'."

Arnie slid his puckered lips from side to side and let out a deep sigh. "Well, I know I keep important telephone numbers on my cellphone. But I also keep a file on my computer that I print out and keep in my desk drawer. That seems to be the handiest place for me. Where's Edie's cellphone? Do you know?"

Sonny scratched his head. "That's a good question. I know she took her purse with her in the ambulance, but whether her phone was in it, beats me. Prob'ly though."

Arnie glanced around the room. "She does have a home phone, doesn't she?"

Sonny raised both his hands. "I don't know. I guess we'll find that out first." His eyes focused on the table next to the chair where Mrs. Mercer watched her television. He saw a black telephone atop another off-white doily. The table had a small drawer in the front. Opening the drawer, a myriad of junk lay scattered inside—pencils, pens, buttons, coins, pins, scraps of paper with notes on them.

"Ah ha! An address book! That was easy enough. Now the trick is to find her daughter's number."

Arnie tilted his head and tapped his tight lips. "You know, I also keep important stuff on my fridge. If she only has one daughter, maybe it would be handy for her to keep her daughter's number on her fridge. Well, unless she knows it by heart. It's worth a try to look there first before going through that address book."

Sonny placed the address book back in the drawer, and they walked into the kitchen. He suddenly stopped when he saw the condition of the room. "Oh, I forgot the mess I left behind after Mrs. Mercer's accident."

Bloody paper towels he used to wipe her head lay on the sink countertop. One of her kitchen chairs was toppled over on its side. Dried blood also streaked the linoleum floor. Before he looked for the daughter's number, he wanted to clean up the mess somewhat. He threw the blood-soaked towels in the trash and picked up the chair. Looking under the sink, he found an aerosol cleaner, spraying it on the blood on the counter and wiping it with clean paper towels. Then he tackled the blood on the floor in the same manner, using additional paper towels as needed. He didn't want Edie to come home to find that mess still in her kitchen.

With that chore accomplished, he stepped over to the refrigerator. Arnie was already searching for the number among the many notes and photos on the door.

Sonny asked, "Did you find it?"

Arnie squinted through his bifocals. "Well, there's a Bridget here with a phone number on a piece of paper. Uh, another paper has Martha's phone number. Then there's one with a Fran on it."

Sonny checked all the papers and saw a list of numbers on another sheet, consisting of the police, the fire department, Dr. Zeldon, the Oak Street Food Mart, and others that must have been important to Edie. "Wait a minute!" he said. "This list has Bridget's office on it. Maybe Bridget is her daughter. Lemme look in the address book to see if there's a Bridget in it."

They went back to the table next to the living room chair, and Sonny retrieved the address book. "There's not a lot of numbers in it, but I'll look under each letter of the alphabet." He started with A, then B, C, D, E, and F. "Hey! I got lucky. She's Bridget Gardner!"

"Yay!" Mr. Hathaway clapped his hands, satisfied with their success.

"And she lives in Texas," Sonny mentioned. He took out his notepad and wrote down her name and number. He slipped the notepad back in his pocket and turned to Mr. Hathaway. "How about that tea now?"

Chapter Eight

It was late when Sonny got back to his basement unit. He debated if he should call Bridget Gardner, Mrs. Mercer's daughter, at that hour or wait until at least daylight. Hell, this was her mother. If his mama was hurt like Mrs. Mercer, he'd sure as hell want to know right away. He took out his phone and his notepad, dialing the Texas number he had written down.

It rang several times before going to voicemail. *Hi, this is Bridget. I'm unavailable to take your call right now. Please text me or leave a message, and I'll get back to you as soon as possible.*

Hmm. He didn't want to simply leave a message. Wouldn't it be rude to suddenly hear something as serious as your mom being severely injured on a phone message? Or worse, a text? He decided to try the number again. It went to voicemail for the second time. That time, he had no choice. He left a message. "My name is Sonny Dankovic. I'm the super in your mom's apartment buildin'. Your mom had a nasty fall and is in the hospital. She's gonna need somebody to take care of her when she comes home. Please call me for more information." He left his phone number and hung up.

Afterwards, he went into his kitchen to clean up the mess he'd made from his second, failed suicide attempt. He threw away the booze still in the glass; he put the salvageable pills back in their correct containers; and for the time being, he found a place under the sink for all the bottles of cheap whiskey. Maybe he'd see if any of the tenants would want them. However, wouldn't they wonder what he was doing with all that booze when he didn't even drink that stuff? How could he explain? He'd have to think about that a little more. He proceeded to wipe up the smelly pill and booze mess on the table and floor.

After all that was cleared away, he glanced around his kitchen. Breathing a heavy sigh and shaking his head, he muttered aloud, "Well, I'll try again after I know Mrs. Mercer will be taken care of. I guess my number isn't up yet. I'll deal with killin' myself another time." Before walking out of the kitchen he repeated once again, "If at first you don't succeed, try, try again."

And he would some other time.

When he woke up the next morning, the first thing he thought about was not how to perform his next suicide attempt but how poor Mrs. Mercer was doing. She was lying in her hospital bed more of an invalid than she was before. Who could he get to care for her when she came home? He waited until eight o'clock and tried calling her daughter again, but it went directly to voicemail without even ringing first. He knew he had to find someone very soon. If Mrs. Mercer came home and nobody was available to care for her, then what would happen to her? She couldn't afford to pay for help for as long as she required it. He knew for a fact that Mrs. Mercer didn't have money to spare.

Years ago, she had told him she spent most her savings when she remodeled her apartment to allow for her disability. Since she had never had a job outside the home, she had no pension of her own coming to her monthly. Currently, her means of support consisted of the survivorship social security she collected on her dead husband's account and a small pension from his work at the car dealership. And without family nearby, what would happen to her? They'd probably stick her in an old folks' home and take that social security away from her. He knew it was up to him to get her some help with or without speaking to her daughter.

Coffee always aided Sonny's thinking ability. He made a pot and sat at his kitchen table, drinking a strong cup of coffee and eating a couple of pieces of toast while contemplating the situation. Who did he know who might possibly take the job? Anybody in the 10-10? What about Linda Abbott?

He knew Al and Linda didn't make a lot of money, or like all the tenants, they wouldn't be living in the 10-10 in the first place. Maybe Linda could use some extra cash. Maybe she'd like to help out Edie. Of course, he couldn't ask her to do it and not get paid. Nobody wanted to work for free. He didn't have to think for very long about that issue. He knew what he had to do. There was no question about it.

Sonny had a little stash set aside for a rainy day. However, since he planned on meeting the Grim Reaper in the near future, he wouldn't be seeing many more rainy days anyhow. So, what the hell? Might as well put that stash to good use, right?

As he finished his coffee and toast and got ready to take out his phone, it suddenly rang. "This is Sonny."

"Sonny, this is Linda Abbott from 2-0-4."

"Hi, Linda, what can I do for you?" Funny, he was just thinking about her.

"Well, I was talking to Arnie Hathaway this morning. He was saying you are looking for someone to help take care of Edith Mercer when she comes home from rehab. I was working at Cappy's last night and didn't even know she was hurt. What a shame!"

"Oh, yeah. I guess you wasn't standin' outside with the others last night when I got back from the hospital, was you?"

"No, I wasn't. Cappy needed me to work late. Anyhow, I wanted to talk to you about maybe helping Edith out for a while. I can look after her in the daytime and those evenings I don't have to work. Do you know how much care she's going to need?"

All he knew was what the doctor had told him. "Well, the doc told me she was gonna go to rehab. But when she came home, she'd still need to stay in bed for a while. She didn't exactly say how long. She'll also need help goin' back and forth to the doctor, too."

Linda didn't say anything immediately, but then she offered, "Well, like I said, I'd like to help out."

He thought about Edie's daughter. "I'm tryin' to get in touch with her daughter in Texas, but she don't answer her phone. I don't wanna wait till the last minute to get Edie some help. So if you're willin' to help out, that'd be great."

"Well, then, you can count on me. Let me know when you get more information, and we'll make arrangements."

Linda hung up.

Good. That problem was solved for now.

Chapter Nine

The next time Sonny decided he wanted to take the steps to place himself in that big sleep six feet under the ground happened a few weeks before the holidays. Everybody in the 10-10 was out shopping for gifts and spending time and money to decorate their apartments with every kind of Christmas paraphernalia: garlands, lights, wreathes, tinsel, ornaments, ribbons, holly, and even mistletoe. Every year the residents of the 10-10 had an apartment door decorating contest with the winner having the most unique or spectacular door receiving the prize. Old lady Feingold was always the judge and gave the winner fifty dollars off their January rent.

Yeah, old lady Feingold, a Jewish lady judging Christmas decorations. What a hoot! Right? But the tenants loved it. Seemed they didn't much care if they got the fifty dollars off their rent or not because they usually spent more than fifty dollars on all the decorations to put on their door display. It was all about coming in first place.

Each year, Feingold decided on the theme. It never was anything religious—can't say I blame her, being Jewish and all. No Baby Jesus with Joseph and Mary. No wise men trekking through the desert to see Jesus. No shepherds standing with their sheep by the manger bed. More like Christmas trees, Santa Claus, or snowmen. The tenants didn't care. They were just so happy to do the decorating so they could be called the winner.

That year's theme was "Winter Fun." Sonny never did his door. Since he was an employee, he didn't think it was appropriate for him to participate. Plus, he wasn't very talented in that respect either, so he left that activity to the tenants. Everyone else started planning and buying their materials before Thanksgiving. They had to finish their door by two weeks before Christmas when the big reveal was scheduled. To keep their displays a secret while they worked on them, every single tenant tacked a large sheet over the door until the deadline so nobody else could see their handiwork. As far as Sonny knew, nobody cheated and peeked under the sheets to see what their competition was doing, although it was all left to the honor system. If anybody cheated, who would even know? One thing for sure— no duplicate designs ever showed up.

Sonny planned to kill himself while Feingold was judging the contest. Everyone in the entire building would be on pins and needles, waiting for her to announce the big winner.

On judgment day, the tenants uncovered their decorative door, then roamed the building observing, critiquing, and comparing their competition. After doing their own judging of the participants, which really had no bearing on Feingold's decision, they gathered in the hallways, impatiently waiting for Feingold's arrival. When she finally came and started her judging, they'd follow her from door to door while she marked her opinion on a paper form attached to her clipboard that listed the apartment numbers and the qualifying attributes needed to win. She had devised some sort of point system, and the door receiving the most points would win the prize. The contestants would be given their critique sheets after the winner was announced.

Since everyone would be preoccupied with the door contest, Sonny surmised they wouldn't even notice he was not among the spectators as he usually was for all the other years. His absence probably wouldn't be discovered until someone needed him the next day.

He had thought long and hard about his method of destruction for this end-of-life experience. His plan this time was to slit both of his wrists and bleed out, becoming weaker and weaker until he quietly slipped away. While everyone was hustling and bustling on the floors above him, he began his preparation. The first thing to consider was where to do the deed. He couldn't do it while sitting on his favorite, and only, comfortable but tattered living room chair. What a mess that would create!

Thus, to avoid getting blood all over any of the cement floors of his apartment, on any of the area rugs scattered about, or on the meager furniture he possessed, he opted to let his life's blood slip away in his crusty bathtub, avoiding the necessity of a major cleanup. Whoever was unlucky enough to get that task only had to rinse the mess of tissue and blood down the drain. Although he was fairly sure there would be more blood than tissue since he didn't plan to take slices of flesh off his arms, the clean-up person still might have to strain out a few globs so the drain wouldn't clog. He'd no longer be around to clean out any clogged drains.

As far as what clothes he would wear, like the time he tried to off himself with the gun, he didn't want anyone to find him naked. Thus, since it was December and cold, he wore his sweats. You might think that was a mean trick to play on whoever had to clean up the mess he left in the tub after the slashing. It'd be a lot easier to wash the blood off a naked body than one wearing pants, T-shirt, and underwear. But he still had his pride, you know. That person would have to deal with it.

Sonny procured the knife from the kitchen drawer next to the stove. He went into the bathroom and over to the sink. He tested the knife against his wrist by gently sliding the edge over his skin. Damn! The blade wasn't sharp enough to penetrate the skin of a peach. It hardly even put a dent on his flesh, let alone cutting through it. What should he do? He had no knife any sharper than the one he had chosen. Maybe he could find something among his tools.

He exited the bathroom, entered the kitchen, placed the knife on the table, left his apartment, and went to his tool room. Through the ceiling and the furnace vents, he heard people laughing and talking on the floors up above. They were probably going from door to door at that very moment looking at all the colorful decorations. Old lady Feingold had arrived a couple of hours ago and had a cup of tea with the Jackson family beforehand. She possibly had begun to do her judging by then.

Sonny unlocked his tool room and pulled the dangling cord to turn on the ceiling light. Going to the tool cabinet that held most of his small tools, he opened the third drawer and removed a whetstone. After closing the drawer, he turned out the light and closed and locked the tool room door.

Back in his apartment, he took the whetstone and the dull knife from the kitchen table into the bathroom. Filling the sink with water, he placed the whetstone in the sink until it was fully submerged. He left it there for ten minutes while he put a hand towel on the closed toilet lid. Then he removed the whetstone and placed it on the hand towel. Retrieving the knife from the edge of the tub, with even and gentle pressure, he drew the knife over the whetstone several times from the edge of the handle to the very tip of the blade. He worked for several minutes at sharpening the dull knife. When he thought it was sharp enough, he dried off the knife and took a sheet of paper from the notepad in his pocket. Using the knife to cut the paper, he determined the knife had become razor sharp. It was ready to do the job that he intended it to do. And at last, so was Sonny.

He dried off the whetstone and returned it to the tool room drawer. Coming back to the bathroom, he climbed into the chipped tub. Leaning with his back to the rear of the tub, he slowly eased himself into the tub until his butt landed on the cold porcelain bottom. Wouldn't you know, his legs were too long to straighten them all the way? Who cared? Not him. He didn't need to be comfortable just to kill himself. Right? It would all be over in just a few minutes, and he'd soon be comfortable in his own coffin for eternity.

He figured he'd slice his right arm with his left hand first. This way his stronger hand could be used when he felt weaker. He clasped the knife tightly in his left hand and bent his right arm forward at the elbow. Gently placing the blade against his right wrist and putting just a small amount of pressure on the knife, a tiny droplet of blood oozed up on the blade. Good. It was sharp enough. He was ready to draw the sharpened blade across his wrist. He lifted his head, closed his eyes, and took a deep breath. Once again, he placed the knife on his wrist, ready to press down on the blade with all his might and pull it deeply across to cut through the veins and arteries carrying the blood back and forth to his heart. One… two… thr—

Suddenly, he heard a massive commotion coming from somewhere up above. It was much louder and more intense than everybody simply walking around looking at the door decorations. He opened his eyes and sat upright in the tub, unmoving with the knife still on his right wrist, but not digging in deeper. He held it there while he listened intently.

Next, he heard screaming and people running on the stairs, sounding like out-of-step marching soldiers. Oh-oh, he'd better stop his suicide attempt to find out what was happening. He dropped the knife into the tub and scrambled out of it. He grabbed a washcloth from the rack and dabbed away the little bit of blood on his wrist.

Just as he came out of the bathroom, somebody pounded frantically on his apartment door. "Sonny, Sonny! Are you there? Sonny?"

"Hold on, hold on. I'm comin'."

He opened the door to see Theresa Amato from 3-0-1 standing on the other side. "Oh, my God! Oh, my God! Sonny. Arnie collapsed on the steps going up to the third floor. You have to do something, *quick!*"

Sonny grabbed his keys and followed her out the door toward the cellar steps. "Call 9-1-1 right now and unlock the main door."

Theresa moved out of his way and took out her phone while Sonny scaled the steps up to the third floor. Everybody stood in the hallway crowding around Arnie Hathaway, who was lying face down near the top of the stairs. "Everybody out of the way," Sonny yelled. "Give him some room."

Arnie had collapsed on the top step. He was on his stomach, moaning and turning pale. Sonny lifted him onto the floor of the hallway and turned him on his back so he could give him better attention and yelled at the people gathered, "Move back some more. Somebody get some pillows to prop him up."

Arnie was still moaning. Sonny asked, "Are you havin' a heart attack, Arnie?"

He sluggishly nodded his head up and down. It was probably too difficult for him to speak with all the pain he felt.

Sonny loosened Arnie's belt and unbuttoned his pants and shirt to make him more comfortable. "Arnie, where's your medicine? Is it in your pocket?"

Sonny could tell Arnie was in extreme pain and having a hard time breathing.

Arnie slowly shook his head back and forth and mumbled something Sonny couldn't understand. He put his ear closer to Arnie's mouth. "Say that again."

Very faintly, he said, "Sink."

Sonny jumped up, yanked his master key from his pocket, and threw it to Tony Amato, who was standing closest to him. "Hurry! Get his heart medicine near his sink."

Tony latched onto the keys and rushed down the stairs.

Then Sonny yelled once more, "Somebody get some pillows and a blanket. Everybody else move back. Give him some room."

Sherry Sweet soon returned from her apartment, carrying three pink pillows and a heart-covered blanket. She dropped the pillows near Sonny, who put them against the wall and propped Arnie's upper body on the pillows. Sherry covered his legs with the blanket.

Then Tony came rushing up the stairs with Arnie's medicine in his hand. He handed the bottle to Sonny, who took off the lid and pulled out one tiny pill. He opened Arnie's mouth and placed it on his tongue. He was still breathing and awake, but obviously in severe pain.

Within a few minutes, commotion echoed from the bottom of the stairs. Four paramedics came tromping up the staircase. Two of them carried a stretcher. Sonny stood up and moved out of the way. All of the tenants also shuffled down the hall to free up space for the paramedics.

One of the medics addressed Sonny, "Are you the person who called 9-1-1?"

"No sir, but I gave Arnie—this is Arnie Hathaway—one of his heart pills right before you guys got here."

"Okay. We'll take over from here."

They put Arnie on the stretcher, took care of his emergency medical needs, and hooked him up to a portable machine. Then they carefully maneuvered him down the two flights of stairs and out to the waiting ambulance.

"Mind if I follow you to the hospital?" Sonny asked the paramedic.

"We're going to Saint E's on Belmont."

Before Sonny took off after the paramedics, Tony Amato handed him his keys. As he ran down the stairs, somebody yelled after him, "Sonny, when you get back, let us know what's happening with Arnie."

Chapter Ten

Sonny Dankovic had made three attempts to meet his maker. Three unsuccessful attempts. First, he tried shooting himself, then he tried a combination of booze and prescription drugs, and lastly, he tried to slash his wrists so he would bleed to death. Each one was interrupted in one way or another by tenants in the 10-10 who needed his immediate and undivided attention. You might think by now he'd either give up or finish the job of killing himself. Honestly, he still planned to kick the bucket. He had things to take care of first.

Take Addie Thompson in 3-0-3. After Rusty Morris' sentence to prison, Addie knew she had to get a roommate to help her pay the rent. With her working five, sometimes six, days a week at the medical clinic and taking a second evening job at Cappy's Bar to manage her rent payments temporarily, it was difficult for her to be available for the screening needed to find someone that could share her lease. She knew better than to try to keep the apartment all on her own. She knew she'd be evicted for not paying her rent if she went too much longer without help. Plus, the two jobs were taking their toll on her health, energy, and concentration.

Thus, although it really wasn't Sonny's responsibility, he felt obligated to help her find someone compatible to share the rent with her. Between the two of them, they came up with the following to place in the ad section of the *Youngstown Vindicator*: *Roommate Needed—2 Bedroom-1 Bath-3ʳᵈ Floor Apartment on Youngstown's East Side—Straight, career woman looking to share lease with another career woman. Half rent; half utilities.*

Addie received several responses to her ad, all types of women. She knew at once the ones who wouldn't be suitable with her personality. A few of them were much older than she was. Her feeling was she would have nothing in common with them. Still others came to view the apartment already with a hangover, smelling of booze, or worse, high on drugs. Eventually, Alexis Madden, a Youngstown State University senior studying pre-law and working at a Boardman law firm, moved into Addie's apartment about two months after Rusty Harris had unintentionally vacated the place. Sonny and Addie helped Lexi move in her personal items.

The two women seemed a good fit for each other. Anyone would be better than Rusty. Well, almost anyone. The important thing was Addie had no more fears about being evicted because she couldn't pay the rent. She cut her second job to just Friday and Saturday evenings when Cappy needed her the most.

Edith Mercer from 2-0-3, who had fallen in her kitchen and broken her leg, came home from the hospital three weeks after Halloween. Linda Abbott kept her promise and cared for her during Edie's convalescence. Edie refused to let Sonny pay Linda, as he thought he would have to do. She told him she had some money set aside for a "rainy day." Her convalescence became that rainy day. Sonny didn't know the financial arrangements the two ladies had made. He did know that Linda was very conscientious in her care. She went as far as to put a baby monitor next to Edie's bed and one in her own apartment, so if Edie needed her at any time when she wasn't in Edie's apartment, she'd be able to get to her within a couple of minutes. Cappy was aware of Linda's arrangement with Edie, and he was on board with it, especially since Addie Thompson was now helping out at the bar also.

It took Edie eight weeks before she made a full recovery and was able to be completely on her own again. She and Linda had become special friends during that time period. As a result, Linda visited her on a regular basis, often bringing her meals so Edie didn't have to cook as much.

Sonny never got a call back from Edie's daughter, Bridget Gardner. He didn't know if she eventually got in touch with her mother. All he knew was that he never talked to her, and she never showed up at the 10-10. If she called her mother, Edie never mentioned it to Sonny, and he didn't bring it up. Something must have been going on in their relationship. Oh, well, none of his business, anyway. He and Edie were both lucky Linda stepped up to the plate. His only concern had been knowing Edie had good care.

Arnie Hathaway in 2-0-1 was not so lucky. After his week in the hospital, he spent a few months in a rehab center in Austintown. However, he was lucky in one way. He had a good pension and good insurance, so he had no worries about paying for his special care. As it worked out, around the end of February, Arnie called Sonny to ask him if he could pick him up at the rehab center. He was finally permitted to go home.

When Sonny received the call, he had just completed fixing a leak in LaWanda Jackson's kitchen sink. "Hey, LaWanda. Okay if I leave my tools here till I get back from pickin' up Arnie Hathaway? He's comin' home today."

LaWanda's face showed a big smile. "Oh, that's great! So glad for Arnie. Well, you sure can leave the tools here until you get back. Tell Arnie that I'm glad he's coming home. I'll make him one of my sweet potato pies tomorrow. "

At the healthcare facility, Sonny helped Arnie into his pickup truck. "Hey, Arnie. Welcome back. I'm so glad they're allowin' you to come home. I didn't have nobody to shoot the breeze with."

"You and me both. I'm so ready to get out of this place. Not that I wasn't treated okay. It's just that, well, you know, it isn't like being at home. I always had to be at their beck and call. I'm not used to that. You know how independent I am. I'll be glad to get my life back to normal."

"I sure can understand that, Arnie. I know exactly how you feel." Sonny really could identify with Arnie, being that he had his own problems to deal with. But he realized his life would never be normal again.

Sonny noticed that Arnie's skin still looked a bit sallow, and he had lost a considerable amount of weight. Otherwise, he seemed to have recuperated and was in good spirits.

On the ride back to the 10-10, they participated in a bunch of small talk. "So, Sonny, how are things going around the place since I've been gone? Anything new happening?"

"Oh, you know. Same old, same old. We missed

you, though."

"Believe it or not, I missed you guys, too."

When they arrived at the 10-10, and Sonny helped him out of the truck, Arnie asked, "Uh, you think you have time for a cup of tea with me and bring me up to date on the goings-on in this place? I can't have a beer. You know, doctor's orders; no alcohol, and he wants me to go light on the coffee, too. Decaf he says. Ugh!"

"Sure, Arnie, I got time. Just give me a coupla minutes to put my tools away, and I'll come up to your place. I just finished workin' on LaWanda Jackson's sink when you called."

They were standing at the bottom of the staircase. "Arnie, are you allowed to do steps now?"

"Yeah, yeah, not like before. The doc said to go slow for a couple of weeks. Then I can get back to my regular routine. I'll tell you all about it when you come up to my place."

Sonny watched as Arnie started up the stairs, but Arnie wasn't making much progress. He was stuck a few steps from the bottom. Sonny walked up the few steps and touched Arnie's shoulder. "Here, lemme take your arm. I think you outta lemme help you for a coupla weeks, okay?"

A tear fell down Arnie's cheek as he looked over at him. "Sure, Sonny, sure. You know, Sonny. You're a good fella. You really are."

Sonny helped Arnie into his room and settled him on his living room chair to rest while he went to the Jackson's apartment for his tools. After he put them away in the tool room, he returned to Arnie's place and spent an uninterrupted two hours talking and enjoying their herbal tea and conversation.

Chapter Eleven

Sonny ended up doling out the cheap liquor he'd purchased for his whiskey-pill overdose attempt to a few of the tenants. The Abbotts, the Jacksons, the Amato's, Addie and Lexi, and sweet Sherry Sweet. They all thanked him and invited him to have a drink with them, which he emphatically refused. Mrs. Mercer didn't drink, and Arnie Hathaway still wasn't supposed to drink, so he didn't give any to those two.

When he knocked on Sherry Sweet's door to give her the bottle of whiskey, she seemed very surprised to see him, "Hey, Sherry, I got these bottles of whiskey as a gift, but I don't drink this stuff. I've given some of them out to the other tenants. Would you like a bottle?"

Sherry's eyes grew wide. "Oh my, oh my, Sonny. That's really nice of you. Sure, I'll take one. Uh, too bad you don't like this kind, or I'd invite you in for a drink."

Damn! What a jerk he was! Now he didn't know what to say. He should've just given her the bottle and not told her he didn't drink that crap. Then what did he do? He acted more stupid with his response. "Uh, yeah. Uh, maybe we could have a beer together sometime."

"I'd like that," she cooed as she thanked him and closed her door.

He stood staring at the door before going back to his apartment. Was that a yes? Would she really have a beer with him? What a hottie she was! Should he ask her again sometime?

But he never approached Sherry again about having a beer together. He simply continued on with his mundane life.

By the end of March, the 10-10 seemed to be running smoothly. Edie in 2-0-3 was capable of living without supervision. Linda still helped her out now and then when needed. Arnie in 2-0-1 was taking his walks up and down Oak Street and maneuvering the 10-10 staircases quite well, although very slowly. Addie and Lexi in 3-0-3 appeared to be very compatible roommates. No noise, drama, or trauma escaped from their apartment anymore.

Sonny made his Sunday trips to see his mother in the nursing home. She was about the same—no worse, no better—still repeating over and over about Saint Vincenca. He had also found out more about his problem, and it was worse than what he expected. He decided it was time to get serious and once again find a method to see what that wrong side of the grass felt like. But hell, he wouldn't *feel* it anyhow. He'd be dead. Just the same; it was time to join that great majority on the other side.

About ten that Sunday night after he had returned from visiting his mother, he sat on his living room chair, staring into space and contemplating what method he should use this time. Not the gun to the head; not the knife to the wrist; and not that gawd-awful whiskey and prescription drugs. He wasted too much money on that stupid attempt.

How about drowning? No lake or river was located near the 10-10. He'd have to drive too far to get to them. Maybe that wasn't a good idea. He began talking out loud. "Awe shucks! I have water right in my own apartment. What about my bathtub? I could drink a coupla beers to relax myself or maybe a coupla shots of that cheap whiskey from the open bottle I didn't give away. No, I think I'll stick with the beer."

He sat upright in the chair and began to plan his demise in his mind. *Yeah, that's it. I'll fill the tub with nice, hot water, take off my clothes... Wait! Do I want to be naked when they find me? Do I want my junk layin' out for the world to see? I was gonna avoid that all the other times, right? Problem, though, if I wear all these clothes, will I be able to relax enough in the tub to keep my head underwater long enough to drown myself?*

He shook his head. This time, he spoke out loud. "Oh, what the hell? I'll be dead. What'll I care if they find me butt naked?"

That was it. Death by drowning in his bathtub. He grabbed a bottle of beer, turned on the television, and got comfortable in his chair. After the first beer, he downed another, then another. By the time he drank the third beer, he didn't feel totally drunk, but relaxed, sleepy, and a little tipsy. He thought he was now ready for the bath to end all baths in his tub. He got out of his chair and threw the beer bottles in his recycle bin. No use leaving a mess for somebody else to clean up. He took a fourth beer out of the refrigerator, opened it, and staggering slightly, he teetered into the bathroom.

He placed the open bottle of beer on the floor beside the tub. Then he looked at himself in the mirror above the sink. "You can do this, Victor Anton Dankovic. You *got* to do this, man. There ain't no other way out. It'll be better for everybody. You got to believe that."

Turning away from the mirror, he stripped off his T-shirt, then he pulled his legs out of his sweatpants, throwing both items in the nearby clothes basket. Standing next to the tub with only his boxers on, he turned on the water and adjusted it to the correct hot temperature for a relaxing, steamy bath. Stepping out of his boxers, throwing them in the clothes basket, and placing his hands on the side of the tub, he lifted his left leg into it, then the right leg. The water was a perfect temperature. He slowly eased his naked body to the bottom of the tub. The feeling of the hard porcelain on his butt was unfamiliar to him, being that he always took showers instead of baths.

It wasn't a bad feeling as the water reached higher and higher, covering his body. When it neared the top of the tub, he stretched to turn off the faucets, causing some of the water to slosh over the rim onto the bathroom's cement floor. After the water stopped flowing, he put his right hand over the edge, searching for the open bottle of beer. Grabbing it, he lifted it to his mouth and slowly drank half its contents.

Now he was feeling a little woozier. Time to take the plunge. He replaced the beer bottle on the floor. It tipped over, and the beer inside spilled into the water already on the floor. Closing his eyes and mouth and clogging his nose with his thumb and forefinger, inch by inch he began to slowly sink his body into the hot water, more of which overflowed and soaked the bathroom floor as he lowered himself into the tub.

Except for his knees, he was completely immersed in the water. He was too tall to submerge his entire body. While underwater, he wondered if he should unclog his nose and open his mouth. It was getting harder and harder to hold his breath, and he was about to open his mouth and release his nose from its grip when he heard a muffled, weak sound coming through the open bathroom door. He was getting close to losing all the air stored in his lungs. He wanted to complete this thing and finally end it all, but that nagging sound came through the door again.

Someone yelling his name? Maybe. Hell, he couldn't drown himself if somebody needed him. How would that look?

He quickly shoved his body out of the water to a standing position and gulped air into his hungry lungs. Water splashed everywhere. Now he could plainly hear pounding and somebody's voice coming from outside the apartment door. Swashing water all over the floor and stumbling out of the tub, he grabbed the bath towel from the rack and wrapped it around his waist. "I'm comin', I'm comin'. Hold your damn horses."

Since he was naked beneath the towel, rather than opening the door wide, he unlocked it, kept his body behind it, and peeked out a couple of inches of space to see Al Abbott standing before him. "Hey, Sonny, I hate to bother you this time of night, but water is dripping like a faucet from the ceiling in our bathroom. It's really bad. A pipe must've burst or something."

Sonny was a little confused. No way could the water he slopped over his bathroom floor be causing any issues on the second floor. "Uh, okay. Come on in. I, uh, was jut takin' a shower. Lemme throw a pair of pants on, and I'll come check it out."

He hastened into the bathroom, retrieved his

sweatpants from the clothes basket that was doddering in a puddle of water, slipped them on his naked body, and dashed out the bathroom door. With his beer belly overlapping his waistband and his bare feet soaking wet, he joined Al Abbott, gripped his master key from the hook, and the two of them ascended to Al's 2-0-4 apartment. Al led Sonny into the bathroom with Linda, who had been waiting at the door, following close behind.

The bathroom floor had about an eighth inch of water gathering on it. "Wow!" Sonny exclaimed. "What the hell! I don't know. This is a heck of a lot of water."

He looked at all of the pipes and fixtures in Al's bathroom but found nothing to account for the huge amount of water on the floor. Then he glanced up at the bathroom ceiling. Water was dripping down from several places. "Oh, oh, somethin's goin' on upstairs. Lemme go check out Sherry Sweet's apartment. Maybe a pipe burst in her bathroom. How 'bout you comin' up with me, Al?"

Both Sonny and Al trudged up to 3-0-4 on the third level. Sonny knocked on the door. No answer. "She's prob'ly sleepin'."

He knocked a little harder. Still no answer. He loudly called out her name while he continued to bang on the door. "Sherry, it's Sonny and Al. Can we come in? It's kinda an emergency."

Still no response.

"I'm gonna use my key to go in, but can you get Linda up here? It don't look so good just two guys bargin' into a lady's apartment."

Al called Linda on her cellphone and told her to join them at Sherry Sweet's apartment. Sonny continued loudly pounding on the door and calling Sherry's name while they waited for Linda. Addie and Lexi, José and Sophia, and the Amato family all came out of their apartments, a few in their robes and slippers, to check on what was causing the commotion. Tony Amato tapped Sonny on the shoulder. "Hey, Sonny, what's goin' on?"

Sonny stopped yelling Sherry's name long enough to answer. "Not sure, Tony. Al Abbott's got a big mess of water in his bathroom, and nuthin' there is broke or leakin', so I wanna check Sherry's apartment to see if she has any problems, but she really must be sound asleep 'cause she ain't comin' to the door."

"Anything I can do?" Tony volunteered.

"I dunno yet. I'll let ya know once we get a look inside, okay?"

"Sure thing, Sonny." And Tony walked back to wait at his own apartment door with Theresa.

When Linda Abbott reached the top of the stairs to the third level, Sonny put his master key in the lock on Sherry's apartment door. "Sherry, I'm comin' in now. Are ya decent?" As he opened the door, he heard no response from Sherry. He called her name numerous times while he searched the living room and the kitchen.

Finding those rooms void of anyone, he turned to Linda. "Hey, Linda, you wanna go in Sherry's bedroom to see if she's in there? I don't feel right goin' in a lady's bedroom without her permission."

"Okay, Sonny," she said and walked toward the bedroom.

Sonny and Al waited in the living room for Linda's return. Suddenly, they heard a scream and then Linda's hysterical voice yelling, "Oh! Oh! Sonny, hurry! In the bathroom!"

Sonny and Al jumped to action and dashed toward Linda's screams. When they entered the bathroom, Linda stood stiffly with both her hands covering her mouth and her eyes open as wide as ping-pong balls, staring down at Sherry Sweet's naked body, half on the floor and half in the tub.

Sherry lay with her left arm and leg inside the tub, her right leg straddling the rim of the tub, her right arm dangling on her right side, and her head lolling against the spout of the faucet, blood oozing from her scalp and mixing with the flow of water still pouring from the spout, then escaping out of the tub in a transparent shade of pink. Her face itself was also partly in and out of the water, resulting in her taking in the liquid through her mouth and nose.

Al immediately dialed 9-1-1 to get emergency help, and Linda rushed into the bedroom to grab a blanket to put over Sherry's naked body.

Without hesitation, Sonny splashed through the tinted blush water on the floor, gently heaved Sherry's body from the tub, and carried her into the living room. Al, waiting for the 9-1-1 operator, immediately turned off the tub faucets and ran downstairs to open the main door.

In the living room, Sonny gently placed Sherry on her back on the floor. He carefully moved her injured head forward and pinched her earlobes to see if she was conscious. He didn't want to shake her, not knowing what injuries she had to her body or head. When she showed no signs of consciousness, he tilted her chin backwards to help clear her airway. Linda rushed over and covered her with the light blanket she had confiscated from the bedroom. Then Sonny leaned over Sherry and placed his cheek next to her mouth to determine if she had started breathing. He looked at her chest—not her ample bosom—to see if it was rising and falling.

When he determined she was still not breathing, keeping her head tilted back, he pinched her nose again, took a deep breath, covered her mouth with his, and breathed into her mouth. This he did five consecutive times. When she still wasn't breathing, he began to apply CPR. Placing one hand on top of the other, he pushed down firmly right in the center of her chest, two pumps per second, for about a minute. When she still wasn't breathing on her own, Sonny gave her two more mouth to mouths and then started the compressions again.

He continued this treatment over and over again until the paramedics arrived on the third floor. Someone placed his hand on Sonny's shoulder. "Here, sir, we'll take over now."

Sonny moved aside and joined Al and Linda standing near the doorway.

There was a scurry of activity. The paramedic who had taken over for Sonny finally was successful in getting Sherry to breathe on her own. She sputtered and coughed as she spit out water and phlegm and took in large breaths of air. Throughout the hallway, shouts of relief echoed from the bystanders.

The paramedics stabilized Sherry, wrapped her well in blankets, and carted her off down the stairs to the ambulance. Sonny, knowing he was only half dressed, asked the paramedics before they left, "Are you taking her to Saint E's downtown?"

"Yes, sir. Do you want to follow us?"

"I'll change my clothes and be on the way."

Linda Abbott, who was in her robe and slippers said to Sonny, "I'm coming with you, so wait for me downstairs." She and Sonny both left to change their clothes.

Chapter Twelve

Sonny and Linda arrived at the hospital about fifteen minutes after the paramedics. They approached the nurse's station in the emergency area. In a voice besieged with concern, Linda said, "We're here for Sherry Sweet, the drowning victim. How is she doing?"

The nurse looked down at some papers in front of her on her desk. "If you'll have a seat in the waiting area, a doctor will be out to speak with you as soon as possible."

Sonny asked, "Can you tell us anything about her condition?"

"I'm sorry, sir, no, I can't. As I said, someone will be out to speak with you soon."

With nothing else to do but wait, Sonny and Linda sat on two neighboring chairs a few yards away from the nurse's station. With a concerned look on her face, Linda asked Sonny, "Do you think she's going to be okay?"

"Uh, I sure hope so. It took her a long time to start breathin' again. You never know if somethin' like that does any permanent damage to the brain or other parts of the body. And I didn't even get a look at that bump on her head. I was too worried about her not breathin'."

Linda shook her head and observed Sonny with admiration in her eyes. "I tell you, Sonny, you amaze me. You are there any time any of us need anything at all. You never hesitate to help any of us."

"Awe, Linda. It's just my job. Anybody would do the same."

"Oh, no. It's not just your job. You don't have to do all the things you do for us. And, by the way, how do you know *how* to do some of the stuff you do, like CPR? You are truly amazing."

"Well, that's nuthin'. I took a class a while back, and I just remembered it. Other stuff just comes natural to me, you know."

"Well, I *don't* know. I just know we're so lucky to have you as our super and our friend. That's for sure."

They sat quietly for a while. Sonny was getting restless. He had not forgotten what he was about to do when Al Abbott came to his apartment door earlier that evening. Should he continue with his plan when he got home? He was torn. He wanted to get it over with, but who knew what would happen with Sherry Sweet? Would she survive? If she did, would she be okay? He had to find out about those things before he could make a decision about his own demise.

Linda had picked up a magazine and was leafing through it. Sonny got out of his chair. "I'm gonna get a cup a coffee. Want me to get you one?"

"Uh, can you get me a cup of cocoa instead? It's kind of late for coffee for me."

"Yeah, that's a good idea. I'll get cocoa, too." It was after midnight.

He walked over to the drink vending machine, glancing around the emergency area on his way. One man in the corner was holding a bloody towel against his left arm. A young woman holding a crying baby was pacing the floor near the wall. A small child rested her head against a woman while the woman rubbed the child's back. An older couple huddled close together, holding hands. Sonny wondered about the concerns of all these people. That was the way he was. Always looking out for others. Always thinking their problems were his problems. If it were up to him, he'd fix every problem for everybody. But he couldn't do that, could he? He could do his best to help out those at the 10-10. At least until he was finally in that wooden box.

He realized that's what he had to do for Sherry. He had to do whatever he could until he knew she would be okay. He'd postpone his buying the farm until he knew Sherry's prognosis.

At the vending machine, he got the two cups of cocoa and went back to his seat, handing one to Linda.

"Thanks, Sonny."

They each sipped at their cocoa for another half-hour, Sonny, getting up several times to walk around, and Linda, picking up another magazine to scan. The woman with the crying baby was called into the urgent care area. A wheelchair was brought out to assist the older gentleman, and he was taken back into that area with the woman grasping his hand as the orderly pushed the wheelchair.

Sonny and Linda waited another half hour.

Then a tall woman dressed in green scrubs exited the metal door from the emergency area, looking around the room.

"Hey! I know her. She's the doctor who took care of Mrs. Mercer." Sonny rose from his seat to approach the doctor. Linda was right behind him.

"Dr., uh, Dr. Drake?" Sonny called out as he reached the doctor.

The lady doctor stopped looking around the room and focused on Sonny and Linda. "Yes, I'm Dr. Drake. And you are?"

Sonny announced, "We're here about Sherry Sweet, the lady who was drowning."

"Oh, yes, Ms. Sweet."

"How is she doing," asked Linda.

Dr. Drake looked back and forth between Sonny and Linda. "Well, Ms. Sweet is in very serious condition. She is lucky to be alive. Thankfully, for someone's quick action with CPR, she has a chance of recovery."

Linda interrupted, "That would be Sonny Dankovic, here, doctor."

The doctor looked directly at Sonny. "Well, Mr. Dankovic, you saved her life." She paused. "Right now, Ms. Sweet is in an induced coma as her body tries to heal. She had a concussion, and we stitched her head wound, but we're more concerned about the lack of oxygen to her brain during that time she was unconscious and taking in water instead of air. We'll know more about her prognosis later today."

Linda asked, "Can we see her?"

"She's in the ICU. You can see her, but you can't stay by her bedside. There's an area connected with the ICU where you can sit."

The doctor went back through the metal doors, and Sonny and Linda had to decide about their next moves. Sonny suggested, "How 'bout if we both go up and see her? Then you take my truck back to the 10-10, get some sleep, and pick me up later today."

"Are you sure, Sonny? You need to sleep, too."

"Oh, I'll take a coupla cat naps on a chair outside

the ICU while I wait. I'll be okay."

"All right, then."

They followed the nurse's directions to the ICU. They were able to look in on Sherry as soon as they arrived. She looked so fragile, doleful, and extremely pale. With all her makeup washed away, Sonny realized just how beautiful of a woman she really was."

"Oh the poor girl," whispered Linda. "I sure hope she pulls out of this."

Sonny shook his head. "You and me both."

After their allotted time, the two of them went out into the ICU waiting area. "Here are my keys to the truck and the master key for Sherry's apartment," instructed Sonny. "Can I ask you a big favor?"

"Of course. What is it?"

"Not tonight, but tomorrow, could you please mop up Sherry's floor a little bit? You don't have to clean it real good or anything. Just so it don't drip no more into your place. I'll take care of your bathroom ceiling first chance I get."

"Oh, Sonny, of course, I will. In fact, I'm going to do our bathroom and hers tonight. Might as well. I'm wide awake. I'll just sleep in and pick you up about ten. Is that okay?"

"That'll be fine. Thanks, Linda. I really appreciate this."

"Sonny, we are the ones who appreciate you."

Chapter Thirteen

After Linda left the hospital, Sonny settled into one of the comfortable blue, cushy chairs to await his next chance to check on Sherry. He couldn't help thinking about how he felt when his lips encircled Sherry's during the mouth-to-mouth resuscitation. He knew he shouldn't have those thoughts. What kind of a person was he? The beautiful woman was fighting for her life, and just the thought of his lips on hers was doing things to his body he couldn't control.

And those breasts! Oh, if only he could have fondled them just a little bit. *Stop it, you jerk. The poor woman wasn't even breathin', and all you can think about is her smokin' body and the pleasure it'd bring to you if you could take advantage of it. You are really a sick bastard.*

But he couldn't help himself. Ever since Sherry moved into the 10-10, he had a major thing for her. Many times, he dreamt about seeing her voluptuous, naked body. And the first chance he got? He couldn't even admire it the way he wanted. *I'm such a son-of-a-bitch. The woman could be dyin', and all I can think about is myself.*

He sat upright and rubbed his hands across his face. Then he stood up. Agitated, he walked around the room and over to the window, looking outside. The streets below were quiet. Glancing at the clock behind him, he saw it was two o'clock. He couldn't sleep. He was too worked up from the attempted suicide, the episode in Sherry's bathroom, and thoughts of her gorgeous nakedness. He looked out the window again. An ambulance was pulling into the emergency entrance. He watched as the paramedics removed an injured person from the back and swiftly wheeled that person into the opening doors. He had to get his head on straight. No more bad thoughts about Sherry. What good would it do him anyhow? He wasn't going to be around much longer. His time was up. He had to kill himself. And soon.

Throughout the early morning hours, Sonny went in to see Sherry several times. According to her nurse, there was no change in her condition. They were going to keep her in an induced coma for a while longer. The nurse told Sonny the doctor said that was the best they could do for now until she showed some improvement.

Sonny had dozed on the chair between visits in the ICU but with no real shuteye. About nine-thirty in the morning, Linda and Al entered the ICU waiting area. Al had driven Sonny's truck, and Linda drove their car. As soon as Linda walked in, she asked, "How is Sherry doing this morning?" Sonny had to tell her there was no change yet. Al and Linda both just shook their heads and frowned.

Al put his hand on Sonny's shoulder. "You go home and sleep. We'll stay here for a while. Sophia said she'd come up this afternoon after José gets home from work to watch little Mateo."

Sonny nodded his head. "That's great. I was hopin' somebody else would help out with keepin' an eye on Sherry."

Linda added, "The others at the 10-10 said they'd take a shift, too. You don't have to handle all of it yourself, Sonny."

"I know, I know." He looked concerned. "Do you know if Sherry has any family that we should contact?"

Linda admitted, "I don't know, but she seems to be friends with Addie Thompson. Maybe she knows something about that."

"Good idea. I'll check with her when I get home."

Linda handed Sonny all his keys before he left the ICU. When he got back to the 10-10, he knew Addie would be at work. He'd have to wait until later to talk to her.

Before he took his nap, he entered his bathroom and observed the mess he had left behind when Al had interrupted his suicide attempt. As he cleaned up the evidence of another failure, emptying his tub and mopping up the bathroom floor, he mumbled to himself as he mopped, "No sense doin' myself in right now; I got to make sure Sherry is okay." He stilled the mop for a moment and sarcastically murmured once again, "Oh, well, here again, 'if at first you don't succeed, try, try again.'" Then Sherry's striking naked body glowed in his vision. He quickly shook it away, finished his mopping, and exited the room.

After the bathroom cleanup, he fixed a quick sandwich and washed it down with a cold beer. Then he set his phone for five o'clock, lay on his bed fully clothed, and almost immediately fell asleep.

When he awakened at the sound of the alarm, he had been lost in a dream, a dream of who else but Sherry Sweet. Groggily, he shook his head and groaned, "I got to stop this stuff right now!"

He had a few chores to do before talking to Addie Thompson, who usually got home about six o'clock. After completing all his tasks and checking that it was after six, he ventured up to Addie's apartment. Lexi answered his knock on the door. "Hey, Sonny, you look tired. You okay?"

Sonny frowned, "Yeah, Lexi, I'm okay. Just a little bummed out about Sherry."

"Oh, how is she doing? Any word yet?"

He explained Sherry's condition and asked, "Is Addie home from work yet?"

"Yeah, yeah. She's in the kitchen. Come on in. I'll tell her you're here."

Sonny went inside the apartment while Lexi walked toward the kitchen. "Addie, Sonny wants to talk to you."

Addie came into the living room, wiping her hands on a towel. "Hi, Sonny. What's up? How's Sherry?"

Sonny once again explained Sherry's condition, then inquired, "You know, I don't know much about Sherry's personal life, her family, and that stuff. I heard you and her are friends. Do ya know if she has anybody we need to get in touch with?"

Addie nodded her head. "Yeah, we've become pretty good friends since Rusty moved out. She has a mother and a sister, who both live in the Cleveland area. I'm not sure if there's anybody else." She hesitated. "Gee, I should've gotten in touch with them. I didn't even think about that."

Sonny responded, "That's okay. I figured I'd let 'em know. Do ya know their phone numbers? I'm sure they'd wanna know."

"Oh, of course, they would." She narrowed her

eyes. "I don't know their address or telephone numbers, but I could tell you their names. Her mom is Christine Sweet. I know her sister and her sister's little boy live with her mom. I'm pretty sure they live in Euclid. I vaguely remember Sherry mentioning that. Her sister's name is Stevie, I think Stephanie, and her little boy is Tate. I think the sister's last name is Hensley or Horsley, something like that."

With concern engulfing his voice, Sonny asked, "Can I ask you a big favor?"

Addie looked puzzled. "Uh, sure."

"I know Sherry didn't take her phone with her to the hospital, so it's got to be in her apartment somewhere. Will you come with me to look for it?"

"Oh, no problem, Sonny. Of course. Let me just put this towel in the kitchen."

Sonny let Addie, Lexi, and himself into Sherry's apartment. The women looked around for the phone. Sonny peeked in the bathroom and noted it was all cleaned up, just as Linda Abbott had promised.

Addie came out of the bedroom, carrying Sherry's phone. "Here it is. I know she doesn't have a password on it. I'll check for the phone numbers." She ambled in while working the phone. "Here they are. Do you want me to call them, or would you rather?"

Sonny thought for a moment, then reconsidered his original decision. "Ya know, why don't you call them? It might sound better comin' from you as her friend. If they have any questions that I can answer, give them my phone number. I don't wanna butt into anybody's business."

"Oh, Sonny," Addie said. "I'm sure Sherry and her folks wouldn't think you were butting into their business, but I'll be happy to call them for you."

They left Sherry's apartment and went back to their own places. Sonny relied on Addie to make the calls. If he then received a call from Sherry's mother or sister, he'd tell them whatever he knew about the incident and Sherry's condition. After all, it wasn't his business. He didn't want to interfere. Right?

Chapter Fourteen

Sherry remained in the hospital for several weeks, having developed pneumonia and other complications from the near drowning. When she came home, she was still recuperating. Sherry's mother, Christine, took her vacation from her job. She and Sherry's nephew, Tate, came to stay with Sherry for the duration of her convalescence, which was very slow and painstaking. The extent of any neurological damage would not be known for months. She would be under a doctor's care perhaps the entire remainder of her life.

Though weak, she was in good spirits on her return home. The first thing she did after her mom and sister got her settled in her apartment was to send Tate down to get Sonny. She had something she wanted to say to him.

Sonny was mopping the ground floor hallway when five-year-old Tate tapped him on his lower back. "Mr. Sonny?"

Sonny stopped mopping, turned around, and looked down at the blond, curly-haired little boy standing several feet below him. "Well, hello, there, Mr. Tate. What can I do for you?"

"My gramma says you have to come up to Aunt Sherry's bedroom 'cause Aunt Sherry wants to talk to you."

Sonny grinned. "Is that so, now? What does she

want to talk about?"

Tate looked at Sonny as if saliva was dripping from the corners of his mouth. "How'm my s'posed to know? I'm just a kid."

Sonny snickered. "Okay, Mr. Tate. You tell Aunt Sherry I'll be right up just as soon as I finish cleaning this floor and put the mop and bucket away. Is that okay with you?"

Again, Tate gave him a strange look. "I guess so."

With a smile on his face, Sonny finished his chore, washed his hands, and proceeded up to Sherry's apartment. Christine answered his knock on the door. "Hi, Mrs. Sweet. Tate gave me the message that Sherry wanted to talk to me. Is she okay?"

"Well, she's resting, but she said she really needed to see you as soon as possible."

Christine led him back to Sherry's bedroom. Much to his dismay, Sonny had never been in her bedroom before. How often he wished he had—and not to just talk to her, either. In fact, as he walked into the room with purple walls, purple carpet, floral purple-and-pink spread on the bed where Sherry's beautiful body lay, he had to admit she did look pale. He hadn't seen her since his last stint watching over her in the ICU weeks before. He had stopped visiting her when her family came to town. He was just a stranger to them; he didn't want to intrude.

Regardless of her health and her paleness, she was still the prettiest thing Sonny had ever seen. He was nervous when he warily stepped into the room. He was always nervous when he was in the presence of this goddess. The only exception was when he saw her in deep distress the night of her near drowning. At that time, all he could think about was saving her life—although he had ogled her naked body for a spell. But now... She just looked so wane and weak. His voice quivered when he spoke. "You wanna talk to me, Sherry?"

Her feeble voice sounded hoarse and gravelly. "Come a little closer, will you, Sonny? You know, I won't bite. I had my chance that night in my bathroom, remember?"

He didn't know how to respond to her little quip, so he dawdled closer to the bed, fearing his very presence might cause injury to her already emaciated body.

"A little closer, please. I can't talk too loud. It hurts my throat."

Christine pushed the chair from Sherry's vanity table closer to the bed. "Sit," she ordered, then left the room.

Hesitating, he finally rested his six-foot-three frame down on the chair next to Sherry's diminutive form in the purple bed.

"Please take my hand, Sonny."

He did as she requested, and an electric shock resonated through his body as he gently grasped her tiny, soft hand. Even in this weakened state, her touch sent wanton desire through him, which he immediately had to curb.

In her strained voice, Sherry turned to him. "How can I ever thank you for saving my life? You are my hero, Sonny Dankovic." Her stunning blue eyes were glassy with tears, and with the little strength she had, she squeezed his mammoth hand.

He was speechless. This adorable angel of his

dreams lay before him, thanking him for something that to him was only second nature. Anyone would have done what he had done. Finally, when he found his voice, that's exactly what he uttered. "Awe, Sherry, I didn't do nuthin' special. Anybody woulda helped you. It's just human nature."

Sherry slowly shook her head. "No, Sonny, it's not. You are a very special person who will do anything for anybody. And we are so lucky to have you in our building. *I* am so lucky that you're here."

She released his hand, grabbed his arm to help prop herself up, reached around his huge chest, and with all the strength she could muster, gave him a passionate hug. He, in turn, wrapped his strong arms around her back to support her and gently squeezed her fragile body.

After a few seconds, she released him, looked directly into his deep brown eyes, and whispered, "Thank you from the bottom of my heart." Before she lay back on the bed, she lightly kissed him on his lips.

Oh, how he ached for more! His heart was pounding out of his chest. Did he see any indication that she might feel for him just a little of what he felt for her? But even if that was the case, it was an impossible situation. First of all, no way could he get involved with her when his life was going to end by his own hand very soon. It wouldn't be fair to her, and it would just keep him from doing what he had to do. Second, she was just so grateful to him. No way in hell could a woman as gorgeous as her be the least bit interested in a man like him. It was only her gratitude for his saving her life that she felt.

He got out of his chair, replaced it back where it

belonged, turned back to Sherry, and said all that he could say, "You're welcome." He paused as he stared at her. Then he turned to go. "See ya later, Sherry Sweet."

She lifted her arm and waved to him as he left the bedroom and sadly trudged down to his apartment.

****

Throughout the next few months, Sonny stopped in to see Sherry quite often, bringing her small gifts to cheer her up as she recuperated. Nothing major or nothing personal. A box of her favorite brand of tea. The chocolate candy bar of her choice. A small flower bouquet from the Oak Street Food Mart. A scented candle from Olga's Discount Galleria. She was pleased with all his gifts and thanked him profusely. "Sonny, thank you so much, but you don't have to do this."

Sonny would shyly admit, "I know. I just wanna help you feel better. You're stuck in your apartment every day. You need some cheerin' up,"

When Christine noticed all the small gifts Sonny dropped off, she shook her head and commented to Sherry, "You know he's sweet on you, don't you, my dear daughter?"

"Yes, I know, Mom." Sherry shrugged her shoulders. "Truthfully, I kind of like him, too. I know he's a little rugged and crude, but he's really a good guy underneath. He'd do anything for anybody."

"Actually, I can see that in him, too," her mother agreed. "You know, you're not getting any younger, Sherry. He wouldn't be such a bad catch, would he? He's stable in his job. Although it might not be some high-paying, white-collar job, at least it's steady."

Sherry looked pensive. "It's not his job, Mom. I'm no big commanding, powerful woman either, you know. Hell, I'm just a glorified retail clerk. What kind of career is that? Sure, I'm a manager now, but that's probably all I'll ever be."

Her mom returned her thoughtful look. "Then what is it? Is he physically unappealing to you? Does he have body odor or bad breath?"

Sherry chuckled, "No he doesn't smell. And even though he's a little overweight, I've noticed this past year he's gotten considerably thinner."

"Well?"

"It's hard to explain. There's something, I don't know, maybe—foreboding? Maybe not foreboding. That's not the right word because he isn't sinister or threatening. Nothing like that. Secretive? Mysterious? It's as if he's hiding something he doesn't want anybody to know."

"Do you have any idea what it could be?"

Sherry slowly shook her head while her mind was contemplating her mother's question. "No. Not a clue."

Chapter Fifteen

Christine Sweet and Tate went back home to Euclid in mid-June after almost three months of helping Sherry out. By then, Sherry was ambulatory but still not able to go back to work. She told Sonny she was hoping she could return the first of July.

In spite of his growing affection for Sherry, Sonny had a job to do. Actually, two jobs. He still had to maintain his duties around the 10-10 until he accomplished his other job. You know, meet his maker. Push up daisies. Become food for the worms. Cross to the other side.

By the middle of June, he knew it was time to start planning his demise again. Ah, but how could he do it this time? He'd prefer something quick and easy. But it actually seemed like nothing was quick *and* easy, as he knew from his other four attempts. If he had been able to accomplish his goal, some of his choices would have been quick. But easy? Take shooting himself in the head. No way was that easy! His hand had shaken so much, who knows if he had pulled the trigger, where that shot would've landed? Quick, but not easy. As for cutting his wrists? Not easy. And death wouldn't have come quickly enough either. He'd probably end up having to stab himself directly in the heart in order to make death come faster. Otherwise, he'd have to wait until his body bled out, a long and painful process.

What about booze and pills? He considered that a fairly easy way to die. It probably would've been somewhat quick, too, once the stuff was in his system. But would he have passed out before he got enough whiskey and pills in his body to actually kill him? What about the bathtub drowning? Quick, for sure, but not too easy either. If Al Abbott hadn't interrupted him, would he have been able to physically stay under that water long enough to drown himself? We won't know, will we? Had he been able to try that method out in the middle of the ocean, it would have worked. Then he wouldn't be in control. There would be nowhere available to swim to safety. His body would eventually be so exhausted that he'd slip beneath the water and drown. But his bathtub? No way.

June of that year seemed to be the vacation month for the tenants at the 10-10. The weather was perfect for taking trips. The Abbotts went to Columbus to spend a week with their daughter, Lisa, who had moved into an apartment off campus. Her parents planned to help her with the move and to get her settled in her new place. Arnie Hathaway left to stay a few weeks with his younger brother in Iowa. His brother tended the family farm, where Arnie had grown up. Sonny had driven him to Pittsburgh's airport. Addie Thompson and Lexi Madden took a girls' trip to Los Angeles for two weeks. They planned to keep track of how many celebrities they'd see. Sonny had also taken them to the airport. Christine Sweet drove Sherry to her home in Euclid to spend her last weeks of recuperation with her family. For the first time ever, the Amato family went to Italy to visit Tony's aunt. Their son, Dominic, didn't want to go, but Tony wouldn't leave him home alone. Even

Alonso closed his barber shop for two weeks to visit relatives in Miami. José Suarez and Sophia Espinoza's baby Mateo was doing better health-wise. Sophia's mother also lived in Miami. José and Alonso rented a van, and they all rode together.

That left only the Jackson family and Mrs. Edith Mercer. As far as Sonny knew, Edie's daughter Bridget never invited Edie to visit her in Texas, and she never visited Edie in Ohio. Sonny felt sorry for Edie, but after all, it was none of his business, whatever their issues with each other were.

Most days, Luther Jackson worked ten-hour shifts. His vacation wasn't until August. Thus, his family was still around the 10-10 that June. Jamal managed to procure a summer job at the nearby fast-food restaurant. He worked late afternoons, slept late in the mornings, and stayed out late at night.

Gardenia wouldn't be starting school until September. She wasn't looking forward to a boring summer vacation. Since the family couldn't afford a sitter or a daycare facility for Gardenia, LaWanda was a stay-at-home mom. That did not mean she didn't work. She took in other people's laundry; she sewed and mended for others; she even sold her casseroles and baked goods to her regular customers. She did her best to keep an eye on Gardenia. But it was difficult to watch an active little girl every minute of the day. If Gardenia played in the apartment, LaWanda was able to check on her often. But if she played outside, it was more difficult to do her work and also monitor her daughter.

As for Gardenia, she was extremely disappointed when Tate, Sherry's nephew, went home with his grandmother. Gardenia and Tate had become inseparable, playing either in the Jackson's apartment, Sherry's suite, or on the grassy area next to the parking lot on the side of the building. Sometimes, they found games to play and things to do in the various hallways of the building. But when Tate went home, he left poor Gardenia without a playmate and nothing to do for the rest of the summer. She constantly complained, "Mama, I'm bored. Play with me."

LaWanda felt terrible. She sighed, "Honey child, you know I can't play with you right now. I got to finish my sewing, and I got pies in the oven. It's a nice day today. Why don't you make a hopscotch on the sidewalk or jump rope? Maybe play with that new ball Jamal gave you."

Dejected, Gardenia grabbed her chalk, her ball, and her jump rope and marched outside.

As for Sonny, he realized since most of the tenants were off on vacation, who would actually need him for anything? The time had come once again to kill himself. But he had the same tired dilemma. How would he do it? He came up with a new idea—by poisoning himself. He spent hours on the Internet, researching what poisons took effect the fastest. He discovered a problem with that premise. The most lethal poisons in that category were too hard to come by for someone like him. He had no idea how to obtain lethal poisons like cyanide and strychnine. Lawn insecticides had poisonous chemicals in them, but they would taste horrible, and he'd have to digest so much of it in order to die quickly. He read about tetrodotoxin, which came from the liver and gonads of the puffer fish and was very deadly whether it was absorbed, inhaled, or ingested. The puffer fish was a delicacy in the Japanese culture. But if it wasn't cleaned properly by removing those organs carefully and completely, then a person could die instantly. Okay. Where was Sonny going to get this fine delicacy? He was not in the habit of eating in fancy Japanese restaurants. Besides, he would hope that the puffer fish prepared there was done correctly. He would never be able to convince the chef to fix it so Sonny could die. Can you imagine him asking some famous chef, "Hey, sir, mister great chef, can you serve me a puffer fish delicacy and include the steamed organs?" He'd get kicked out of that fine dining facility faster than you could say, "teriyaki."

What other choice did he have? With further research, he discovered a poison that he could procure from the local superstore or auto parts store—antifreeze. Yes. Simple antifreeze made with ethylene glycol. The more he drank, the faster it could kill him.

Apparently, it wasn't like a gunshot to the temple where nine times out of ten a person would die instantly. No. With antifreeze, it would be a lingering, painful death. However, Sonny assumed if he'd take a large enough portion, he could hasten that prediction. Maybe he should take some sleeping pills with it, so if he were going to feel miserable, he could be asleep. His research stated that antifreeze tasted sweet. Perhaps like drinking a bottle of pop or eating syrupy candy. That's why so many pets who lick it up in garages or driveways, not knowing it was poisonous, get sick or die from it. The sugary taste made them want to lap it up. Thus, Sonny should not have a difficult time ingesting it. At least that's what he hoped.

Since Sonny had no antifreeze on hand in his

storage area, in order to use it as a means of poisoning himself, he had to go purchase some at the auto parts shop a few blocks away on Albert Street. He went out to his pickup, started it up, and coasted out of the parking lot onto Colleda Avenue, which wasn't too busy of a roadway. Except for Alonso's Barber Shop and Cappy's Bar, most of it was residential. However, the majority of the buildings on Oak Street were businesses, such as small shops, gas stations, fast-food restaurants, churches, and abandoned buildings. The traffic could get very heavy and congested, especially when people were going to and from work. Regular commuters. Large delivery trucks. Shoppers.

Sonny needed to turn left onto Oak Street to get to Albert Street. Since it was lunchtime, traffic was heavy. The only traffic signal at the corner was a caution light, with Colleda having the red light. As he looked back and forth onto Oak Street, waiting for an opportunity to make his left turn, he noticed that Gardenia was bouncing a ball on the sidewalk next to the 10-10. Thinking to himself, *I hope LaWanda is watchin' Gardenia. Wonder why she's letting her play on this side of the buildin'.*

Thinking nothing more about it, he went back to checking the traffic in both directions on Oak Street. Finally, he had a chance to pull out into his left turn. At the same time that he made his turn, he heard the sound of tires screeching on the hot pavement and offensive noises of metal crunching. Across the street from the 10-10 was a service station. He immediately pulled into their parking area and looked in the direction of the clamor. "Oh my God!"

There in the middle of the lane on the other side of

the street lay Gardenia with her deflated ball a few yards away from her. Sonny quickly put his truck in park and jumped out of the vehicle, leaving the driver door gapped open. He ran into the oncoming traffic, yelling and waving his hands in the air, "Stop! Stop!"

He rushed over to Gardenia's unconscious, tiny body. The driver of the beer delivery truck hovering over Gardenia's still form had also exited his vehicle. Sonny yelled to him, "Call 9-1-1!"

The man immediately pulled out his cell phone and, with shaking hands, punched in the number. Patrons from Cappy's Bar also began funneling out of the establishment, curious about what had caused the commotion. Sonny yelled to a familiar patron, "Hey, Patrick, go into the apartment entrance and buzz LaWanda Jackson! Hurry!"

Sonny knelt down next to Gardenia. She was breathing, but to what extent she was hurt, he couldn't tell. Blood was seeping from her right side. The truck driver got off the phone with 9-1-1 and crept nearer to Sonny and Gardenia. "I... I didn't mean to hit her. She jumped right out in front of my truck. I didn't mean it. I didn't see her until it was too late."

The man kept wringing his hands and wiping his forehead with his forearm. "I... I was slowing down to turn the corner to make my delivery to Cappy's, and there she was. Boom! Right in front of my truck. I put on my brakes as fast as I could. Is... is she okay? Is she still alive?"

Sonny cautioned, "She's alive 'cause she's breathin', but I don't know what her injuries are. She's bleedin'. Do you have a blanket, maybe something to cover her?"

"I got a plastic tarp in the truck."

"No. That's too heavy." Sonny had a light T-shirt on. He took it off and laid it over Gardenia. The poor little thing looked so small and frail with her big Afro hair all tangled with blood, grime, and stone particles from the roadway. He wished he could help her medically, but he didn't know the extent of her injuries, and he didn't want to do any further damage to her fragile body.

A crowd began to gather around the accident area. Sonny ordered, "Please stay away from the little girl. She's seriously hurt." They all stepped back and remained on the sidewalk.

Suddenly, Sonny heard screaming and wailing. "Oh my God! Oh my God! My baby! My baby!"

With her hands over her mouth, her eyes like wet saucers with tears weeping from them, LaWanda came running to Gardenia. Sonny immediately got off his knees. "Hold it, LaWanda. You don't want to touch her now. She's alive, but I don't know how bad she's hurt." He restrained LaWanda with his arm around her shoulders as they waited for the medical personnel and police.

The truck driver cautiously approached LaWanda. "I'm really, really sorry ma'am. She jumped right in front of my truck. I tried to stop. I really did."

In her grief, LaWanda was unable to respond to his apology. With tears running down her shiny cheeks, she simply sniffled and shook her head, repeating over and over, "My baby, my baby."

Sonny allowed her to kneel down to be closer to Gardenia. LaWanda kept patting her on her back.

Within minutes, the paramedics and the police

arrived and took control of the scene. The medics transferred Gardenia to a small board before lifting her onto the stretcher and strapping her tightly. Then they hastened her into the ambulance. LaWanda followed. As she rushed forward, Sonny yelled, "I'll join you at Saint E's as soon as I give my statement to the police."

LaWanda stopped suddenly and turned to look back at Sonny. "Oh, Sonny, please turn my oven off. I have pies in it." Then she entered the back of the ambulance to be with Gardenia. The sirens sounded, and the red and blue lights flashed brightly as the vehicle pulled swiftly away toward the hospital.

Police began questioning the bystanders. The truck driver was taken away from the crowd to give his statement. An officer approached Sonny. "Sir, did you witness the accident?"

"Actually, no." He pointed across the street at the gas station. "That's my truck over there with the door open. I made a left-hand turn out of Colleda when I heard tires screechin' and the sound of metal hittin' metal. When I looked out my window, I saw Gardenia lyin' in the street in front of the truck." He pointed at the spot where the child had lain.

"Do you know that little girl?"

"Yes. Yes. I'm the super of the apartment buildin' where she lives." He again pointed toward the 10-10. "The Jackson family are tenants in the buildin'."

"Do you know anything about what happened here? I see you're shirtless. Was that your shirt on the victim?"

"Yeah, that's my shirt. I put it on Gardenia in case she was in shock or somethin', but I only know what the truck driver tole me, that Gardenia ran out in front a his truck. I saw her squished ball lyin' near her, so I suppose it went into the street, and she didn't look if any traffic was comin'. That's what I think happened, but I don't know for sure."

"Where were you headed before you heard the accident?"

"Uh, I was on my way to the auto parts store on Albert Street."

"Having trouble with your truck, are you?"

Sonny wasn't sure what his business had to do with the accident, but he answered anyhow. "No, not really. Just needed to pick up a coupla things."

"Like what?"

How the hell was his shopping any business of this cop? It would be odd to tell him he needed antifreeze in the middle of June. He sure as hell didn't want to tell him the reason he wanted to purchase it. So he lied. "I was gonna check out their floor mats. Mine are gettin' pretty scuffed up."

"Is that so?" The cop stared at him for a few seconds. "Okay then, if you give me your name, address, and phone number, I'm through for now."

Sonny did as the policeman asked. The cop put away his pad and pen, nodded his head, and left to speak with other spectators.

Sonny hurried into the 10-10. He climbed up to the Jackson's apartment. LaWanda had left the apartment door wide open when she had gone down to the accident scene. Sonny didn't need his key to enter. He went into the kitchen and opened the oven door. He wasn't a baker, but to him, the three pies on the oven shelves did not look completely baked. However, he had no time to wait for them. Like LaWanda had asked, he turned off the oven, took the potholders from the counter near the stove, and removed the pies, placing them on some cooling racks LaWanda had already set out on the counter. "She'll have to finish bakin' them later, I suppose. That's up to her," he said out loud.

He made sure the apartment door was locked when he closed it and went to his place to get another shirt. After fitting it over his head and shoulders, he left the building, noticing that the police presence was still on the corner, talking to eyewitnesses and bystanders and directing traffic.

Because of the rapid, unanticipated stop that the delivery truck had made, the car behind the truck had also crashed into it, and the car behind that car had also failed to stop in time. The police were observing the damage done to all the vehicles and talking to each of the drivers. Consequently, the traffic was thick and congested, making it difficult for Sonny to cross Oak Street to get to his own truck. One of the policemen actually stopped the ongoing traffic to assist him. When he reached the opposite side of the street, the front door of his truck still gaped open.

He got in the truck and drove directly to Saint E's Hospital's Emergency entrance, not the auto store. He approached the nurse's station in the waiting area. "I'm here with the lady and the little girl who was hit by the truck."

The nurse gave him a strange look. "Uh, are you family?"

"No, ma'am. I'm their friend. Mrs. Jackson needs somebody with her until her husband gets here."

"One moment, please." The nurse picked up the phone. Sonny assumed she was calling back to the treatment area to verify his identity. She spoke quietly to someone on the other end. When she hung up the phone, she stated, "You can go back now."

The nurse buzzed Sonny through the heavy doors to the treatment area. Walking down the hallway, he tried to spot LaWanda and Gardenia's cubicle. As he was looking in one direction, he almost collided with someone walking toward him. "Mr. Dankovic, is that you?"

Sonny quickly looked at the person into whom he almost crashed. "Uh Doctor, uh Doctor Drr...ake?"

"Yes, Amanda Drake. You're here *again*?"

Sonny shook his head and shyly frowned at the doctor. "I'm afraid so. The little girl in my buildin' was hit by a truck a little while ago."

Dr. Drake smiled, "Since you visit us so often, maybe you should set up a permanent residence here."

Sonny grinned and nodded. "Yeah, I guess you're right. I been here a lot lately, haven't I"

They both chuckled, then Sonny asked, "Do you know where I can find the little girl and her mom?"

"Oh, yes. They are about to take her to surgery. She'll be on the right side, three rooms down."

"Thanks, Dr. Drake. So sorry I almost knocked you over. I should a been more careful."

"That's okay Mr. Dankovic. I'm so sorry I have to see you in this emergency ward so often."

"You and me both, doctor. You and me both."

Just as Sonny arrived at Gardenia's cubicle, the orderlies were in the process of transporting her to surgery. He put his hand on LaWanda's shoulder as she came out of the room. "Did they tell you what her injuries are yet?"

She wiped her tears away with the back of her hand as the two of them followed the gurney. "She has a broken arm, a broken leg, and they're not sure of any internal injuries. They told me they'll find that out in surgery. They don't think she had any brain damage. Her face was scratched and bruised, but it doesn't look like the truck struck her head. The injuries to her face were probably caused from her sliding on the street surface." She stopped momentarily. "Oh, Sonny, this is all my fault. I should've been watching her more closely. She's not even six years old yet. What kind of a mother am I?"

Sonny patted her on the back. "You're a good mother, LaWanda. That's what you are. This was an accident. It was nobody's fault. Not even the truck driver. As terrible as this is, it was only an accident. Don't blame yourself."

"But I should've been watching her more closely. I told her to go out and play. I told her to take that damn ball. Why did I have to tell her to take that ball? What can one kid do with a ball anyhow? When Tate was here, they used to play with it together. But what was she supposed to do with it all by herself?" She was silent again. Then she wailed, "Oh, my baby. My poor baby!"

While they continued to walk, she began to cry even harder. Sonny tried to soothe her anguish and pain, but he knew it was impossible. She was so torn between blaming herself and worrying about Gardenia.

An orderly directed them to a room off to the right. "This is the waiting room for relatives and friends of the surgical patients," he said. "Someone will update you on your daughter's condition as soon as possible."

LaWanda went over to Gardenia's unconscious body. She reached down and kissed her forehead. "I'm so sorry, baby. I love you." Then she backed away as the orderlies proceeded to the operating room.

Still crying with Sonny's arm around her, they entered the waiting room and found seats next to each other. As soon as they were seated, Sonny asked, "Did you get in touch with Luther?"

She looked up at him with the saddest eyes he had ever seen. "Yes. He's on his way. I know he's going to blame me for this. I know it's my fault."

"No, no, he won't. He knows you take good care of Gardenia. He knows everything you have to do. It is not your fault. Get that through you head."

She simply turned away and continued to dab at the constant flow of tears running down her cheeks.

Chapter Sixteen

Gardenia was in the hospital for several days. She came home with casts on her left leg and arm. She had also suffered a bruised kidney and her left lung had collapsed, but she was expected to make a complete recovery. Because she was so young, the doctors also thought she would eventually have normal use of her left leg and arm as she healed and grew.

Of course, LaWanda never forgave herself. From that day on, Gardenia was not permitted to play outside without adult supervision or her brother Jamal. LaWanda determined she could do her hand sewing for her customers while sitting outside and observing Gardenia at play on the side yard. Gardenia liked the new arrangement, too. At least she had someone to interact with while she played. The washing and baking that LaWanda did for money she now did either when Gardenia played in the apartment or in the evening, when it was too dark outside for her to play.

Luther constantly told LaWanda they could manage on whatever money he made. She didn't have to burden herself for just a few extra dollars. But LaWanda insisted on helping out. She simply made sure her child came first. Besides, Gardenia was starting kindergarten soon, leaving LaWanda with more time on her hands. She might even get a part-time job when the girl started school.

Sonny never made it to the auto store to purchase the antifreeze. That form of suicide was soon forgotten. Still, he hadn't given up on his intentions altogether, remembering, "If at first you don't succeed, try, try again." It seemed that quote had become his new motto. When would the "trying" end and the succeeding happen? He couldn't believe it would be a year since his first attempt.

He still remembered the feel of the cold steel from that gun when he had pressed it against his temple. There had to be a better way. It was time to get serious and get the job done. No more excuses. No more fooling around. He had lost more weight. He was having a more difficult time doing his chores around the building. He was told he had to make a decision soon. He couldn't wait much longer.

It was September again. School had been in session for a couple of weeks. The kids in the 10-10 were normally home at least by dark to do homework and get enough sleep in order to be on time for school the next day. Why did this matter? Well, Sonny's next method to make his way to that happy hunting ground was to use his old pickup truck. He had envisioned taking it out on the open road, bringing the speed up to as fast as his truck could go, and then ramming into a tree or a cement wall somewhere.

However, he was a bit afraid that even if he was careful, he might still be putting others in danger. He could lose control of the truck while another vehicle was coming in the opposite direction. He could run into a tree or wall that might fall on some unsuspecting person or occupied property nearby. Thus, he didn't want to take the chance of anything like that happening.

He had to be alone when his time was up. No one else could be harmed in any way, so he nixed that idea.

A large shed occupied a space on the side of the u10-10 building just beyond the parking lot. The shed stored the power lawnmower that Sonny used to mow the small area of grass near the building, the snowblower to clear the sidewalks and parking lot during Ohio's miserable winters, and other outdoor mechanical and electrical tools and equipment too large to store in the basement. The shed had room enough to park a car inside, although no one used it for that purpose. All vehicles were parked in their allotted spaces in the parking lot, Sonny's included.

Sonny used that extra space in the shed for repairing equipment and for other maintenance functions. His workbench took up a large portion of the area. However, if necessary, he could move the workbench and whatever else was in the way to allow the space for a vehicle, which was his plan for late that September night.

It was a Monday about eleven o'clock. Sonny had visited his mother the Sunday before. She must've repeated the Saint Vincenca story five times while he sat with her. Each time, he pretended it was the first. He had talked to her doctor the week before. Basically, all the doctor said was that Sonny needed to expect that kind of behavior occurring because her dementia was progressing.

He did expect it, but he didn't like it. His sister Marta happened to visit their mother the same time that Sunday. She was surprised at her mother's change since her last visit. "Sonny, I didn't know Mama was this bad. Is she ever lucid and making sense?"

Sonny didn't want to tell his sister that if she visited their mother more often, she would know how quickly she was declining. But with her living farther away and with having a family, it was more difficult for Marta to get away as easily as Sonny. He was just a few miles across town from the nursing home. Instead of chastising Marta, he tried to explain what was happening with their mother. "Yeah, she's been like this for a while. But it ain't too bad. She really believes Saint Vincenca saved her and me when I was born. She has always talked about this. Even before she got sick."

"Does she talk nonsense about anything else?"

"Sometimes she asks me when Papa is coming to see her. Sometimes she thinks *I'm* Papa. Her doctor said all that's normal for her condition."

"Oh, actually, she called me Millie when I first came into her room today. Wasn't that her best friend when she was a teenager?"

"Yeah, her, Millie, and Doris. They were like the Three Musketeers."

"So does she ever talk about normal things?"

"Sometimes. Most of the time, it's about when we were little kids or teenagers. She remembers a lot of stuff from a long time ago, just not stuff from today." He smiled as he thought of a particular occasion. "She talks about your yellow prom dress and that goofy kid you went to the junior prom with. What was his name?"

Marta shook her head. "She would remember something like that. That was one of the worse days of my life. The dress was strapless and kept falling down. I spent all night pulling it up so my boobs wouldn't fall out. And as for my date, Henry Elrod, he was the weirdest kid in school. I only went with him because

Donny Beckett and I had this big fight, and the jerk took Christy Douglas to the prom. I could've killed him! He totally ruined my night."

Sonny snickered. "Even Mama thought Henry Elrod was a weirdo. After you guys left, she asked me what happened to your other boyfriend, the nice-looking one."

Sonny had enjoyed spending a few hours with his sister. They even went out to dinner that night. It was difficult for him to see Marta upset over their mother's condition. She promised she'd come to see her mother more often. Sonny felt better about her decision. He guessed his sister just needed to see what was really happening to their mother to realize she should spend more time with her.

That Monday, Sonny assumed all the kids in the building were in their own units, either studying or sleeping by the time he decided to take his forever dirt nap. Dressed in a T-shirt and lightweight sweatpants, he went out to the shed, carrying several old blankets and a six pack of ice-cold beer. He planned to move the workbench and anything else in the way, so he could pull his truck into the shed. Then he'd get out of the truck, tightly close the sliding door, stuff the blankets along the narrow opening where the door did not quite touch the blacktop of the parking lot, and get back into his truck on the passenger seat so he'd have more space. He'd move the seat back as far as it would go. He'd set the six-pack next to him on the driver side, maybe even turn on the radio to listen to some soothing, dreamy music like the old classics—Frank Sinatra, Perry Como, or Tony Bennett. His truck was old. It didn't have many of the modern safety features on it.

Plus, there was a small hole in the muffler which had started to get loud and annoying. Next, he'd turn on the ignition, grab one of the cans of beer, pop open the tab, sit back to relax, and take a big swig of beer.

They said carbon monoxide was odorless. He wouldn't smell it. He wouldn't even know he'd be taking it into his lungs. Maybe after the second or third beer, he would simply drift into oblivion. What could be easier? This could be the ideal way to commit suicide. He'd barely have to think about it because it would just happen. One minute he'd be drinking his beer, and the next minute he'd be dead. Easy, right?

At least, that was the plan he had in mind when he carried those blankets out to the shed.

At eleven o'clock dressed in his T-shirt and lightweight sweatpants and carrying old blankets and a six pack, Sonny walked out to the shed. However, when he got there, he noticed that the lock on the sliding door had been cut off and had fallen onto the blacktop. Confused, he looked around the parking lot. He hadn't brought a flashlight since there was enough light from the streetlamps. He saw no movement or anything strange, but he still was concerned. Did some creep steal the lawnmower or the snow-blower? You never knew about people nowadays. Sometimes they stole just for fun. Or maybe they figured they could sell the stolen property and buy something they shouldn't.

Seeing nothing out of the ordinary in the parking lot, he bent down, picked up the lock, and put it in his pocket. Then he lifted the sliding shed door. He stared into the darkness. Again, he saw nothing suspicious. He walked over to his right and switched on the overhead light. The glare was so bright he had to adjust his vision before he could see properly. Standing at the light switch, he looked around the shed. Nothing out of place. The workbench was in the middle a few yards from the door. The lawnmower was on the right side next to the pegboard holding some small tools. Sonny dropped the blankets and the beer on the workbench.

The shed was deep rather than wide. Most of the storage area was way in the back. The overhead light that he had turned on did not illuminate that area. After a few seconds, he walked farther into the shed to the panel of switches that would light up that space. Before turning on the switch, he listened carefully for any sounds. There were none. He flipped the switch. Nothing moved. He waited a few more seconds. Then he started walking deeper into the shed. Everything seemed to be in order.

Wait! Something was in the far left corner where the light didn't reach too well. Sonny hastened his steps. "Oh, my God!" he yelled out loud.

Dominic Amato, the older son of Tony and Theresa, lay on the concrete floor in a fetal position. Was he sleeping? Sonny stepped over to him. He shook his shoulder. "Dominic, are you okay? Dominic?"

When Dominic didn't respond or move on his own in any way. Sonny reached for his arm to take his pulse. As he turned it toward him, a needle slipped from Dominic's forearm. "Oh, no!" Sonny yelled.

He still grabbed the boy's wrist to check his pulse. It was weak, but at least, he had one. His face was extremely pale, and his lips were bluish-purple. His body was clammy to the touch.

Sonny gently shook the boy's shoulder. "Dominic, wake up. Wake up, Dominic."

There was no response. Sonny pinched his shoulder and called out his name again. But Dominic remained unconscious.

Immediately, Sonny dialed 9-1-1.

"9-1-1. What is your emergency?"

"I think a boy has overdosed. He has a pulse, but it's weak. So is his breathing."

"What is your name and your location?"

"My name is Sonny Dankovic. I'm the super at 1010 Colleda Avenue. The boy is in the shed on the side of the buildin'. His name is Dominic Amato. The family lives here."

"Where is his family? Do they know about this?"

"I was gonna call them as soon as I got off the phone with you. Is there anything I should do while I wait for the paramedics?"

"Have you tried to awaken him?"

"Yeah, but he's not wakin' up."

"Since he is only barely breathing, do you know CPR?"

"Yes, ma'am, I do."

"Can you start CPR on him until help arrives?"

"Sure, sure, I can do that. Maybe you can call his parents since I'm gonna be busy tryin' to get him to breathe better." He gave the operator the Amatos' phone number and then started the CPR.

The operator came back on the phone to Sonny. "Please stay with him until help arrives."

Between breaths Sonny huffed, "I will, ma'am."

He was still administering the CPR when Tony and Theresa Amato came dashing into the shed. Sonny heard Tony roar, "Sonny! Sonny! Where are you?"

Between breaths, Sonny bellowed, "Back in the

corner."

The pounding of their footsteps on the cement floor grew louder as they got closer to Dominic and Sonny. Both Tony and Theresa dropped to their knees as soon as they arrived near the two figures huddled on the floor.

Tony screeched, "Is he breathing? Is he alive? What happened?"

Sonny quickly replied, "He overdosed on somethin'."

Theresa shouted, "No! Dom doesn't do drugs. What are you talking about?"

Sonny said nothing else. He focused on CPR. But Tony reached down to pick up the needle that had fallen out of Dominic's arm. "Oh, God, Theresa, look at this."

Theresa screamed, "No! No! Dom! No!"

Soon, the trio heard the sirens of the emergency vehicles getting closer. Within seconds, they were entering the parking lot. Tony ran to the doorway. "In here. He's back in the corner."

As the paramedics rushed to help Dominic, a police cruiser pulled into the parking lot. The officers quickly exited the vehicle and followed Tony back to the corner of the shed.

Sonny stopped CPR as soon as the paramedics arrived. One of them continued the CPR while another administered naloxone. When Dominic was stable and breathing on his own, they placed him on a stretcher and wheeled him to the ambulance.

As Tony and Theresa rushed after the paramedics, Tony yelled back at Sonny, "Sonny, please keep an eye on Vito. Tell him what happened. We'll be in touch as soon as we know more."

Theresa went in the ambulance with Dom and the paramedics while Tony followed them in his vehicle.

Sonny looked around the shed, shaking his head.

Chapter Seventeen

When the ambulance and police had left the area, Sonny decided to clean up the mess in the corner. He filled a large bucket in the utility sink in the shed with hot, soapy water. He grabbed the mop hanging nearby and cleaned up the vomit and urine left behind. After putting the cleaning articles away, he searched for another padlock and threw away the mangled one. He checked his set of keys, exchanging the old padlock key with the new one and tossing away the old key. When everything was back to normal, he seized the old blankets and six pack from the workbench, turned out the lights, closed the shed door, and attached the new padlock. Back in the 10-10, he put away the old blankets in the tool room and the beer in the fridge.

It was time to tell Vito what happened to his brother.

Sonny always had misgivings concerning the type of friends with whom Dom Amato hung around. More than once, he found them skipping school and hanging out in the Amato's apartment when Dom's parents were at work. Of course, it was none of Sonny's business, so he never mentioned it to Tony or Theresa. He also never mentioned to them Dom's attitude whenever Sonny would see him around the 10-10, always aloof and antisocial. At first, he thought Dom was perhaps a little shy, maybe an introvert, while Vito was more of an extrovert and more easy-going. But no. As time went on, Sonny realized Vito was a friendly, responsible kid while Dom really was a jerk who thought he knew all the answers and hung out with the wrong dudes.

After putting everything away, Sonny went up to 3-0-1, the Amato's apartment. He knocked on the door, but no one answered. He was torn between banging harder while yelling Vito's name and using his master key to let himself in the apartment. He hated to burst in with his key when someone was actually home. Who knew? They might take him for a burglar and shoot him. He hoped if Tony had any guns on the premise that he kept them away from the kids. Sonny opted to use his key.

The boys slept in the second bedroom, which was a little smaller than the master. Sonny went to the bedroom door. He knocked and called out, "Vito? Vito? Wake up."

Vito didn't stir.

Sonny opened the door, turned on the overhead light, and called out a little louder this time, "Vito, wake up. It's Sonny. Somethin' has happened to Dom."

Vito jumped to attention, sitting up with fists drawn. He looked at Sonny with utter confusion all over his face, eyes and mouth wide open. "What the h— what are *you* doing here, Sonny?" He unclenched his fists and relaxed.

"Somethin' has happened to Dom."

Looking even more befuddled, Vito protested, "What are you talking about? He's right over th—" He pointed to the other single bed on the opposite side of the room. When he saw that Dom wasn't in the bed, he blurted, "Where the hell is Dom? He was here when we went to bed."

Sonny gazed sympathetically at the kid. "Your mom and dad wanted me to tell you Dom is in the hospital. They wanted me to stay with you until they can get home."

"In the hospital? What do you mean? What time is it? He was here when we went to bed. What happened to him?" Vito kept babbling questions almost without expecting any reply.

"Take it easy, kid. Get hold of yourself. Lemme explain."

He stared at Sonny with eyes wide, waiting.

"It's like this, kid. I found Dom in the shed out in the parking lot. I guess he took too much drugs. He's really sick. The ambulance took him to the hospital. Your mom went in the ambulance with them. Your dad followed in his car. They're gonna let us know how he is as soon as they find out more."

Vito continued to stare at Sonny as if he were talking a foreign language. For several seconds, he was silent. Then suddenly, he put both his hands over his face and began to sob and mumble at the same time.

Sonny couldn't understand him. "Talk to me, Vito. What are you sayin'?"

Vito took his hands away from his tear-streaked face. "I told him not to hang out with those druggies. I told him they were no good. But he just told me to mind my own business." Then with concern all over his face, he asked, "Is he gonna be all right, Sonny? He has to be. He just has to be."

Then he broke down with heavy deep sobs and tears.

Sonny went over to the bed and sat down beside

him. He put his arm around the kid's shoulders. The two of them sat there for several minutes until Vito's sobs finally subsided a little. Sonny then suggested, "Why don't we go in the kitchen and get somethin' to drink while we wait? I tole your mom I'd stay with you awhile."

Sonny stood up and turned to face Vito, who seemed to be in a daze. "Come on, kid. Nothin' we can do now but wait."

Like a zombie, Vito got off the bed and walked to the kitchen with Sonny following him. Sonny went to the fridge. "Do you want some water? Maybe a pop or a cup a tea?"

Vito just stared at Sonny as if he hadn't heard him. Then he sobbed, "A million times I told him to stay away from those guys. But he just told me I didn't know what I was talking about. Why wouldn't he listen, Sonny? Why?"

Sonny reached in the fridge and took out two waters. He placed one on the table in front of where Vito had sat. "I don't know, Vito. Sometimes there's nuthin' you can say or do to make a person do what they should do. They're gonna do what they wanna do every time. It's not your fault. You tried."

Vito stared at the water bottle in front of him.

Sonny wanted to get Vito to talk about his feelings, instead of holding them inside. He wasn't sure if Vito would talk to *him* about it, but he figured there was no harm in trying. "Did you know Dom was doin' drugs, or did you just suspect it?"

Vito slowly raised his head and looked at Sonny. "I... I had a bad feeling he was. He never brought any home with him." He paused, covered his eyes, and sighed. After a few seconds, he took his hands down, his voice cracking. "I admit I searched his dresser drawers and his stuff in the closet a couple of times. I know it wasn't right, but I was worried about him, Sonny. But there wasn't any there. So if he had them in the house, he hid them somewhere I couldn't find them."

"Did he ever act like maybe he was high?"

"Yeah, he did. And I asked him why he was acting weird. He just told me to mind my own business."

"Did you say anything to your mom or dad?"

Vito frowned and shook his head. "I tried to hint around about it, telling them things like I thought Dom was acting weird sometimes. But they just said he was having issues at school." He looked down at his water again. "Hell, how could he have issues with school when he hardly ever went? We'd walk to the bus stop to catch the school bus, and before the bus came, he'd take off somewhere with one of those gangbanger friends of his. And, no, I didn't tell Ma and Pop this. I guess I should've. But I don't know if they'd believe me. When it comes to Dom, they don't believe he could do anything wrong."

Sonny was surprised to hear Vito admit this relationship between his brother and his parents. He never gave Sonny even a hint of animosity or jealousy in their many conversations. He didn't even say it now with a resentful tone to his voice. It surprised Sonny that the Amatos didn't realize what an observant and nice kid Vito was.

Sonny responded to Vito's confession. "Well, kid, you did all you could."

About a half hour later while Sonny and Vito were

mindlessly staring at whatever was on the television, Tony called Sonny's cell phone.

"Hey, Sonny. They finally got Dominic stabilized. How can I ever thank you? The doctor said you saved his life. Man, you are the best."

"That's great, Tony. I'm so glad he's gonna pull through." He looked over toward Vito, smiled, and gave him a thumbs-up. Vito let out a huge sigh of relief.

Tony continued, "I'll be coming home to be with Vito. Theresa is staying in the hospital. Is Vito okay? Did you tell him? What did he say?"

"Yeah, I told him. I'll let you talk to him." He handed his cellphone to Vito.

Vito burst into tears while talking to his dad. It seemed like all his emotions finally broke loose. When he was done with the conversation, he handed Sonny back his phone. The boy's face had instantly relaxed at the moment he had heard the good news about his brother. "Dad says I don't have to go to school tomorrow. He'll call them and explain." He took a couple of deep breaths. "I'm ready for a can of pop now, Sonny. How about you?"

Chapter Eighteen

When Dominic Amato was released from the hospital after his drug overdose, his parents sent him to a wilderness therapy treatment center located out-of-state. They knew Dom needed the help they were unable to give him. The Amatos hoped this type of therapy would aid Dom in his recovery. The doctor warned them it wasn't right for every kid. But they hoped by removing him from his current caustic environment and the negative stimulus from the wrong type of associates that he could focus on building more self-confidence and self-worth. As long as Sonny had known Dom, he never thought of him as a friendly, good-natured kid with a likable personality. Maybe he just wasn't happy. Sonny also hoped this therapy would work—for Dom's sake *and* the rest of the family.

Tony and Theresa thought it best to avoid visiting Dom at the retreat for the duration of his residency, but they did keep in touch by phone whenever Dom was allowed to call or take calls. Vito made sure he was always available to talk to Dom during those phone conversations. The great kid that he was, he never spoke negatively to Dom, but always in an upbeat, loving way. He missed his brother and wanted him home as soon as possible.

****

Life for the rest of the residents of the 10-10

moved on as always. Halloween came and went without any incidents similar to what had occurred the year before. However, Sonny knew he was just wasting time. Had he lost his nerve? Did he decide not to take his last bow? No, it wasn't that at all. He was simply getting frustrated.

Every attempt he'd made was thwarted by unforeseen events over which he had no control. His last attempt with carbon dioxide barely had gotten started when he had been interrupted. With each suicide attempt, he'd spend days before it working up the nerve, squelching his anxieties, and talking to himself about the necessity of killing himself before he could actually do the deed only to have something not within his power stopping him from completing his urgent task. No one could blame him for being so frustrated. But he had to get on track.

What was next for him? He ran through the gamut of all the ways to kill oneself. Ha! He had already tried most of them. Shooting himself in the head. Slitting his wrists and stabbing himself, if necessary—but it never even got that far. Poisoning himself with booze and pills. Poisoning himself with antifreeze. Drowning himself in the bathtub. Poisoning himself with carbon monoxide. What the hell was left?

He thought there was always starving himself or dying from dehydration. Were those even possible with food and water so readily available? He didn't think he could commit suicide in that manner unless someone locked him in a room for weeks without food or water. He was back to the old problem—who would actually do that for him? No, there was no way he could die in that manner without help.

Maybe he could go to the Cleveland Zoo and jump in a cage of lions. Or would the cats be so well fed and docile that they'd ignore him? He also wouldn't want his death to be on display for any young children visiting the zoo. How traumatic would that be for their poor little psyches? That was a bad option.

A few houses up Colleda Avenue lived a guy who took his two Doberman Pinchers for walks almost every day. According to many movies Sonny had seen, two vicious Dobermans, who were often used to guard properties, would savagely attack anyone trying to infiltrate their domain. Perhaps Sonny could climb the fence in the man's backyard and allow the dogs to attack and maul him to death. There was a problem with that scenario. Every time Sonny saw the man walking the dogs, he would stop to greet them and bend down to pet them. The dogs didn't bite or growl at him. No. They gave him kisses. Guess being mauled by the neighbor's vicious Dobermans wouldn't work either.

So what was left? Ah-ha! What about suicide by hanging? Yep. That's just what he'd do: he'd hang himself.

Other than in Sonny's apartment, the basement of the 10-10 had gas lines, electric conduit, and water pipes meandering below the ceiling. He could throw a strong rope over a couple of these, stand on a stool, wrap the noose of the rope around his neck, and then kick the stool out from under his feet. He would dangle in the air for a few minutes before his carotid arteries and jugular veins were crushed, and he collapsed, strangling himself to death. Or would that really happen? Would those water pipes be strong enough to hold all his weight? He was a big man. Would the pipes break and cause massive flooding in the basement? Worse than that, what if he had the rope slung over a gas line and it broke, sending natural gas throughout the building? Or if the electric conduit snapped creating flames that would set the rafters on fire? He might cause the death of everyone in the entire building. He had to find a better, more sturdy way to hang himself.

It was early November, about ten at night. Many of the trees still had their leaves, but most of them weren't vibrant shades of orange, yellow, and red. Most were now dull tan or brown and dry, covering neighboring yards like thick carpet. Since he ruled out tossing the noosed rope over the pipes, he had to find another, sturdy support. Walking around the basement and looking up at the ceiling, he scoured the space with his eyes and noticed that in his tool room, a couple of round holes had been burrowed out of a few rafters. The 10-10 was built way back in the late 1930s. The gas, electric, and water lines probably were updated several times over the years, leaving behind those holes in the wood. One of these would be the idea for Sonny's ingenious plan. Its diameter was plenty wide enough to fit Sonny's thick rope through it. Then he'd wrap the rope around the rafter itself to make sure it would be strong enough to hold a man of his girth.

He searched the tool room for a length of rope strong enough for the task. Finding a bundle of eight-mm nylon rope on the shelf, he used it to tie a noose at the end. Taking the step stool from its place in the corner and setting it up in the middle of the room, he mounted the stool and measured the length of the rope he'd need to hang himself. Then he cut off the portion he would use and tied it firmly through the hole and around the rafter, wrapping it several times. He grabbed the noose and got off the stool, pulling on the rope to test that the rafter and the short length of rope would hold his weight. When he was satisfied, he placed the stool directly under the rope and went back into his apartment for his final preparation of psyching himself up to prepare to take his very last breath. It wasn't every day that a guy tried to kill himself, although Sonny began to feel like he was having an episode of déjà vu over and over again.

He took two cold beers from the fridge. Walking into the living room, he set the beers on the side table and plopped down in his ratty chair. He turned on his television to keep his mind off the vision he was having where his body dangled in midair, legs kicking wildly in all directions, and his hands inadvertently clutching at the rope as it grew tighter around his neck.

He shook his head and argued with himself. "No! I can't think of it like that. I just have to concentrate on getting it over with, once and for all. This will be quick. I can do this."

He turned the channel on the television to some dumb sitcom rerun. He always liked that type of entertainment. Something to take him away from his own misery. It was helping because he even chuckled during a few of the scenes. He finished his first can of beer and opened up the second during the commercial break.

When the comedy episode finished, so had his beer. It was time. He got up from his chair, turned off the television, went into the kitchen, and threw his empty beer cans in his recycle bin. Walking out of his basement apartment without locking the door—why bother?—he entered the tool room. His body was shaking, but he kept repeating, "You can do this, Sonny Dankovic. You can do this. This one will be quick."

Holding the back of the three-step stool, he climbed to the top step, stationing his head so as not to bump it on the rafters. The noose dangled in front of him. With his hands shaking, he took the noose in his hands and lowered it over his head, down his face to his neck. It felt scratchy and irritating. He tightened it securely around his neck to be sure his head wouldn't slip out of it when he kicked away the stool.

He took a deep breath. Another deep breath. He softly counted to three. "One... Two... Thr—"

Before he finished his countdown with number three, he heard a voice coming from outside the closed door of the tool room. "Sonny, are you in there?" A pause. "Sonny?" Another pause. "I tried your apartment. You weren't there. Your truck is still outside. Sonny? There's an emergency!"

"Shit!" Sonny murmured as he slipped off the noose from around his neck and jumped off the stool as he yelled, "I'm comin'," closing the door behind him as he exited it.

To Sonny's surprise, Sherry Sweet stood a few feet outside the door. She quickly insisted, "Sonny, you have to come help. Mateo is choking, and Sophia can't seem to get him to breathe. José is still at work. She's on her way down with the baby right now."

He and Sweetie had been spending time together the last few months. Nothing sexual. Meeting for coffee. Enjoying a couple of cans of beer together. Maybe a quick peck on the lips when he left her apartment. She had gone back to work after her near drowning and so far, no complications. Sonny wanted to take their relationship further, but he didn't feel it was fair to her, being that he would soon be dead. Several times he thought she was coming on to him and wanting more than casual kisses, but as difficult as it was, he ignored her advances.

Now he had to focus on how to help Mateo. He heard Sophia scrambled to pick him off the stairs, screaming, "Sonny, Sonny! Help!"

When she reached the basement floor, Sonny swiftly grabbed Mateo from Sophia's arms. The child was not breathing, but he was conscious. His face was flushed, his eyes were bulging, and his body was stiff. Sonny rushed into his open apartment and sat on his couch.

In the meantime, Sherry dialed 9-1-1. "Please hurry to the 10-10 building on Oak Street. A baby is choking."

She gave them her name and Mateo's name and was told to wait on the line until the paramedics arrived. Still holding her phone, she dashed up to the first level to unlock the building door.

Although Mateo was now over a year old, he was a very small child. Sonny laid the toddler on his lap, face down along his forearm. He held the child's chest in his hand and the jaw with his fingers, pointing Mateo's head downward, lower than his body. With the palm of his other hand, Sonny gave the child five quick, forceful blows between Mateo's shoulder blades. Whatever was blocking his trachea still did not clear. Sonny then placed the child on his back atop the area rug on the floor and put two fingers in the center of Mateo's chest, giving him five chest thrusts, similar to what he would use on an adult, only with slower and sharper compressions.

Finally, after the fifth compression, the blockage had come loose, and Sonny was able to remove it from Mateo's throat with his little finger. Then he put Mateo on his side with his head tilted down as Sonny, Sophia, and Sherry listened to the boy breathe on his own.

Mateo began to cry. Sophia rushed to pick him off the floor. "My baby, my baby!" She cuddled him close to her bosom while she joined the child in crying.

Sherry, who had returned from unlocking the building door, placed her arm around Sophia's shoulders and hugged both her and Mateo. Sonny sat on the couch, breathing heavily after avoiding one more catastrophe.

They soon heard the paramedics enter the building. Sherry rushed to the stairs. "Down here! The baby's down here."

The rescue crew stomped down the stairs, and Sherry led them into Sonny's apartment. "He's breathing now. Our super was able to dislodge the food."

Mateo and Sophia were still crying as she handed the baby to the female paramedic, who put the child on the gurney to check him over. Mateo's cries had reduced to whimpers by this time, as had Sophia's. She took out a tissue from her pocket to dab her nose and eyes.

The medic addressed Sophia, "We'd like to take him in to the hospital to make sure he is okay. Would that be all right with you?"

Sophia sobbed, "Yes. Yes. Of course. I can come with you, right?"

"Oh yes. You can accompany the child in the ambulance."

Sherry immediately spoke, "I'll follow you in my car, so you have a way to get home."

Within a couple of minutes, the entire entourage was out of Sonny's apartment and on their way to the hospital, leaving him still sitting on the couch, his breathing finally subsiding after another averted tragedy. He leaned his head back and rested it on the couch. Closing his eyes, he whispered, "What is wrong with me? Why can't I ever accomplish what I have to do?"

It had been over a year of unsuccessful suicide attempts. He was becoming seriously frustrated. It wasn't that he didn't try. Oh, how he tried. But every single attempt was ruined by some unforeseen emergency. Why? He could not understand.

He got off the couch and went to his refrigerator. "Might as well have another beer. I'm not gonna hang myself tonight. Somethin' tells me it ain't supposed to be tonight. Might as well enjoy another beer till Sweetie comes back. Maybe she'll join me. Maybe we'll get a little more acquainted." He took his beer to his chair, snapped open the tab, and took a large swig. Then he rested it on the side table. "Wouldn't that be nice? Me and Sweetie. Yeah. Maybe we'll get hot and heavy tonight. Yeah, maybe."

But Sonny and Sherry did not have those beers together that night. By the time Sherry and Sophia got back to the 10-10 with Mateo, Sonny was sound asleep in his chair with the unfinished can of beer beside him.

Sherry had peeked in the open apartment door, softly called out Sonny's name. When there was no answer, she tiptoed into the apartment, saw him snoring on his chair, went over, and kissed him gently on his forehead. She left the apartment, lightly closing the door behind her.

Chapter Nineteen

The day after the unsuccessful hanging, Sonny went about his business as usual. Why not? Just like all the other times, he'd have to come up with another plan. But for today, he had work to do.

Addie Thompson in 3-0-3 had asked him the day before to check out her bathroom sink. The water flowed down the drain very slowly. First thing after breakfast, he gathered his plumbing tools in his tool sack and ventured up to the third level. Addie and Lexi had already left for work but had given him permission to use his master key to enter the apartment. Everyone trusted Sonny. They knew he was one of the most honest and helpful people they'd ever met.

As he was turning the key and opening the door, Sophia came out of her apartment, holding little Mateo, who seemed happy and content in his mother's arms— nothing like the night before. "Sonny, how can I ever thank you for saving my baby's life last night? Those paramedics would never have arrived soon enough. They even told me so. They said Mateo and I were lucky you were around." She approached Sonny and gave him a big hug, squeezing little Mateo in the process as the boy broke out in big giggles.

After she released him, Sonny looked at the toddler. "I guess the little guy is doin' okay then?"

"Oh, yes. He's as good as ever. They said he won't

have any reactions from the choking. Maybe a scratchy throat for a day or so. And as far as his other problem, his obstetrician said he probably can stop taking his medication and be clear of all signs and symptoms by the time he starts school."

Sonny gave her a quizzical look. "Actually, Sophia, what is wrong with Mateo? I know he seems small for his age, and I know you and José worry about him, but I didn't know what his problem is."

"Oh, I'm sorry. I guess we never told you. His blood was tested after his birth. They found that he was born with neonatal hypothyroidism."

This time Sonny raised his eyebrows, crinkling his nose, "Uhh, what is *natal hyperroidism*?"

Sophia chuckled and Mateo joined her. "No. It's neonatal hypothyroidism. It means that his thyroid gland wasn't working right when he was born. Even though he wasn't born prematurely, he was underweight at birth, and his thyroid didn't fully develop properly. Remember when I first brought him home how he was so cranky, wouldn't take his bottle, and was kind of weak? He used to sleep a lot and had trouble with his bowels. Well, that was all caused from his thyroid not working right. Thankfully, he'll eventually be just a normal little kid. You notice he's finally starting to put on some weight."

"Yeah, I did notice that. Good for him." Sonny reached over and tickled Mateo under his chin. The toddler responded by giggling again.

After Sophia gave him another quick hug and went back into her apartment, Sonny entered Addie and Lexi's unit and spent about twenty minutes unclogging the drain in the bathroom sink. Then he wanted to stop in to see Sherry Sweet, but he knew she was at work. He had a couple of chores to complete before running a few errands. A few stair treads had come loose, and he tacked them down. He replaced a couple of light bulbs in Mrs. Mercer's apartment. Arnie wanted a small shelf put up in his closet. He took care of that next. The task that took him the longest was fixing a few potholes in the parking lot before they got worse.

After finishing the work, he drove to the superstore to pick up some cleaning supplies for the building and a few groceries for himself. He usually placed an order for supplies with the janitorial service, but it wasn't due to arrive until next week, and he was running low on a few items. By the time he completed all these jobs, it was around five o'clock. Sweetie would be home in about a half hour. He'd been thinking of her a lot lately. Then seeing her last night brought her more into his mind. Sure, he was going to kill himself soon, but not tonight. Tonight he wanted some company. And she would be the perfect evening companion for him.

He put all his purchases away, took a shower, washing off all the grimy dirt from his hair and body that he had accumulated throughout the day. Since he hadn't shaved that morning, after putting on clean underwear, he accomplished that chore, splashing some spicy, fragrant aftershave lotion on his cheeks. His hair, which was well past his ears didn't often get much attention. He found his brush under the sink and stroked it through the strands, brushing it back and behind his ears. Then he put on a nice pair of black pants and a clean, buttoned-down, light-blue shirt, tucking it in at the waist. He found his only leather belt, ran it through the belt loops on the pants, and fastened it. He was going to ask Sherry Sweet to go to dinner with him that evening.

From the closet, he grabbed his good leather jacket that he seldom wore and went out his door, locking it behind him.

He was nervous as he left his basement apartment to walk up to the third level to Sherry's place. Would she think he was being way too assuming, thinking she, a gorgeous, alluring babe like her would stoop so low as to go out with a crude, dull individual like him? But she had always been kind to him, never giving him the impression that she thought he was some kind of jerk. They had actually exchanged those light kisses over the last few months. Surely, she wouldn't kiss him or let him kiss her if she thought he was some scumbag. Right? The closer he got to her apartment, the more he felt the sweat accumulating on his back and hands. Luckily, he had put on a thick layer of deodorant under his shirt.

At her doorway, he almost turned around and went back to his apartment. But he took a huge breath and knocked on the door. Within seconds, he heard Sweetie ask in that smooth, sexy voice of hers, "Who is it?"

Even to himself, Sonny's reply sounded nervous and insecure. "Uh, it's Sonny from downstairs." How stupid! She knew he lived downstairs. Why did he have to say such a stupid thing like that?

"Oh, one second, Sonny."

After a short while, he heard the door unlock. "Sorry for the wait. I just got home from work." Then she stared at Sonny, casting her eyes over the way he was dressed. "Wow, Sonny, you look great? What's the occasion?"

Looking down at his feet and clutching and unclutching his hands, Sonny finally looked at her and stammered, "I... I know you just got home from work. I was wonderin' if you'd like to go out to dinner with me tonight. Uh, that is, if you ain't got other plans, I mean."

Sherry's eyes opened wide. At first, she didn't speak. She was so astonished by his request that she didn't know what to say. Then, stumbling over her words, she sputtered, "Oh, uh, yeah, I'd really like that. Sure." She still was flustered and kept staring at him for a few seconds. When she realized the two of them were simply standing there, looking at each other, she finally remarked, "Come in. Come in. Uh, do I have time to change my clothes? You look so nice, and I'm just in my work clothes."

Sonny thought she looked just fine. She had on a pair of dark, blue-green slacks and a fluffy sweater in a lighter shade of the same color. Shyly, he answered, "You look beautiful. You don't have to change nuttin' if you don't wanna."

She opened the door wider, and he entered her living room. "Well, let me just touch up my face and comb my hair a little." She pointed to her couch. "Please. Have a seat. It'll only take me a couple of minutes. You aren't in a big hurry, are you?"

"Oh, no. Take your time." He sat on the couch, brushing his pants after he was seated. "I ain't in any hurry."

"Okay. I'll just be a minute." She left the room.

When Sonny got nervous, his right leg had a tendency to shake. The leg was doing just that as he waited for Sherry, but he had a huge smile on his face.

He couldn't believe it. Sherry Sweet was actually going out to dinner with him. He was the luckiest guy in the whole world.

As she predicted, Sherry returned in a few minutes. To Sonny, she didn't look much different. How could something so perfect get more perfect?

When Sherry had come home from work, she left her coat on the back of the couch. Sonny picked it up and helped her put it on. "Thank you," she said as she looked at him with her radiant blue eyes.

They left Sherry's apartment, and Sonny followed her down the stairs. On one of the warmer days the week before, he had cleaned his truck. Since the seats were tattered and worn, he had placed a clean, gray blanket over the passenger seat—just in case Sherry agreed to go out with him. Lucky him. He opened the truck door for her and helped her enter the truck. Then he went around to the driver's side and got in himself. He turned the motor on and let the truck warm up for a minute. "I hope you like Italian food. I was gonna take us to Thomasino's Restaurant in Struthers. Is that okay with you?"

She smiled at him. "I love Italian food, and I think Thomasino's is a great choice."

For a few minutes after Sonny started driving, the two of them were silent. They both felt a little strange in this new situation for them. Then Sonny decided he had to say something. It was getting awkward. Timidly, he asked, "So how was your day at work today?"

She took in a huge breath, letting it out slowly. "Do you really want to know?"

He quickly glanced over at her before turning his eyes back on the road. "Yeah, I do."

"Well, there's this one girl who works for me. She is literally driving me nuts!"

Sonny glanced at her again and snickered. "How is she drivin' you nuts?"

"You know I work at the Southern Park Mall, right?"

"Uh, no. I knew you worked at some store, but I didn't know where."

"Yes. At the mall. The store is Lena's Fashion Box. It's not a huge store, but we carry high-end clothing for older women. We don't carry the type of fashions that teenagers or young adults would usually wear. If those shoppers stop in the store, they usually turn around and go directly back into the mall. And that's okay. We know we cater to a certain clientele. You would think our sales personnel would realize this."

Sonny questioned, "They don't?"

"Well, I have to say, most of them do. And they're good workers. Always on time. Always cordial to the customers. But a couple of months ago, I had to hire a new girl because one of the clerks went on maternity leave. So I hired this girl, well, not so much a girl. She's actually twenty-two. At first, she was okay. Nice to customers. Friendly to the other clerks. But lately, several other clerks have told me she's getting combative and argues with them constantly. And that isn't the worst of it. Seems like when she waits on a customer, she tries to turn them off shopping in our store, telling them our line of clothing is frumpy and out-of-style. Like I said, we cater to the more mature woman. You wouldn't expect her to be wearing strapless tops with her bulging midriff sticking out, would you?"

Sonny was smiling. This was the first time Sherry had opened up to him in a real conversation. He was enjoying this. He had to say something even though he was the last one to ask about ladies' fashions. "Uh, no, I guess not."

Satisfied with his response, she continued, "Sure, there are some older women who could wear the short shorts, the tight jeans, the scanty tops, but not most. It's our management's prerogative to choose the type of customers they want to cater to and please. It's not this woman's place to discourage any customer who comes into our store."

Sonny thought he would contribute more to the conversation. "Did you talk to her and tell her how you felt?"

Sherry looked toward him, her eyes vivid. "Oh, yes, I did. You know what she said to me, that little twerp? She had the gall to tell me I didn't know what I was talking about and that I should talk to management about getting a different line of clothing."

Sonny was not going to tell Sherry how much he was enjoying her little fit of rage. She was so cute when she was angry. Instead, he asked, "So how did you end your little chat with her?"

She shook her head back and forth, still upset. "I told her as long as she worked at this store, her job was to invite the customers into the store and give them reasons to buy our clothing line, not to go elsewhere for something more youthful. I told her if I ever saw or heard she was backstabbing our store, she could find a job elsewhere."

He reached over and patted her on her shoulder. He

realized he didn't have to come up with another conversation topic. She was on a roll. "Good for you."

She got control of her emotions and continued talking. "Overall, though, I like my job. Management is good to me and my clerks. And aside from fashionista Kristen, all my girls are good."

"How long have you worked there?"

"Oh, it's about fourteen years now. I started as a clerk when I was still in high school and just stayed on after I graduated, working myself up to a manager position."

"That's awesome," Sonny replied as he pulled into Thomasino's parking lot. "Well, here we are."

As he stopped the car, Sherry apologized, "Hey, Sonny, I'm sorry I went off like that. I don't normally get so upset, but that woman just rubs me the wrong way."

"No, no. Don't apologize. I'm glad you opened up like that. I was beginnin' to think you were calm and cool all the time."

She laughed as she opened the truck door. "Oh, you'd be surprised. I have a temper. Just ask my mom and my sister."

Sonny turned off the truck and quickly went around to assist Sherry out her door. They walked into the restaurant and were seated in a corner booth, facing each other. The waitress gave them menus and asked what they wanted to drink. They both opted for water with lemon as they perused the menu.

Sherry glanced up from the menu. "What's good, Sonny?"

He pointed at his selection. "I'm a red sauce kind of a guy. I like the cavatelli with meat balls, but everything is good here."

"I'll have the same."

The waitress returned with their water and took their order. They sipped their water while they waited for her to bring their meals. Sherry had one hand on her water glass and the other resting on the table. Sonny reached over and placed his hand on top of hers. He wasn't sure how to say what he had planned to say, but he tried. He focused directly into her glowing blue eyes when her eyes met his. "You know, Sherry, I don't know how to say this, but I'm just gonna say it." He hesitated. "I like you a lot. Really a lot." He hesitated again. "I know I'm not good enough for you. You're so pretty and so, so perfect. You're like first-class. Then there's me, a big oaf and… and third-class."

Before he could utter another word, Sherry interrupted him. "Oh, Sonny! Don't sell yourself short. You are definitely not some big oaf." She let go of her water glass and clasped his hand with both of hers. "You are the kindest man I've ever known. You have a heart as big as a mountain." She lifted up his large hand with her two tiny hands, bent her head toward them, and gently kissed the back of his hand. She then raised her eyes to his face. "And you're not so bad looking either."

At a loss for words, Sonny began to blush. Before he could speak, the waitress returned with the meals.

Silence and small talk, mostly about the tenants in the 10-10, took place during the dinner. They topped off their meal with tiramisu and coffee, then drove home with more casual conversation.

In the parking lot, Sonny helped Sherry out of the truck. Before going into the building, Sherry suggested,

"Sonny, would you like to stop in for a beer or a night cap?"

He thought to himself, *Well, she must've had an okay time if she invited me back to her apartment.*

"Sure. I'll take a beer," he said, forgetting that he shouldn't be drinking the stuff.

Sonny didn't stay late at Sherry's place. They each had two beers. They sat on the couch next to each other. At first, they talked. It wasn't exactly that Sonny ran out of things to say. It was just that he had something else on his mind. He thought about the things she had said about him at the restaurant. Maybe she did like him a little. Maybe.

With a lull in the conversation, he put down his almost empty bottle of beer and took Sherry's hand. Turning to her, he whispered, "Can I kiss you? Not just a 'friend' kiss. A real one?"

Sherry didn't answer. She didn't have to. She placed her beer bottle on the coffee table, turned toward Sonny, put her arms around his neck, and gave him the sweetest, most passionate kiss Sonny had ever had. And that was the first of many. They kissed. They groped. Their breathing was heavy and lustful. But their clothes stayed on. Neither of them were ready to take their petting to the extreme.

When Sonny realized that he couldn't take it anymore, breathlessly he murmured, "I got to stop, or I'm gonna burst."

Sherry, also panting, warned, "Good idea, 'cause I'm about to tear both your and my pants off."

The two of them had been laying intermingled on the couch. Sonny slowly extracted his body from atop Sherry. Then she gradually rose. She walked him to the door. He gave her one more fervent kiss before he hurried out the door, whispering back at her, "Thank you."

Chapter Twenty

Unless something came up, Sonny and Sherry began getting together every Friday night. Sometimes they went out to dinner. Sometimes they went to a movie. Sometimes they simply hung out in her apartment. Each time they ended their date with passionate lovemaking, but never getting naked or going all the way. Sonny had too many things on his mind.

He figured if they actually had sex together, it would really screw up his mind and be unfair to Sherry. Reason being, he still needed to complete his suicide, which kept being postponed over and over again by himself, sometimes by others.

His decision to follow through with the suicide came to him shortly after Christmas. He had been keeping more in touch with his sister Marta lately, and they had both visited his mother on Christmas day. She was extremely agitated that day. It didn't appear to Sonny to be her advancing dementia causing it. She just seemed extra worried and concerned about Sonny and Marta. She definitely recognized them and kept asking them if they were okay. She talked about Saint Vincenca coming to her in more visions, this time warning her of some fateful event expected in the near future. Both Sonny and Marta tried to appease her and convince her everything was fine with them. Of course,

Sonny never mentioned to his mother or Marta what his eventual plans were. He did tell her about dating Sherry, and his mom wanted to meet her. He didn't think that was a very good idea, being that the relationship could not progress any further than it already had. Even Marta wanted to meet Sherry, inviting them to Canton to visit her and her family, but Sonny gave excuses about why they couldn't go.

His visits with his mom always made him melancholy and indecisive about his suicide decision. He worried how his mother would react to his death. Sometimes that fear was enough to keep him from thinking about how to do it. But he knew, in the end, it was for the best. Marta would take care of his mother. Sherry would find a new love interest. Because she was so beautiful, finding a new boyfriend wouldn't be the least bit difficult for her. And the 10-10 would find another superintendent to take care of the building. Mrs. Feingold knew all types of people. It wouldn't take her long to replace him. Maybe that guy would even be more skilled than Sonny. Feingold would be better off.

So why not carry out his plan? He was determined this time it would work. Nothing could stop him or get in his way.

But how should he do it? He was running out of options.

The 10-10 had a flat, asphalt and gravel roof. Sonny had repaired it and given it a protective coating two years ago. He expected it would need another maintenance check next year. But that would be the next super's responsibility, not his. However, debris, such as leaves, branches, and paper, often accumulated on its surface and had to be removed. One time Sonny actually found a broken picture frame up there with the picture of a pretty, dark-haired woman in it, scratched and torn. How it got there, he couldn't say. He and Mrs. Feingold were the only ones with a key to the door leading to the roof.

On a blustery day after Christmas and his visit with his mother, Sonny decided it was time to clean off the rubble from the roof. He hadn't done it since last spring. The weather had been fairly mild for this Ohio week in December, and any snow that had fallen onto the roof had melted and dried. It was a gloomy day, but rain or snow weren't predicted for several more days.

The roof had a small metal shed attached on top of it adjacent to the door leading into the building. This structure held Sonny's supplies—a push broom, a regular broom, a large dustpan, leaf bags, plastic leaf claws to pick up the trash, clean rags, cleaning spray, a large garbage container, a bucket of gravel, and a five-gallon bucket of sealer for any quick repairs, and other useful paraphernalia to clean a flat roof. At one point in time, renters must have also lived in the attic of the 10-10 because a small working bathroom complete with sink, tub, and toilet had been built off in a corner. Sonny kept a bucket and heavy-duty soap in there.

The day he decided to clean the roof, he filled the bucket in the attic bathroom with hot, soapy water and carried it up the steps to the roof entrance. Setting the bucket on the top step, he unlocked the door. When he opened it, he could feel a brisk wind blowing. He grabbed the bucket and set it on the roof's surface, still holding the handle on the door so the wind wouldn't whip it shut or wide open. Once he set the bucket down, he was able to go through the opening himself and close the door.

Knowing it was going to be windy and cold, Sonny wore his heavy zippered sweatshirt. He pulled the hood over his head, tying it under his chin, and shoved his hands into the deep pockets of the sweatshirt. He walked around the roof, observing what he needed to clean up. Scraps of paper and dried leaves thrashed across the surface, flying in the air, then touching down at uneven intervals like skipping stones on a lake. A deflated balloon with a string attached was caught on one of the pipes protruding from the roof. A large branch with withered maple leaves still clinging to it huddled in a corner, held captive by the parapet wall, which prevented its escape from its sanctuary. An old, disintegrating newspaper was embedded in a soft tar spot on the rooftop.

Sonny walked over to the edge of the roof facing Oak Street. He watched as the traffic drove by. He glanced at the gas station across the street as customers filled their gas tanks, used their credit cards to pay, and then drove away into the traffic. A few people bundled in winter gear walked briskly along the sidewalks, hurrying to their destinations. He saw Arnie Hathaway come across Colleda Avenue, making his way to the entrance of the 10-10 Apartments and carrying a small tan, plastic grocery bag from the Oak Street Food Mart. Arnie didn't notice Sonny looking down on him.

Sonny walked the perimeter of the roof along the parapet and looked down at Cappy's parking lot in the back of the building. The lot had a few cars parked here and there. The parapet was about three and a half feet in height, hitting his body just below his waist. He rested his palms on the cold edge of the parapet, bent over, and looked down below. He was surprised how far down it appeared. Directly below where he looked was a pile of cement blocks hovered fairly close to the building. Hmm. That heap of concrete caused his mind to create a plan.

He needed another means to make those gravediggers at the cemetery shovel a spot for him. Right? This roof could definitely supply that need. Calculating, he figured the building, including the attic was probably about thirty-eight or forty feet high. That height was a substantial drop from the roof top to the ground below. What if he chose the exact spot where he stood with that pile of cement blocks directly below to dive over the edge headfirst off the parapet? Kind of like an Olympic diver who stoops on a diving board before diving into a huge pool filled with clear water. Only Sonny wouldn't bother putting his arms out in front of him, but he'd keep them tucked firmly at his side. Then he'd dive headfirst into those blocks.

No one parked in that spot because of the cement blocks taking up most of the space. Therefore, he wouldn't damage or destroy anybody's vehicle. It would be quick. Probably instant death. It would also be very messy and bloody. That couldn't be avoided. And he wouldn't have to be naked, like when he was going to drown himself in the bathtub.

His melancholy feelings melted away. He couldn't say he was happy or full of joy, but he was satisfied he finally had his plan. He would commit suicide by jumping off the roof of the 10-10.

His decision gave him the incentive to directly start cleaning the roof. It took him two hours to have everything accomplished including throwing out the trash and putting his supplies away. He was back in his apartment, enjoying a beer to celebrate his decision—his New Year's resolution.

Yes. New Year's Eve was a few days away. The perfect time for him to jump. Everyone would be out for a night on the town or partying at home. They would be eating and drinking and enjoying the camaraderie with friends and family. No one would have a thought or concern as to where Sonny was. Who knew how long it would take anyone to even find his body? After his sky dive, he'd land close enough to the building that the rays from the street and parking lot lights wouldn't reach his bloody corpse. People would come and go in and out of the parking lot for hours without noticing his grisly, mutilated body lying dormant on the cement blocks, its view being obstructed by darkness and vehicles.

He was invited to the Abbotts for a party on New Year's Eve. He told Al he'd be there, but he'd probably be a little late. All the other tenants were also invited. Once everyone started drinking, they wouldn't know who was there and who never showed up. A perfect cover for him.

When New Year's Eve arrived, Sonny completed his everyday chores early. He heard movement in most of the apartments as the tenants prepared for whatever event they were attending. Al Abbott promised he'd get José Cortez to help him bring Edie Mercer across the hall to the party. Al also said his daughter Lisa would be home from school, bringing one of her girlfriends with her. It sounded to Sonny as if the party would be a blast. Too bad he'd miss it.

The party started about eight o'clock. Sonny

actually helped Al and José with Edie. Since her wheelchair would be hard to maneuver through the Abbotts' doorway, he and Al made a kind of seat for her with their crossed arms clamped together. José helped Edie onto their arm seat and followed them across the hall with the folded-up wheelchair. It was easier than they thought it would be. Edie was a small woman, not frail but on the thin side. Therefore, the two men had no trouble transporting her. After Sonny helped put her back into her wheelchair in the Abbotts' living room, he went back to his own apartment, saying, "I'll see you guys in a coupla hours." It was a lie, except nobody but Sonny realized this.

Back in his apartment, Sonny dressed all in dark clothing: black pants, black turtleneck sweater, black socks, and black shoes. He had a black cap, but he didn't want to wear it. He didn't want anything hindering the damage to his skull as it hit the cement blocks.

After he was dressed, he straightened up his apartment, so no mess was left for someone else to clean up. He would, however, leave quite a mess in the parking lot, which would be much worse than any mess in his apartment. Then he did his usual pre-suicide kickoff: a couple of beers to build up his nerve, deep breathing to relax, and a self-lecture to convince himself of the necessity of his actions. He planned to jump exactly at midnight. Everyone in the entire city would be so busy welcoming in the New Year they would not see, hear, or care what Sonny was doing.

To be sure he'd be in position at exactly midnight, he left his apartment at eleven forty-five. As he reached the first floor, through the walls he heard the drunken, cacophonic noises from Cappy's Bar. It was apparent that the partiers were definitely enjoying themselves. On the second level, the sounds of merriment were even louder coming from the Abbotts' unit. On the third level, things were quiet. He knew Sherry would be at the party, waiting for him. Would she be disappointed he hadn't arrived yet? He felt a pang in his heart, knowing how much he cared for her. Was it fair to do this to her? He knew it was better to do it now rather than if their relationship had gotten even more serious.

He climbed the stairs to the attic. Here, he took a huge breath. This was it. At last. No turning back now. His feet mounted the final staircase to the roof, and he unlocked the door.

Again, the wind was blustery. He had to hold on to the handle lest it whipped the door away and slammed it wide open. He trudged up the final step onto the black surface of the roof. Immediately, he could see the lights of the city surrounding him. The sounds of the party revelers were more muted now—faraway laughter, heavy dance music, even screaming and shouting. He heard the traffic on Oak Street more clearly. Some revelers' horns were beeping prematurely. He walked over to the spot he had chosen for his final descent. This time, Cappy's parking lot below was filled with vehicles, even some double parked. However, he didn't have to worry about landing on any of them because his projected destination was not a marked parking spot.

He checked his watch. Eleven fifty-five. He looked over the edge of the parapet, searching around the area. He precariously lifted one foot onto the parapet, readying to hoist his entire body up to the edge for his fatal plunge.

But he hesitated. Suddenly, he stood perfectly still with his leg over the edge of the wall. He breathed in heavily as he cast his head from side to side. Did he smell smoke? He took another deep breath, drawing the air through his nostrils into his lungs.

Yes, he did smell smoke. Quickly, he pulled his leg back to the roof and looked over the edge again, scrutinizing the back of the building. *Smoke was coming out of a window on the second level!* That would be the Abbotts' apartment where everyone was gathered for the party. The smoke was billowing out of the kitchen window. Sonny immediately took out his phone and dialed Al.

It rang several times, then went to voicemail. Al probably couldn't hear the phone with all the raucous and celebrating going on. He left a message. "Hey, Al, there's smoke comin' from your kitchen. I'm gonna call the fire department."

No sense trying him again. It would just go to voicemail and waste precious time. Sonny dialed 9-1-1. When the operator answered, he quickly blurted, "There's smoke comin' from a second-floor apartment of the 10-10 buildin' on Colleda Avenue. They're havin' a party there. I don't think they know what's happenin'."

"Sir, are you okay?"

"Yeah, I'm not in the apartment. I'm, uh, at another part of the buildin'. I'm gonna go tell them about the smoke right now 'cause they're not answerin' their phone."

"Sir, you shouldn't go in that apartment. Wait for the fire department. It could be dangerous."

"Uh, that's why I gotta go. I gotta make sure those

people get out of there." He didn't take time to hear the dispatcher's response. He hung up the phone, shoved it back in his pocket, and ran to the rooftop door.

Sonny took the steps two at a time down all three staircases. When he got to the second level, he grabbed the fire extinguisher from the hall wall unit and hastened over to 2-0-4, the Abbotts' apartment, and pounded on the door. By that time, he heard the smoke alarms beeping out their deafening warnings.

So much noise was coming from within the apartment, he didn't think anyone heard his pounding or the loud clanging of the smoke alarms. If they did, they probably assumed it was just the sound of the celebration. Sonny pounded harder, but still no answer. On the chance the door might be unlocked, he tried the doorknob. Sure enough, it opened immediately. He rushed into the living room, seeing a crowd of people shouting and holding glasses of champagne and other drinks raised into the air, ready to usher in the New Year. Everyone turned to him. "Where've you been, Sonny?" "Hey, Sonny, get in here." "Oh, Sonny, it's about time you got here."

Sonny paid no attention to them. He pushed through the crowd to the kitchen, yelling back to the crowd as he made his way. "Get out now! There's a fire in the kitchen."

At first, no one moved. They were stunned or too drunk to realize what he had said. Al, who was not as drunk as the others, quickly placed his glass of champagne on a nearby table and followed Sonny into the kitchen. The sight they saw horrified both of them. The entire side of the one wall above and around the stove and the window was engulfed in flames. The window curtain was ablaze with pieces of burning fabric floating away and landing on other surfaces in the kitchen to ignite a new fire. Sonny immediately began squirting the fire extinguisher on the blaze. Al grabbed an empty pot sitting on the counter, quickly filled it with water, and began splashing it on other parts of the fire. Some of the guests came to the kitchen doorway. Sonny yelled again, "Get out, get out of the building, now!" The women started screaming and scurrying toward the front door.

Sophia and José had left little Mateo in their apartment with Sophia's fifteen-year-old niece. She yelled to José, "The baby, José. And Carmelita. We have to get them out, too."

José quickly glanced at Edie Mercer, who had the most terrified look on her face. How would she get out? He switched his vision between Sophia and Edie. What was he to do?

Tony Amato realized the dilemma facing José. He yelled over the noise and confusion, "José, you go get your baby and niece. Vito and I will take care of Edie."

Sophia and José rushed out of the apartment on their way to the third level. Tony and Vito made a seat with their arms like Al and Sonny had done earlier. Luther Jackson lifted Edie onto their arms, and then turned to get Edie's chair. As that foursome left the apartment, Luther yelled back to LaWanda, "Take Gardenia and Jamal outside away from the building."

Linda Abbott and Sherry Sweet clutched Arnie Hathaway by his elbows. Sherry softly instructed, "Come on, Arnie. We'll help you out."

Lisa Abbott and her college friend followed Theresa Amato swiftly out of the apartment. Addie and

Lexi had brought two young gentlemen to the party. The four of them made sure everyone was ahead of them before they exited the apartment. The parade down the staircase to the first level and out the building exit was orderly and swift. No one panicked. No one said much as they nervously concentrated on their departure. The fire trucks arrived as all the party guests were funneling out of the building and moving to the far end of the parking lot. Linda yelled to them, "The fire is on the second floor. Two men are still in the building trying to put it out."

The merrymakers in Cappy's Bar realized there was an emergency when they heard the fire alarm sound. They, too, exited the bar and gathered across the street away from the building.

From the parking lot, the tenants stared at the flames and smoke flowing from the Abbotts' kitchen window. The women were softly crying from emotions and smoke, dabbing at their eyes. Neighbors from the houses on Colleda Avenue began to assemble with the crowd. Someone had brought some coats and blankets and passed them out to the tenants, who wrapped themselves in the welcomed warmth. The temperature was below freezing.

Linda looked up at her apartment and started to walk toward the entrance to the building. "Where's Al? Where's Sonny? They should be coming out. Where are they?"

Theresa gently grabbed Linda's arm. "Wait here, Linda. They'll be out soon. They'll be okay."

But Linda wasn't sure Theresa was correct. They should've exited the building along with the others. She tried again to go back into the building, but both

Theresa and Tony restrained her. Her sobbing got heavier, and the seconds ticked away. Lisa and her friend came over to her mother. "Mom, Dad's going to be okay. He's probably just helping the firemen." But Lisa also had a very anxious look on her face. She, too, was very concerned.

Another minute passed before the outside crowd finally saw Sonny and Al helped out of the building by two firemen. Their faces and hands were covered with blackened and red skin, and they were coughing and spitting out smoke-filled phlegm. But they were on their feet. As soon as they were out of the building, paramedics rushed over to them, setting them on two gurneys, removing their burnt clothing, and cooling and treating their burned and reddened skin. After the initial emergency treatment, the medics escorted them to two waiting ambulances. Both men remained upright as they continued coughing and entering the ambulances.

Linda moved forward to follow Al and turned to her daughter. "Lisa, I'm going with Dad. I'll call you as soon as I can."

Sherry left the crowd of spectators and followed Sonny, expressing to anyone who was listening, "I'm going with Sonny."

At the hospital, the paramedics directly led Sonny and Al into the emergency treatment area. Linda and Sherry followed close behind. The men were treated more extensively for their first- and second-degree burns and given pain medication. Luckily, during the fire, Al had had the presence of mind to douse both of them with gallons of water that he poured over their heads and bodies. The ER doctor commended Al for his quick thinking. It really helped reduced the severity of their burns.

The patients remained in the hospital overnight and were told to see their primary care doctor as soon as possible for further treatment. It was undetermined whether or not either one of them might require skin grafts to their arms, but the doctors were of the opinion that they would not be needing them.

As for the 10-10, luckily, the fire was mostly confined to the Abbotts' apartment, primarily their kitchen area. However, smoke and water damage was significant in other areas of the 10-10. The restrooms of Cappy's Bar had a good deal of water damage. Sherry's apartment, which was above the Abbotts had fire, smoke, and water damage, also. All the other apartments had minor smoke damage that didn't destroy any property. Mrs. Feingold called in a professional cleaning team to fumigate, sanitize, and deodorize all the smoke smell and damage. The tenants were very thankful to Mrs. Feingold for her quick action. Most of them only had to spend a few days at the Belmont Motel in Liberty, which Feingold's insurance covered.

As for Sherry Sweet and the Abbotts, since their apartments had more extensive damage, the construction crew took a month to get their suites into livable condition. Their temporary living bills were footed by Feingold's insurance also, even though the fire was actually caused by the partygoers. Tony Amato had made his famous Italian sausage and lentil dish, which he cooked every New Year's Eve. It required a couple of hours of simmering time. Tony combined the ingredients in advance and brought it down to the Abbotts' apartment, placing it on their stove's burner to cook when he, Theresa, and Vito came to the party. Dominic was still at his camp retreat. Tony had turned the gas burner on low when he arrived but should have turned it off around ten o'clock. He and everyone else at the party forgot that task. Consequently, the mixture bubbled over, then boiled dry, the gas flame igniting the food that had spilled onto the surface of the stove, eventually enveloping the pot and the burnt, dried food within, and ultimately the surrounding wall. The fire was deemed an accident, but Tony was distraught for months, knowing it had been his fault.

Chapter Twenty-One

Sonny Dankovic did not commit suicide that New Year's Eve or on the seriously close New Year's Day. Like always, he was busy. Busy helping others. Par for the course, right? Where did that leave him? He was out of options. Perhaps he could have caused himself to be enveloped by the fire and smoke in Al's apartment. Easy enough. However, not so easy to do if he needed to actually fight the fire. Then when the firefighters arrived, do you think they'd allow him to burn up in the flames while they watched? No way.

Once again, he was out of luck—or perhaps, better said, in luck again. Saved by the bell, so they say— whoever "they" is. What was next for him? What was he to do? Eight failed suicide attempts. That had to be a record of some sort for anyone. He was out of ideas. He tried that old expression, "If at first you don't succeed, try, try again," way too many times. He was tired of trying.

He spent the next several weeks recuperating, getting his burns to heal and his breathing back to normal. He did only light duties around the 10-10. Besides, for a time, there wasn't much he could do, with the cleaning and construction crews taking over the entire building. Luckily, the smoke hadn't funneled down to his pad too much, and he was able to stay in his own apartment. He could slightly smell it at first, but it didn't take long for it to dissipate. It helped when he ran the humidifier for a few days.

During those days when Sonny was the only soul in the entire building and after the work crews left for the day, the 10-10 had rather an eerie feeling about it. The wooden floors seemed to creak a little more. The wind seemed to whistle in and out the spaces in the windows more than usual. He swore he heard rodents scampering in the walls. He went as far as to lay out traps throughout the building, but he never found any vermin in them.

By the end of February, everything was mostly back to normal. The Abbotts and Sherry settled back in their apartments with replaced appliances for their kitchens. New. Not secondhand, as they expected. Since the insurance covered all the damage, they didn't come out of Mrs. Feingold's pocket full of money. She was happy; they were happy—although Sonny had a feeling her insurance rate for the building would go up. Not his business.

Sonny didn't see much of Sherry during the refurbishing period. She would go directly to the motel after work each night. On Friday nights, he'd pick her up, and they'd go out to dinner. But since he was still sore, he went back to his own place after spending a short hour or so with her at the motel. Their relationship neither blossomed nor withered, but Sonny knew he had to make some important decisions soon. Sherry wasn't going to wait around forever for a commitment.

On a Saturday at the end of February, Sonny was drinking a ginger ale while sitting on his dilapidated, comfy chair, watching some TV sports program to which he paid no attention. He was trying to ease off the beer. His mind was on his future, or lack of. He was confident Sherry would get tired of their stagnant love life and search for something better.

But Sherry wasn't the only issue with which he had to make a decision. After all his failed suicide attempts, he really didn't have the heart or energy to try again. Not only that. He noticed since the fire that his physical strength had diminished. Would he be able to continue on as the super of the 10-10 much longer? Would he end up becoming his mom's roommate in the home for the disabled?

He set his ginger ale on the side table, letting it get lukewarm. He paid no attention to the sports program on the television. He was more despondent than he had ever been, feeling like he had no options left. What was he to do? As he grew deeper and deeper into a depression, he knew he had to come up with another plan.

"But what?" he proclaimed out loud.

Tomorrow, he'd go to see his mother. Marta was not going to be there. She had some event to attend with her son. Maybe he should talk to his mother about his problem. It wasn't that she would actually understand or be able to give him advice. During his last two visits with her, she barely spoke at all, and he wasn't sure if she even knew he was sitting beside her. Therefore, he really didn't expect any advice from her. But maybe just voicing his problems out loud to someone other than himself—just maybe that would help him make his decisions even if she couldn't advise or answer him.

He grabbed his tepid ginger ale and took a big swallow. Yes. That's what he'd do.

The next morning on the way to the nursing home,

he stopped at the donut shop and picked up two coffees, one black for him and one with double crème for his mother. She loved her coffee. He also bought a couple of French crullers, her favorite donut. He normally only took coffee with him. Due to her diabetes, the home frowned on giving her extra sweets. Sonny figured one time was not going to hurt her. Besides, maybe it would perk her up a little.

"Hi, Mama, I brought your coffee." He set his cup down and took the plastic tab off hers. It had cooled enough on the ride to the home, so it wasn't too hot for her to drink.

She was sitting in her chair next to her bed. Sonny had placed the cup on the small table he had pulled in front of her chair. She stared at the cup but did not reach for it.

Sonny then reached in the red-and-white paper bag he was carrying and pulled out one of the French crullers, placing it, and the tissue paper attached, on the table next to her coffee.

She looked down at the donut. Her eyes brightened up as if she were a kid given a brand-new toy. With a shaking hand, she reached for it, lifted it to her mouth, and took a huge bite. She set the remainder of the donut back on the table and looked at Sonny while she chewed, still with her eyes wide and bright. "Mmm, that's good."

Sonny smiled widely. He should've thought of this before. What harm would a single donut each Sunday do to such an old lady who was nearing the end of her life?

His mother picked up the donut again and devoured the entire thing without putting it down a second time. Then she took a gulp of her coffee.

Sonny went into her bathroom and brought out a wet washcloth. "Here, Mama, let me wipe the sugar off your face."

He gently wiped her mouth and her fingers. She smiled at him the entire time he was cleaning her. When he was done, she looked into his eyes. "Thank you, my boy."

He wasn't sure if she knew his name, but she knew he was her "boy." That was good enough for him.

Sonny pulled the lightweight chair on which he was sitting closer to his mother so he could use her table to drink his coffee and eat his donut. He didn't say much while he was chomping on the donut. Neither did his mother, but she still had a contented smile on her face. When his donut was consumed, he wiped his hand and mouth, took a few swigs of his coffee, and decided it was time to talk to her. She had said nothing more since she had thanked him for the donut. He moved the table holding their coffee aside, and he took his mother's hand in his. She stared into his eyes.

"Mama, I wanna talk to you. I'm kinda in trouble."

Saying nothing, her smile disappeared, and her face took on a worried look.

"I got a coupla serious things on my mind, and I need some help. I love you, Mama, and I know you prob'ly can't give me answers, but I need to get this stuff off my chest." He paused. "I hope it's okay."

He cleared his throat, which was still a bit irritated from the smoke inhalation. "Mama, I'm sick. I have CKD, which is short for chronic kidney disease. I'm sure you don't know what that is. Oh, hell. I don't even know what it is. All I know is that my kidneys ain't workin' right, and I'm gettin' sicker and sicker, My doc tole me I got to go on dialysis, which I guess is not a picnic. Somehow it cleans the blood, but I'll have to do it a coupla times a week. And that ain't gonna cure this CKD stuff. He says I'm gonna need a kidney transplant. If I don't get one, I'm gonna die soon."

Did his mother's expression change a bit? He wasn't sure. Whatever, he had to go on. "All kinds of crazy things are happenin' to my body. I'm havin' a hard time sleepin'." He pushed up the sleeve of his sweatshirt. "See my arms. They're real puffy. My legs are, too. Sometimes I don't feel like eatin' anything. And lotsa times I've been throwin' up what I do eat. It's gettin' worse and worse."

Still not speaking, his mother reached up and patted his cheek.

"Mama, I see this special doctor. He's a nice guy. He's called a nephrologist. He only treats people with kidney disease. I've been seein' him for a coupla years now. He says I got to go on dialysis until I can get a transplant. Problem is that transplant kidney has to match my body. If it don't, it ain't gonna work. So I either have to wait until somebody out there dies with my type a body or somebody who's alive is willin' to donate one of theirs to me. First, whose gonna die that matches me? Hell, I don't wanna keep wishin' for somebody to kick the bucket just so's they could gimme their kidney. What kind of guy would that make me? Besides, there's this list of other people who also need new kidneys, and they're ahead of me on the list. And second, what person who's livin' would wanna gimme one of their kidneys? What if they caught CKD or some other kidney disease in their good kidney? I sure would feel like crap that they gave me somethin' they really needed." He paused and sighed deeply. "Can ya see why I'm so confused, Mama?"

Sonny didn't expect his mother to answer him, but just the same, he looked into her eyes. To his surprise, he saw tears accumulating in the corners of her narrow, clouded eyes. Did she understand some of the things he said?

His confession was having an emotional effect on him. He got out of his chair and walked over to the window. It was a sunny but cool February morning. The snow from earlier in the week had all melted. Rain was expected for tomorrow. Outside the window, he looked at the barren trees highlighted against the clear, blue sky with branches like witches' fingers reaching toward heaven for forgiveness. A few patients bundled in heavy coats and hats were being pushed in wheelchairs around the property by loved ones or caregivers. He often took his mother outside when the weather was nice. Probably a little too cold today for her.

He turned back and gazed at his mother. She had been staring at him as if waiting for him to continue with his confession. He walked back to his chair, sitting down again, took a deep breath, and resumed his narrative. "The doc tells me if a dead person gives me a kidney, I'll prob'ly live for ten or fifteen more years. If somebody who's alive gives me one of theirs, maybe I'll live for twenty or twenty-five more years. Nobody really knows for sure."

Sonny was silent for a while longer, staring somberly at his mother. She stared back, unspeaking, the tears now channeling down the creases in her withered cheeks.

He leaned back in his chair. "Ya know what that means, Mama?" He hesitated again. "It means I can't do my job no more. I can't work at the 10-10 no more. What good is a super who can't do his job?" He paused. "No good. That's what. So how'm I gonna live? I can't do nuthin' else, even if I didn't have CKD." He covered his face with his large, rough hands and sighed heavily. "Takin' care of the 10-10 is all I know how to do."

A couple of minutes passed in silence, Sonny and Blanca, both overwhelmed and overwrought. Finally, he looked up and glanced directly at his mother. "And, Mama, I didn't even tell you about the worse part yet 'cause I don't know if you'll ever forgive me for what I tried to do." He was having difficulty finding the words he needed to say. "I ain't a good person. I did somethin' really, really bad. Not once but many times." Again, he struggled for words. "Mama, I tried to kill myself."

Blanca's face became as blank as a slate. Sonny knew she was upset. He knew she understood what he said. But as he shook his head and frowned, he continued, "Yep. Because of this stupid disease, I figured life wasn't worth livin' anymore. I just didn't know what to do. So that's why I did it. You know, Mama, I tried to kill myself eight times. *Eight times*! Can you believe that? But you know what happened? Every single time before I was able to do it, somebody in my buildin' needed my help. So I didn't do it. Can you believe that, Mama? Somebody stopped me from killin' myself every single time. They didn't see me doin' it, so they didn't know that they stopped me. But they did."

He leaned back in his chair, tilting his head and

closing his eyes. He sat without moving for about a minute or two. Suddenly, he felt a hand on his upper arm. He opened his eyes. His mother had grasped his arm, and in her raspy, feeble voice, uttered, "You go see Father Novak. Saint Vincenca saved you. Father Novak will get Saint Vincenca to help you again."

Sonny was shocked. His mother was actually listening to him. She knew what he had said. She knew what he had done and the dilemma he was in. And she didn't condemn him for it. She was the best mother a guy could ever have.

"Oh, Mama, I don't know. Father Novak is d—" He stopped himself. Father Novak had died several years ago. But his mother didn't remember that.

However, maybe his mother wasn't so wrong after all. Maybe Sonny should go talk to a priest. He hadn't been to church in so long he couldn't remember the last time he stepped inside one. But how could it hurt? As a kid, his mother took him and Marta to Saints Peter and Paul Church over on Covington Street every Sunday and sometimes during the week. His father would drop them off because his mother didn't drive. Sometimes her younger sister, Aunt Klara, would drive them. They didn't miss a Sunday unless someone was very sick.

But time and events turned Sonny away from the church. Maybe now was the time for him to go back. It couldn't hurt, right?

He turned to his mother. "Mama, maybe you're right. Maybe I should go see Father Novak."

Chapter Twenty-Two

Sonny kissed his mother goodbye and left the nursing home. He was amazed that she had responded to his admission. He'd have to bring her a French cruller with every visit. Despite his own issues, he was elated that she was so responsive. It made him feel so much better.

He knew he couldn't contact Saints Peter and Paul on a Sunday. The priests were much too busy with saying masses all day. He also didn't want to go to confession. He wanted to talk face to face with the priest so they could see each other's expressions. This was not a matter for the confessional. He had to be honest and open about everything. Perhaps down the road all his transgressions could be addressed. Right now, he needed advice in making decisions. Forgiveness was for later.

When he got back to the 10-10, although tired, he had a few things he had to accomplish. Arnie Hathaway's toilet was clogged. It probably only needed a few plunges, but Arnie wasn't strong enough. Sonny hoped he still had the strength to do the job. It should only take a couple of minutes. Arnie often had this problem. Some people are just more full of crap than others.

He also needed to replace a mini-blind in the Jackson's apartment. Then he thought if Sherry was home, he'd like to spend a little time with her. It would give him a chance to explain a little bit about what was happening to him. Just a little. He wanted to talk to the priest before he revealed too much to anyone.

Arnie invited Sonny to have a sandwich with him after he unclogged his toilet. As Arnie prepared the ham and cheese sandwiches, he asked, "So what's going on with you these days, Sonny? Haven't seen much of you lately."

He shrugged. "Nuthin' much. With those cleanin' and construction crews spendin' so much time here, they took care of some of my jobs for me."

Arnie paused while putting the cheese in the sandwiches. "Well, you know, Sonny, you don't look so good these days. Are you feeling okay?"

Sonny was not yet ready to tell anyone the truth. "I think I had a touch of the flu. I'm startin' to feel a little better today."

"Are you sure that's what it is? You've been looking a little peaked and puffy lately."

"Yeah, well, I'm gonna see the doctor at the end of the week." It wasn't a lie. He had an appointment with his nephrologist on Friday.

"Good. You got to keep up with your health, you know. You're a young man. Not like me. I'm going to be eighty-six this year. Can you believe it? I sure can't. Seems like yesterday, I was your age working with my dad at Youngstown Sheet & Tube." He paused. "My, how the time flies, doesn't it?"

Sonny and Arnie enjoyed their sandwiches, and then Sonny went to the basement to get the window blind and his tools to replace the Jackson's broken blind. After retrieving his gear, he went up to the

Jackson's apartment and knocked on the door. LaWanda answered it. "Hey, LaWanda, are you busy? I was gonna put up that blind of yours if you don't mind."

"Come on in, Sonny. No, I'm just cooking dinner, but I got it in the oven already."

As he followed her back into the master bedroom he said, "Sure smells good in here. What're ya cookin'?"

"Oh just a pork roast, potatoes, and carrots. It'll be done soon. Would you like to stay for dinner?"

"Awe, wish I could, but I just had a ham sandwich at Arnie's place."

"Well, how about if I fix you a serving for later?"

"Yeah, I'd like that."

Since the apartments in the 10-10 only had two bedrooms in them, the Jacksons' had cordoned off an area of their master bedroom to create a small room for Gardenia. Sonny had helped Luther build a removable, collapsible wooden structure to give both the married couple and the little girl privacy. Gardenia's side was painted pink, and LaWanda had drawn and painted princesses on the temporary wall on Gardenia's side. The other side was painted the same color as the bedroom walls, a boring beige. Luther and Sonny had even attached a sliding door to give them more privacy.

After LaWanda led Sonny into the bedroom and pointed to the broken blind, she returned to the kitchen to check on her roast. It took Sonny only a few minutes to tighten the brackets and replace the broken blind with a new one. By the time he'd gathered his tools and the discarded material, LaWanda had a container filled with dinner for him.

"Here you go, Sonny. Just put it in the microwave for a few minutes when you're ready to eat it."

"Thanks so much. I'm lookin' forward to eatin' it. Everything you make always tastes so good."

As she handed the dish to him, she tilted her head to the side with a worried look on her face. "Are you feeling okay, Sonny? You look sick?"

"Yeah, I got the flu or somethin'. Got an appointment with the doc at the end of the week."

She walked him to the door. "You'd better take care of yourself. You know, we can't do without you around here."

He meekly smiled back at her. "Oh, that's not true, ma'am. Anybody can do what I do."

At the doorway, she clasped his arm. "No, Sonny. Nobody can take your place. You remember that. You are one of a kind."

LaWanda watched him as he walked down the stairs, the concerned look still on her face.

Sonny threw away the trash from the blind replacement, put his tools away, and set the pork roast in the refrigerator for later. He decided to call Sherry to be sure she was home before making the trip up to the third level. Lately, the stairs were starting to get to him.

Sherry answered on the first ring. "Sonny, this is a surprise. What's happening?"

Shyly, he inquired, "Uh, are you busy with somethin'? I was just thinkin' of visitin' with you for a while."

Sherry thought his suggestion was rather odd. Sonny usually just came to her door. If she was busy, he'd come back later. Otherwise, she'd invite him in, and they'd hang out for a while. "No. Of course not. I was just relaxing and listening to some music. Come on up."

Sonny trekked up the stairs, a little out of breath when he arrived at Sherry's door.

"Come in. Come in. You look beat. Are you okay?"

"Oh I'm just a little tired today."

She looked more closely at him. "Sonny, you're more than just tired. Something else is wrong. What is it?"

He walked into her living room and sat on her couch, shaking his head. "Sit with me, please. I've got somethin' to tell you."

She turned her music down and sat beside him. "Sonny, you've got me alarmed. What's the matter?"

He was all worked up. How much should he tell her? She deserved to hear everything, but was this the right time?

She took his face in her tiny, soft hands. "Sonny, tell me. What's the matter?"

He knew he would be talking to the priest soon. Should he wait to see what he thought he should do? Oh, hell. Why should it depend on the priest? Sonny had to make up his own mind. It was his life. It was time Sherry knew the truth. Then, if she wanted to end any relationship they had, he'd know he wasn't keeping any secrets from her. He wouldn't blame her for ending it. After all, he had some troubled times ahead of him— one way or another. He didn't need to pull her into them without her knowledge.

At first, he didn't look at her when he started to speak. "Sweetie." He lightly shook his head from side to side. "I haven't told you everythin' that's goin' on in my life."

She became more concerned. "What do you mean?" Confused, all kinds of scenarios wrestled in her head. Was he going to admit he was married and had a kid? Had he spent his younger years in prison? Did he have an STD? Is that why they never had sex? What had he kept from her all these months?

Sonny turned to her and took her hand. "I'm sick, Sweetie. Really sick."

Oh God! She was right. He had an STD. Warily, she asked, "Uh, what do you mean, you're sick? Do you have the flu? I'll take you to the doctor. He'll give you some medication. You'll be fine after a few days."

He shook his head. "No. It's not the flu. I'm really sick, and I won't get better."

She dropped his hand and covered her mouth. "Oh, my God! What's wrong with you?" She started to cry.

He took her hand again and spoke in such a soft voice she had to strain to hear him even though they were sitting right next to one another. "I have CKD."

Confused, her face contorted. "What the hell is CKD? I never heard of it."

"It's, uh, chronic kidney disease. It means my kidneys have been damaged, and they're shuttin' down."

Her mouth dropped open, and she was silent for a few seconds. Then with more tears, she begged, "The doctors can fix it, right? Please tell you'll have surgery, and you'll be fine afterwards."

He slowly shook his head. "No. It don't work that way."

"What do you mean, it doesn't work that way? How does it work then? Do you have to take more medicine? Do you have to quit your job? What?"

"Well, I'm gonna see my kidney doctor this Friday."

She interrupted, "You've been seeing a kidney doctor, and nobody knows about it?"

Timidly, he nodded his head. "What good would it do if I tole anyone? It can't be fixed."

"Oh, Sonny. No. You should've told all of us. We could've been there for you all this time like you've been there for every one of us."

"I… I didn't wanna burden anybody with my problems. That's all."

She huffed crossly, "You didn't want to burden us? Sonny, the people in this building are not just people for whom you fix their sink, change their lightbulbs, or scrub their floors. They're your friends, and they all love you. You have done so much for all of us. You saved my life, damn you! How could I not care what was happening to you?" She started to cry very heavily.

Sonny put his arms around her and held her close to him. When the sobs subsided, she looked up into his walnut brown eyes, softly whispering, "So that's why you never ask me to have sex with you."

He slowly nodded his head again. "I didn't want to make a commitment to you, not knowin' how long I'd be able to keep it. I'm sorry. Oh, babe, how I wanted to rip your clothes off and touch every part of your body with every part of mine. But I didn't know…"

She understood. Sitting upright, she asked, "So what happens now?"

"Uh, I'm not sure. The doc says I need to go on dialysis for three days a week. That means I'm not gonna be able to be the super of the 10-10. I'm not gonna be healthy enough to do the stuff I need to do."

The look she gave him was not only one of sadness, but also of commiseration. "Oh, Sonny, how long would you need to go for dialysis? A couple of weeks? A couple of months?"

He shook his head and looked down. "For the rest of my life."

She jumped up. "What? No! That can't be. That just can't be!" She sat back down and put her arms around him, crying into his chest.

He patted and rubbed her back. "It's okay, sweetie. I'm okay with it. I knew about it for a while now."

She moved slightly away from him and tilted her head up to look at his face. "How long have you known?"

"Oh, prob'ly a little over a year. Maybe a year and a half."

"And you never told anyone?"

He simply shook his head, casting his eyes downward. She clutched him to her body once again and sobbed softly. He held her closely and continued gently rubbing her back, comforting her as much as he could. She broke away from him again. "I'll drive you to your dialysis. From what I've heard about it, you're weak, and you don't feel well afterwards. You'll be in no mood to drive."

"Awe, no. I can't ask you to do that."

"You didn't ask me. I told you I'd do it. It's not up for discussion."

"What about your work?"

"Hey, I'm the manager. I'll switch my lunch hour and take you then." She kissed him gently. "It's the least I can do for somebody who saved my life."

Chapter Twenty-Three

Sonny's appointment with the nephrologist was for nine o'clock Friday morning. He arranged to meet with Father Pavic, the current pastor at Saints Peter and Paul Church at one in the afternoon. Sherry insisted on accompanying him to his medical appointment. Dr. Demaris examined Sonny, then called Sherry in for the consultation. He explained to them that Sonny's condition warranted him starting dialysis as soon as possible at the dialysis center on Belmont Avenue. He put Sonny on a strict diet to help alleviate stress on his kidneys—avoid avocados, bananas, oranges, orange juice, apricots, tomatoes, spinach, potatoes, sweet potatoes, only no-salt canned foods, no dark-colored soda, stay away from wheat bread and brown rice, go light on dairy products, no processed meat, no pickles or olives, keep away from packaged and instant meals, avoid dates, raisins, and prunes and stay away from pretzels, chips, and crackers.

"Hell, what can I eat, Doc? There's nuthin' left."

Dr. Demaris responded, "Mr. Dankovic, these things are all bad for you because they are either high in phosphorus, sodium, or potassium, all of which will have an adverse effect on your condition. Try to avoid these as much as possible."

The doctor grabbed a leaflet from the cabinet behind him. "This booklet recommends the food items you *should not* eat and advises you of the foods you *should* eat, such as cauliflower, blueberries, sea bass, red grapes, egg whites, garlic, cabbage, bell peppers, skinless chicken, onions, radishes, turnips, and pineapples. All of these foods are low in the three minerals your body should not be digesting."

"Hell, Doc. This is gonna be really tough, man."

"I know, Mr. Dankovic, but we must preserve what health you have in your kidneys for as long as possible. As I recommended at your last visit. I think you are a candidate for a transplant. Have you considered this?"

Sherry, who had been quiet through all this discussion, finally queried, "Wait. Doctor, are you saying that Sonny should have a kidney *transplant?*

The doctor looked over toward Sherry. "Yes, uh, Miss…"

"Sweet. Sherry Sweet," she offered.

"Mr. Dankovic is definitely a candidate for a transplant. I recommended that he suggest to his family and friends to be tested for potential compatibility. That is the first step. If he cannot find a donor for whatever reason, either there is no match or no one has the desire to donate one of their kidneys; if that is the case, he will be placed on the center's transplant waiting list and will be notified when a compatible one is available for him."

"Does that mean he gets a number and has to wait until his number comes up?"

"Not exactly. He is in line with first come, first serve, but compatibility becomes the deciding factor. For example, if the available kidney is not a match to the person before him on the list, then it will be offered to him."

"How long does it take to get to the top of the list?"

"Well, that's hard to say. It often depends on the geographical area in which you live. However, on the average, it usually takes three to five years."

"Three to five years! Oh, my God! He could die before a donor is found."

Dr. Demaris didn't respond immediately. Then he offered, "That's why dialysis has become necessary for Mr. Dankovic."

****

For a while on the way back to the 10-10 in Sherry's car, neither Sherry nor Sonny spoke. Both were spinning what Dr. Demaris had told them in their heads. Sonny knew Sherry was upset that he hadn't told her anything about the transplant. After all, he had finally confessed about the CKD. Why didn't he tell her about the transplant possibilities? Well, he had his reasons.

Sherry certainly was upset. She had feelings for this man. And suddenly she found out that he'd been suffering with his secret for over a year. She simply could not understand how he could keep his pain and suffering to himself for so long. Didn't he know she cared for him? Didn't he know that every single person in the 10-10 was indebted to him and would do anything they could to help him through this crisis? Well, she would have a surprise for him. His secret is out.

As she drove, she briefly glanced over toward him. He was staring out the front window. "I can't believe you didn't tell me any of this, Sonny. I thought we cared for each other."

He took his eyes away from the scene outside and turned toward her. "I do care for you, Sweetie. That's why I didn't want to tell you any of this. It ain't your problem. It's mine."

Now she was angry. "Oh, don't you say that to me. That's where you're wrong. Maybe I don't have bad kidneys. Maybe I'm not stuck on never eating the food I love. Maybe I don't have to have my blood cleansed three times a week. But damn you, Sonny…"

She started to cry, tears blinding her and making it difficult to see the road. She quickly pulled into the service station on the right and stopped the car in a spot beside the road. She whipped her body toward Sonny. "Damn you! I love you, you big oaf, and it pains me to no end, knowing how you already suffered and the suffering that lies ahead for you." She covered her face with her hands. "And you shut me out of all that."

Sonny moved closer and grabbed her, clutching her tightly in his arms. "I'm sorry, Sweetie. I'm really sorry. I just didn't want you to get hurt."

She clung to him. "Oh, Sonny, it hurt me more not being able to help you." She released her arms around his body and tightly clasped his shoulders. She peered deeply into his eyes. "You have to promise me you won't keep anything from me ever again." She kept staring into his eyes. "Do you promise?"

He reached down and gently kissed her. "I promise."

They sat in the car at the service station for several more minutes, not speaking. Then Sherry broke away. "I'm going into the station and get us some coffee. Luckily, you like black coffee, since Dr. Demaris said to limit your dairy intake. I'll be right back."

While Sonny waited for Sherry to return, he thought about the last year and a half—all those suicide attempts and the stress associated with them. He sure as hell wasn't going to tell Sherry or anyone else about those. He could only imagine how she would react if she knew what he had gone through. That would be his and his mother's secret until the day he died, whether it be in the next few months or, if he was lucky, when he was eighty-six like Arnie Hathaway.

Sherry came back with the coffee. Sonny reached over and opened her door. They sat quietly for a while, sipping the coffee while the thoughts of the last hour bounced privately in their heads.

"Well, let me get you back to the 10-10. I have to get back to work. What time is your appointment with the priest?"

"One o'clock."

She glanced at him again. "Okay. I don't expect you to tell me what you two talked about. That's something that really doesn't concern me. But if he gives you any advice or any revelations concerning your CKD, I expect you to tell me exactly what he says. Is that a bargain?"

He touched her arm and smiled. "That's a bargain." He was silent for a few seconds. "Man, you are one pushy broad."

"Get used it, fella."

They both chuckled.

Chapter Twenty-Four

Sonny was a few minutes early for his meeting with Father Pavic. He went inside the church sanctuary before going to the church office. It brought many memories back to him. He even sat in the same pew that he, Marta, and his mother normally would sit in when they attended mass. He remembered the old priest, Father Novak, standing at the pulpit, his scraggly white beard that always needed a trim, his rugged face always showing emotions when he spoke. He remembered when Father Novak gave his homily how anxious Sonny was for it to end. He wanted to go play baseball or hockey with his friends. Why did his mother insist on making him listen to that boring speech? To this day he couldn't remember one single homily that stuck in his mind. He wondered if others felt the same.

When did he stop attending mass? He couldn't remember. Probably when his mother stopped forcing him to go, which actually wasn't until he had moved out of the house and was on his own. He just never had the time after that. Something else was always more important to do.

And now he sat in the same seat where he had sat so many times all those years ago. Years ago, when things were much different. His dear father was alive, and his mother was jovial, active, and very alert. And he was not dying from CKD.

He looked at his watch. Time to make his way to the church office for his meeting with Father Pavic.

The priest looked to be somewhere in his fifties. He was tall, muscular, but he gave the impression of being a gentle man. He was handsome with dark hair and finely chiseled facial features. Sonny assumed many of the female parishioners probably had a crush on him. Sonny hoped neither the priest nor the ladies ever acted on those crushes. It was a strange world he lived in.

Father Pavic greeted Sonny with a warm handshake. "Good afternoon, Mr. Dankovic. Please have a seat."

"Call me Sonny, okay, Father?"

They were in a small parlor with comfortable, upholstered gray chairs. Sonny took a seat near the window. Father Pavic sat in one next to him and tilted toward Sonny's chair. "What can I do for you, Sonny?"

Sonny wasn't sure how to start the conversation. This man was a stranger to him. He was able to talk to his mother about his illness because he had not thought she would even understand him. He was taken by surprise when he realized that she had understood. As for Sherry, he had a hard enough time talking to her, and he knew her quite well. Now he had to talk to this man. Actually, he didn't have to—it was his choice. But he really needed some spiritual advice. Thus, he had to get on with it.

"Well, Father, first off, I haven't been to mass in ages. It's been longer still since I've been to confession. But that ain't why I'm here. I'm sure you'll tell me to come back another time for that. But right now, I got some huge problems I'm dealin' with, and I'm havin' a hard time figurin' what to do about 'em."

Sonny looked down at his clenched hands.

Father Pavic suggested, "Why don't you just start from the beginning?"

"Yeah, you're right." He paused. "Good idea."

Sonny actually started with his birth and what his mother always claimed about Saint Vincenca, how the saint saved both his and his mother's lives. He went on to tell about his uneventful youth. He hadn't been a bad kid, but he didn't actually excel in anything either. He talked about his job as super at the 10-10. How he was good at it. How he enjoyed the work and the tenants. Then he told him about his mother's dementia and how it also affected and depressed him.

The priest continued to listen, not interrupting with any comments or critiques.

Sonny then brought up CKD and how it had worsened over the last year and a half. Finally, even though he swore he wouldn't, he told Father Pavic about all of his suicide attempts. With each attempt he told the priest how they were thwarted from being completed by some emergency with the tenants in the 10-10, mentioning his own responses to these emergencies that were often life-threatening.

Father Pavic had a very quizzical look on his face during that part of the narration, but he still said nothing. He thought it best not to interrupt Sonny. Questions and comments would come later.

Sonny told him about his relationship with Sherry and how he was afraid to proceed with it because of his disease. He told him he had just recently confessed this disease to her, that she was very upset, and wanted to be by his side during his treatment and even his debilitation. He also told the priest how his mother credited his foiled suicide attempts to the divine intervention of Saint Vincenca, and even with her dementia, she empathized with him and directed him to the church.

Sonny probably communicated his issues to the priest for about a half hour. When he finished his dissertation, he sat back in the chair, placing his feet flat on the floor. "So that's it. That's my story. I'd like you to help me make sense of all of this."

Sincere compassion shrouded the priest's face as he placed his hand on Sonny's shoulder. "Sonny, I am so sorry you've had to endure such pain and suffering over your lifetime."

He paused as he drew his arm away and folded his hands together. "Let's first address your birth and your mother's interpretation of it. I'm sure you're aware of how medical technology has definitely advanced over the years. How old are you? You look like a man in his thirties."

"Yes, Father. I'm thirty-six,"

"I thought so," confirmed Father Pavic. "It is possible that during childbirth, you and your mother were saved by these advancements in technology. It is also possible that Saint Vincenca intervened. However, I am a man of God. I know the powers of His hands. I cannot neither deny nor confirm that what your mother believed on that day was a miracle through the hands of Saint Vincenca with God's guidance." He paused again. "However, from your account of your experiences over the last year and a half—your suicide attempts, their abrupt failures because of the needs of others, and your actions to immediately alleviate those needs—this suggests to me, as your mother believes, that it is definitely possible that some divine involvement has been interrupting your attempts to kill yourself."

He leaned back in his chair. "Now you may choose to embrace Saint Vincenca's interference in your life, or you may choose to refute and ignore it. But, Sonny, you seem to be a reasonable and alert man. Don't you think after all you've gone through, it would seem unlikely that all those botched suicides simply happened by chance?"

Sonny looked bewildered. "I... I guess I never thought of it that way."

"What were your thoughts when all your attempts were cut short of fruition? Did you think they were all just coincidences?"

"Uh, I guess so. Uh, actually I never thought about it one way or the other. I only felt frustrated that I couldn't get it done and over with." He paused and looked down at his folded hands. "Yet at the same time I was glad I was still alive. And when that stuff happened, you know, all the emergency stuff, I just figured I needed to help those people no matter what. I guess what went through my mind was that after the emergency was over, I could go back and kill myself some other time. It's just that I never was successful. In the end I didn't feel like doin' it no more 'cause I was gettin' sicker and runnin' out of ideas on how to kill myself."

"And why is that? Couldn't you have repeated some of the methods you had tried before but was interrupted? Wouldn't your sickness hasten your desire to end your life?"

"Uh, I don't know. I guess so. But usually it took a

long time to get the critical situation under control. By the time I took care of it, I think I was just too worked up that killin' myself wasn't as important right then as fixin' the other person's problem. And, like I say, I just kinda gave up on it each time for a coupla months."

"You never thought to yourself perhaps there was a reason why you couldn't complete the task? Perhaps that something was stopping it?"

"Uh, no. Not really. I just knew that whenever somebody needed me, helping them was more important at the time than killin' myself. I could always kill myself the next day. Only I never did."

"Exactly!" Father Pavic raised both his arms and firmly shook them once. "You never did. You never completed your task."

Father Pavic nodded his head while looking into Sonny's eyes. "I believe you never finished the job for two reasons. Number One: Deep in your heart that desire to kill yourself was won out by your desire to live. Although you thought your future was bleak, there was something in you that said, 'No, I can't do this.' It was an unconscious thought, but it was always there. You knew your life was important to yourself, your family, and those many friends you have in your building."

Again Father Pavic stretched out his arm and placed it on Sonny's shoulder. "Do you see that, my man?"

"I... I don't know."

The priest removed his arm and nodded his head. "I think you do, Sonny Dankovic. I think you do."

Sonny bent his head down and placed both of his hands on the top of his head. He mumbled, "I guess so."

Father Pavic didn't speak for a while. He let his words enter into Sonny's head. Then he continued, "Number two, Sonny: I am convinced that God also intervened in circumventing your suicide attempts. Perhaps your mother did see Saint Vincenca at your birth. Perhaps God worked through her. It is totally feasible that God has other plans for you, and He assigned Saint Vincenca to help Him out. You may choose whether or not to believe this, but it is my belief that Saint Vincenca will also help you through the pain and suffering you are about to endure because of your CKD."

He leaned back in his chair again. "I know we are not in the confessional right now, but what I'd like for you to do is to go into the sanctuary and pray. Pray to God to help you with your impending battle with your disease, whether you ask for Saint Vincenca's help or not. God will guide you. Just ask Him."

Sonny removed his hands from his head and looked up. Tears engulfed his eyes and flowed gently down his cheeks. After a few seconds, he rose from the chair. He reached over and briefly hugged Father Pavic. After he released him, he held out his hand. Father Pavic clasped it in his. Sonny quietly said, "Thank you, Father. Yes, I need to ask God to help me. That's the only way I'll get through this."

As Sonny left the church office on the way to the sanctuary, he called back to Father Pavic, "I'll see you at mass next Sunday, and I hope to have you officiate at my wedding someday."

Sonny felt much better as he made his way to the sanctuary. He still didn't know exactly what he would do about anything—his CKD, his relationship with

Sherry, his mother's debilitating health, his job—but with God's help, he knew he would find answers.

He entered the sanctuary, sat in his familiar pew from long ago, and prayed.

Chapter Twenty-Five

After dropping off Sonny at the 10-10, Sherry went back to work at the dress shop in the Southern Park Mall. Her mind wasn't in her work. Her thoughts kept bouncing back and forth with what Sonny had told her, as well as what Dr. Demaris had predicted for Sonny's future. She had to do something. She had to do it soon. Like right now. But what could she do?

She knew Sonny had to start dialysis as soon as possible. She would be able to use her lunch hour to take him to the dialysis center, but Dr. Demaris said the treatment would last for three to four hours. She couldn't wait at the facility until he was done with the treatment. And she couldn't go back to work and come back later either. That just wasn't feasible. She needed to work. Her family had never been lucky to be financially independent. Her dad worked in the Youngstown steel mill until it closed. For a time, he commuted to Pittsburg to work in one of their steel mills, which was where he worked when Sherry was born. But eventually, those mills also shut down. After all the mills in the area closed, he worked odd jobs wherever he could find them. Money was scarce during those times. He passed away from a heart attack when Sherry was sixteen.

Her mother Christine worked at their cousin's restaurant on Belmont Avenue on the north side while

Sherry and her sister Stephanie were growing up. After her husband died, Christine had to work two jobs until her girls were old enough to get their own jobs and help out with family expenses. Enough money never suddenly showed up to pay for the girls to go to college. On a few evenings and weekends, Christine cleaned houses for the wealthy residents in Poland and Canfield.

Thus, Sherry had no choice but to work her forty-hour-a-week job at the mall. She started out as a clerk in a dress shop when she was still in high school. She worked herself up to assistant manager by the time she was twenty-one. Within a few years, she was promoted to manager. In that position, she made decent money, but no way could she take off work three days a week to transport Sonny back and forth to dialysis. It just didn't work that way for people like her who weren't independently wealthy.

But she had really come to care for Sonny. He was the kindest, most helpful man she had ever known. Sure, he was a little rough around the edges, but who didn't have their faults? Take herself, for example. She could have gone to college like she had wanted to after her high school graduation. She could have applied for scholarships or grants. Her math teachers always told her she was intelligent and caught on to facts and figures very quickly. But after graduation, she knew it was more important to help out her mother and sister by working full time. She probably could have taken a college class or two at night at the community college. But she didn't. And that was on her.

As she sat in the office of the dress shop, looking over some orders that had just arrived, she finally realized what she had to do. Yes. She was very fond of Sonny. But she wasn't alone. Every person in the 10-10 was equally fond of him. Well, maybe not exactly in the same way as she was. But each of them owed Sonny big time for helping them out of some type of difficult situation, all of which were very serious.

She thought back to the last couple of years: Sonny saved Addie Thompson from being killed or seriously maimed by her whacko boyfriend. Sonny kept Arnie Hathaway alive after a heart attack until the paramedics arrived. Not only did he take Sophia Espinoza to the hospital to have her baby, but he saved little Mateo when he was choking on a large bite of hot dog. What would Edie Mercer have done if Sonny hadn't rushed to her apartment to call the paramedics and go to the hospital to make sure she was okay, then even arranging for Linda Abbott to care for her during her convalescence?

And little Gardenia Jackson, Sonny tended to her broken body until the paramedics arrived to take her to the hospital. Then he followed LaWanda there to sit with her until Luther arrived. Then there was the Amato family. If Sonny hadn't found Dominic in that back shed, he would've died from a drug overdose. He never would've had the chance to enter his successful treatment program.

As for Sherry herself? She was so indebted to him for saving her from drowning in her bathtub after being knocked unconscious. What about the Abbotts? Actually not just them, but everyone else in the 10-10, as well as Mrs. Feingold—they owed their lives and their homes to Sonny. Had he not seen that fire coming out of the kitchen window, they might have all been burned alive or very seriously injured.

Her thoughts focused on that night, going back to all that happened. Everyone had been in the Abbotts' apartment partying and having a good time. Except Sonny. He wasn't there. He had told her earlier in the day he'd be at the party by ten o'clock. But he wasn't. Nobody had seen him until he burst through the Abbotts' door and rushed to put out the fire. How did he know that their kitchen was on fire? He had told her later that he saw smoke billowing out the window and drifting up into the sky. Just how could he have seen that? He either had to be back in Cappy's parking lot and looking up, or he had to be on the roof looking down. Neither location made any sense to her. If he were in the parking lot, he must have been planning to go to the tenants' parking lot and get in his truck to go somewhere. Somewhere other than the Abbotts' party. As for being on the roof, what possible reason could he have to be up there at midnight on New Year's Eve? It didn't make sense. She filed that thought in the back of her mind to investigate at a later time.

After revisiting all the ways Sonny had helped every single person in the 10-10, she knew what she had to do. She finished checking in the new orders and then went out onto the floor to make sure everything was going smoothly with the shoppers and the clerks. Then she told Tammy, her assistant, she'd be back in her office. If she needed her for anything, just give her a buzz.

When she returned to her office, she took out her cellphone. She had numbers for several of the 10-10 tenants, but not all of them. One she did have was LaWanda Jackson's number. They had communicated several times when LaWanda wanted to change her laundry day with Sherry. A couple times a year, they went out to lunch with each other when Sherry was off work. Sometimes Gardenia would join them. Sherry dialed LaWanda's number.

"Hey, LaWanda, this is Sherry."

"Hey, Sherry, how are you doing?"

"I'm doing okay, but Sonny isn't."

LaWanda's voice sounded worried. "Why? What happened?"

"Sonny has been keeping a very serious secret from everyone. I just found out about it myself."

"What is it?"

Sherry took a deep breath. She wasn't sure if Sonny would be angry with her for releasing his confidential health information, but at this point, she didn't care. He needed help, and she was going to get it for him. Like it or not. "Sonny has CKD?"

"What? What the heck is that?"

"It's a very serious kidney disease."

"Oh!" Temporarily, LaWanda was at a loss for words. How could something seriously be wrong with a man that was so strong and so kind? But she knew bad things do happen to good people. Finally, she lamented, "Oh, no! What will happen to him? Is there any treatment?"

"According to his kidney doctor, he needs to start on dialysis as soon as possible. He will have to go to the dialysis center three times a week, and the treatments take about three to four hours."

"Oh, that's awful! Is there anything I can do?"

"Well, actually, that's why I'm calling. I want to get in touch with everyone in the 10-10—maybe have a meeting with all of us—to come up with a plan to help him out."

LaWanda immediately responded, "How about if we have the meeting at my place? I'll make my sweet potato pie. That'll convince everyone to come."

Sherry agreed, "That would be great. Your pies will definitely be an incentive to everyone, although I'm pretty sure the people in this building would want to help Sonny in any way they can."

"Yes, I think you're right. Everyone in the 10-10 loves Sonny and appreciates all he has done for each and every family here."

Sherry asked, "The thing is... I don't know everyone's phone numbers. I remember when we had the issues with the laundry room, you called all of us. Do you still have all those phone numbers?"

LaWanda hesitated momentarily. "Uh, yes, I do. How about if we split the list? You call half of them, and I'll call the others."

Sherry replied, "I have Addie, Sophia, and Theresa's numbers. I'll call them. If you'd call Edie, Arnie... Oh, I think I have Linda's, too, but if you could call her, too, that would give us three each. Would that be okay?"

"Sure. No problem." There was a pause. "When would you like to meet?"

"Probably as soon as possible. I have a feeling Sonny will be starting dialysis maybe as early as next week."

"How about tomorrow night at seven?"

Sherry thought that would work for her. "Yes. That would be great. I'll bring snacks. Let me know if you don't get in touch with anybody. I could always ask them in person."

"Okay. That's our plan then. See you tomorrow night. And thanks, Sherry, for bringing this to my attention."

Chapter Twenty-Six

The next night, everyone—yes, everyone—met at seven in the Jacksons' apartment, adults and children. Dominic had completed his drug treatment program and was happy to be home. His return had brought a change in him. He was not so surly and aloof. Now he'd greet neighbors in the hallways or stairways with a friendly hello. His school grades had definitely improved, and it was hopeful he'd be able to graduate with his own class this June.

Tony and Theresa were so thankful they had sent him for that treatment and that it seemed to have worked for him. However, they remained vigilant in keeping a constant watch on him, hoping to catch any suspicious behavior before it got a chance to flourish. Dominic and Vito had also renewed their brotherly bond with each other that had waned during Dom's drug use. Their parents were extremely happy about this new relationship also.

Small talk took front stage as everyone arrived at the Jackson's apartment. Then LaWanda asked the guests to take seats in the living room. In addition to the regular furniture, folding chairs were set up to form a crooked circle so everyone faced each other. LaWanda and Sherry served the pie and coffee with Gardenia's assistance. Snacks were laid out so the guests could nibble on them during the discussion.

LaWanda and Sherry took their seats and ate their pie. As others were finishing up their plates, Sherry greeted them over the soft conversations going on in other parts of the room. "Uh, I'd like to interrupt to discuss why LaWanda and I have asked everyone here tonight."

All eyes and attention turned to Sherry.

"You notice there is one member of the 10-10 family who is not present this evening."

Everybody looked around the room. Someone asked, "Where's Sonny?"

Another said, "Oh, yeah, Sonny isn't here."

Sherry nodded her head. "That's right. He isn't here."

Several voices interrupted, "Where is he? "Why isn't he here? He's part of the building, too." "What's going on?" "Why wasn't he invited?"

Sherry said, "I've heard several of you comment lately that Sonny looked like he lost weight, or Sonny looked and acted tired lately. Well, all this is true. And his weight loss wasn't by choice." She paused and looked around the room, knowing everyone contemplated her with anxious eyes. "Sonny is very sick."

More comments of surprise and disbelief emanated from the tenants. Arnie said, "What's wrong with him, Sherry? He told me he just had the flu."

Theresa put her hands over her mouth. "Oh, my gosh. I knew something was wrong with him. I knew it. He hasn't looked well for a couple of months now."

With sadness in her voice, Sherry revealed, "Sonny has CKD, chronic kidney disease."

Again, comments flowed from the guests. Vito,

who really looked up to Sonny and hoped he could be as good a man as him someday, asked, "Wow! What is that? Can some kind of medicine cure it?"

Others asked similar questions.

Sherry put her hand up to halt the questioning. "I don't know the answers to a lot of your questions. But this is what I do know. Sonny's disease has progressed to the point where he needs to have dialysis treatment three times a week. This process uses an artificial kidney to remove extra fluid and waste from the blood. Sonny's kidneys no longer do this sufficiently. What the procedure does is remove his blood from his body, filter it through the artificial kidney, then return the filtered blood to his body with the help of a dialysis machine. This process takes about three to four hours and must be done three times a week for Sonny."

Again, expressions of alarm filled the faces in the room.

With an austere look, Sherry shook her head. Then in an imploring tone, she interrupted, "It comes down to this…" She paused. "Sonny desperately needs our help. He has helped each and every one of us in so many ways and so many times. It's payback time for us. What I need from you is a commitment to help transport him back and forth to the dialysis center. I know most of you have full time jobs, but somehow, we can make this work. I'm willing to take him on my lunch hour, but I can't stay for the treatment. So if some of you will step up and agree to pick him up when the treatment is completed, I'll appreciate it as I'm sure Sonny will also."

A cacophony erupted as every single person raised his hand and volunteered. "Put me down." "I can do it."

"Give me a day." And so on.

Both Sherry and LaWanda couldn't hold back the tears. These good people wanted to somehow pay back Sonny for all that he had done for them. Many of them had wanted an opportunity such as this. Tragically, here it was.

Sherry held up her hand again. "Okay, okay. Now that I know I can count on you, I'll tell Sonny his transportation to and from the center is covered."

A "yes" was proclaimed by everyone.

Sherry continued, "As soon as Sonny goes through all the paperwork and his schedule is set up, I'll get in touch with each of you to check your availability. I'm sure it will be within the next couple of weeks."

Thinking Sherry had completed her request, the group started talking and discussing among themselves. But she had more to say. "Uh, can I have your attention again? There's something else."

The room became silent, and everyone focused on Sherry once more.

"I regret to inform you that Sonny's kidneys will not improve. The dialysis is basically done to keep him alive. The average life expectancy for someone on dialysis is five to ten years, although many have lived longer. It's unpredictable."

Murmuring could be heard resulting from this discouraging disclosure. Sherry continued, "And his quality of life will drastically change. He's not sure if he'll be able to be the super of the 10-10 any longer."

Sherry wanted to boost their morale and also give them something more serious to think about. "Sonny is being placed on the list for a kidney transplant, which is essentially the last resort to save his life. I've done some research on this and also talked to Sonny's doctor. The life expectancy of a recipient of an organ from a deceased donor is eight to ten years. However, the life expectancy of a transplant from a live donor jumps up to twelve to twenty years. Of course, the donor has to be tested to see if he or she has matching blood typing, tissue typing, and cross matching. Just a few simple tests can determine if a prospective donor is a match. So that procedure is rather easy."

She paused as she looked around the room. She had everyone's undivided attention. "Why am I telling you this?" She looked down at her folded hands on her lap. "I'm telling you all this on the off chance that you might want to be tested to see if you are a match to donate one of your kidneys to Sonny."

The room was completely silent. The participants looked around the room at one another. Several seconds went by with no one uttering a single word.

Sherry interrupted the silence. "I know this is asking a lot from anyone. It's not like asking someone to loan him money that he could pay them back. This is something beyond anything else you could ever give him, and no one could pay back in kind."

More silence.

Sherry circled her eyes around the room. "Anyone?"

Still, no one broke the silence.

In hopes to invite others, Sherry attested, "I plan to get checked as soon as possible."

Then Luther Jackson cleared his throat. "Sherry, I'd like to find out more about this donor thing. Do you know what I have to do?"

Sherry's face lit up. "Actually, I have an

appointment myself with Dr. Demaris, Sonny's kidney doctor, to find out if I'm a match. If you're interested, I can see if you could accompany me on the appointment."

Tilting his head to the side, Luther looked at his wife. LaWanda nodded her head. "Put me down for that appointment, too, Sherry."

Soon, all the adults were telling Sherry to include them. She huffed out a short laugh, shaking her head in disbelief. "I can't believe the overwhelming support from you guys." She abruptly stopped for a second. With happy tears breaking from her eyes and her voice cracking with emotion, she sobbed. "Oh, yes, I can. I knew you'd all come through for Sonny. I knew it."

Sherry promised the group she would check with Dr. Demaris to see how they could all get tested for compatibility with Sonny.

The meeting broke up, and Sherry immediately went down to Sonny's apartment to tell him the good news.

Chapter Twenty-Seven

When Sherry went down to Sonny's suite to give him the good news she gleaned from the tenants' meeting, his door was slightly ajar. She gently knocked on the door, calling out his name. "Sonny? Can I come in?"

There was no response, but she tapped the door open and walked inside.

Sonny was sitting on his living room chair. His body was bent forward with his elbows on his knees and his head resting in the palms of his hands.

"Sonny?"

As Sherry grew closer to him, he took his hands away from his face and looked up at her. She was torn with emotion and concern when she saw the look on his face. She had never seen him like this before. He looked so defeated and sorrowful. "What am I gonna do, Sherry? What am I gonna do?"

Sherry immediately knelt down before him. She took his face in her two hands and lightly pressed her lips to his. "I'm so sorry for all you have been through and for all the anguish you have felt since you found out about this. I wish you would've told me about it sooner so I could have helped you deal with it. But now I know, and I'm going to help you through this, no matter what it involves."

She stood up and went over to sit on the couch. "I

just had a meeting with all the tenants in the building."

He raised his head and stared at her vacantly.

"Everyone in the building is going to help you out. We've all agreed to transport you back and forth for the dialysis. As soon as you find out your schedule, we'll take care of your transportation."

His eyes opened wide. "They'd do that for me?"

"Of course, they would. We all love you, sweetheart, and we want to help you. You've done so much for all of us, and we'll be honored to help you out for a change."

Sonny shook his head but said nothing.

Sherry suggested, "Come sit beside me, please."

She moved over to the edge of the couch. Sonny slowly arose from the chair and sat next to her, clasping his hands together and staring down at them. She turned to him, taking his clutched hands into hers. "That's not all, sweetheart." She paused as she looked into his deep, dark eyes. "We are all going to get tested to see if any of us are a match—"

Sonny jerked to attention; Sherry finished her sentence. "To donate a kidney to you."

He broke his hands loose, covered his face while his body became overwhelmed with loud, uncontrolled sobs. Sherry put her arms around him and held him close to her as he broke down. The two of them sat, unspeaking and unmoving, for several minutes. Finally, Sonny's body relaxed. He removed his handkerchief from his pants pocket, dabbed at his eyes, and wiped his nose.

Then he turned to Sherry. "How can I ever thank you and all the others? I can't believe that all of you are willin' ta gimme part of your bodies so's I can live longer. That's so much more than anybody could ask for."

She hugged him tightly. "Hon, you have done so much for all of us. You deserve our help."

They remained on the couch for over an hour, just enjoying the comfort of each other's company. Around ten o'clock, Sherry said to him, "Sonny, sweetheart, come up to my apartment and share my bed with me."

He faced her with a startled stare. "Are you sure?"

She threw her head back and laughed. "I'm sure, but do you think you're up to it?"

"Hey, I'm up to it. Whatever happens, I'm up to it. You'll know soon enough how much I'm up to it."

The couple meandered up to Sherry's apartment, holding hands while climbing all three flights of stairs. Sherry unlocked her door. She turned to Sonny, "Would you like something to drink?"

"No, no. I just want to take you up on your offer before you change your mind."

She smiled her sweetest smile at him as she led him into her bedroom.

Chapter Twenty-Eight

After a referral from Dr. Demaris, Sonny made an appointment with the Cleveland Clinic for a more comprehensive evaluation than Dr. Demaris performed. He was given additional laboratory, radiographic, and cardiovascular testing. Based upon these tests, the clinic placed him on the wait list for a donor kidney. If a living donor would be identified as suitable, he'd proceed to living donor transplantation.

Dr. Demaris also set up an appointment for the adult tenants of the 10-10 with a transplant coordinator so they could learn just what was involved with becoming a living donor. That appointment was also attended by Sonny's sister, Marta. It appeared that she and Sonny's last visit with their mother in the nursing home turned out to be quite an event. Mama Dankovic had actually remembered much of Sonny's conversation with her from his previous visit when Marta was not in attendance. And, as the old saying goes, his mother "spilled the beans."

Marta became very angry at Sonny for withholding information on his condition from her for all this time. Then the two of them had a hugging, crying bout with one another and their mother. Marta made Sonny promise to inform her when the tenants in his building were going to meet with the transplant coordinator.

When the tenants and Marta eventually met with

the coordinator, they learned all they needed to know to make their decision whether or not to get tested. As it worked out, each of them made an appointment with the Cleveland Clinic to see if they were a match to be a donor for Sonny. The first step was to determine their blood type. Sonny's blood type was O positive, which is actually the most common type, but also the type most in demand since it is compatible with all other blood types. His problem with having this type of blood was that his body would only accept a kidney from a donor also having O positive blood. His sister Marta tested A positive, eliminating her directly as a possible donor.

The others also had their blood tested for typing. As a result, most of them were eliminated also. Those whose blood type matched Sonny's were Arnie Hathaway, Tony Amato, and LaWanda Jackson. Sherry was very upset that she was rejected because her blood type was AB negative and not a match with Sonny's blood type. She had wanted to be the one to help Sonny. As for the three who shared Sonny's type, Arnie was rejected because of his age and health issues. It was not necessary to go forward with any more testing on his blood.

Tony and LaWanda took the next blood test, called a crossmatch test. A sample of their blood was mixed with a sample of Sonny's blood to see how they reacted with each other. This made sure their bodies didn't have antibodies that would attack Sonny's kidney. As a result of this test, LaWanda was eliminated as a donor.

The third test, which only Tony was given, was called HLA Typing, or tissue typing. This one looked to see if Sonny and Tony shared certain genetic markers related to the immune system. A high match wasn't necessary, but it would be good for judging the outcome of the surgery. Tony's results were not quite as good as if he were related to Sonny, but thankfully, the transplant team thought they were good enough to continue on with the surgery.

Since Tony was a willing donor with a compatible match, the clinic decided to go ahead with the surgery and not subject Sonny to any dialysis beforehand. Tony had to take several additional medical tests and procedures to make sure he was healthy enough for the transplant. He even saw a psychologist to be sure he was mentally ready for the procedure. He jokingly told his wife Theresa, "Hey, I'm sure I'm gonna be eliminated after I talk to that shrink." But he wasn't. The psychologist cleared him also. Perhaps he wasn't as crazy as he thought he was.

Sonny was so grateful to Tony and had a difficult time expressing his gratitude. "How can I ever thank you, man? In the future, anything you want from me, you just ask. And I mean anything."

Tony put his hand on Sonny's shoulder. "Sonny, do you not remember what you already have done for me? Do you forget if you hadn't found Dom in that shed when you did, my son would be dead from a drug overdose?" Tears were flowing down both Tony's and Sonny's cheeks. "I'm just paying you back for what you did for me. Besides, I got a second kidney. I don't have a second Dominic Anthony Amato."

The surgery was scheduled for the third week in May. Tony had all his tests done by the end of March. As for Sonny, he completely stopped drinking beer and smoking cigarettes. He also started a regiment of healthy eating, thanks to all the ladies in the 10-10 who cooked nutritious meals for him. They set up a schedule as to who cooked and what would be prepared on which days of the week. No more frozen dinners or greasy restaurant fast food. He also started an exercise program and ended up toning his muscles and ridding his body of unwanted fat and toxins. He sincerely wanted this transplant to work if he wanted to live a longer, more meaningful life.

He still kept up most of his duties around the 10-10, but José was also hired part-time to help out with any heavy projects that the doctor advised against Sonny tackling.

On the day of Sonny's and Tony's surgeries, everyone except little Mateo gathered at the Cleveland Clinic to support and rally for a successful and speedy recovery for both of the patients. Only two of them were permitted in the surgery waiting room. The rest remained in the main waiting area of the facility. Sherry and Theresa were the first to go to the surgery waiting area. Then throughout the four-and-a-half-hour procedure, Theresa was replaced periodically by another tenant—friend is a much better word. Since Sherry was now considered Sonny's official girlfriend, the others decided she should be the one to stay permanently in the surgery waiting room until the operations were completed. And since Theresa's husband was donating his precious kidney, it was decided that she, too, should be there more often than the other friends.

After what seemed like an eternity to especially Sherry and the Amato family—Dominic and Vito were also there—both Sonny's surgeon, Dr. Jenssen, and

Tony's surgeon, Dr. Mueller, came into the waiting room. Dr. Jenssen allayed their fears by saying, "The surgeries went well. Both patients are resting comfortably in recovery. Both will be transferred to the ICU when they are stable." Dr. Jenssen turned to Dr. Mueller. "I'll let Dr. Mueller inform you what to expect with Mr. Amato's recovery."

Dr. Mueller stepped forward and addressed Theresa, "Mrs. Amato, your husband went through the operation just fine. He will remain in the hospital for two or three days. He may experience tenderness, itching, and some pain for a few days. This is normal. Those symptoms will gradually dissipate over time. However, he should follow a normal, healthy lifestyle when he is discharged. Upon his release, he'll be given specific instructions on what he should and should not do, but I want to mention a few of these things to you. He shouldn't drive for at least two weeks. No heavy lifting or strenuous physical exercise for six weeks. Otherwise, his normal activity can resume. He should have no side effects after he has recuperated. I want to see him in my office in two weeks. Please call my office to set up an appointment."

Theresa smiled as Dr. Mueller shook her hand. "Thank you, Doctor." She was so relieved that the surgery was over, and Tony was recovering as expected.

Dr. Jenssen directed his words to Sherry. "If Mr. Dankovic has no complications, he will remain in the hospital for four or five days, depending on his medical conditions and needs. We'll get him up walking in a day or two. Once he leaves the hospital, he should start to feel better after about two weeks, but he will need to wait at least eight weeks before he can return to work and other normal activities. No lifting of objects more than ten pounds or exercise other than walking until his wound has completely healed, which is usually about six weeks. I'll want to see him weekly while he is recovering. He, too, will be given specific instructions and several new medications upon his hospital release. We'll discuss those things later in his recovery. As of now, he had no complications from the surgery, but we'll continue to watch him closely during his hospital stay."

Sherry thanked him and asked, "When will I be able to see him?"

"As soon as he is transferred and settled in the ICU, a nurse will inform you they are ready to let you see him."

****

Tony went home after a two-day stay in the hospital. As predicted, he was sore but in very good spirits. The friends in the 10-10 gave him a small welcome home party in the newly renovated apartment of the Abbotts.

Sonny spent eight days in the hospital and also recuperated as expected. For a few weeks after his hospital release, he and Sherry stayed in a hotel near the Cleveland Clinic to be closer to the transplant team for monitoring. When he finally returned to the 10-10, he was escorted home in an ambulance and taken to Sherry's apartment, where she could attend to his needs. She slept in her spare bedroom until he recuperated enough that she didn't think her presence in the same bed would be harmful to him. Of course, Sonny was of a different opinion. He would've been very happy if Sherry shared the bed from day one.

Sonny was given several medications, the most crucial being anti-rejection mediation, which he'd take for the lifetime of the new kidney. He was also given infection-fighting medications to counteract the effects of the anti-rejection medicines.

He had lots of visits from friends in the 10-10. This helped him to pass the time away. Both Vito and Dominic came by often. Sonny was so glad he got to know the "new" Dominic. He discovered Dominic was actually a pretty, good kid after all.

Chapter Twenty-Nine

About one o'clock on a Sunday afternoon a few weeks after Sonny returned to the 10-10, Sherry and he were relaxing on her couch, watching a major league baseball double-header on the television. He heard sirens in the distance that gradually became closer and grew louder.

Puzzled, he turned to Sherry. "Hmm, wonder what's goin' on. Those sirens sound awful close. Nobody called needin' help. Do ya think they don't think I can help them anymore?" He sat upright on the couch as he listened more intently. Sherry didn't respond but continued watching the game as if she hadn't heard his comments.

Soon the clomping of thunderous footsteps resounded from the hallway. Apparently, the apartment door was unlocked, because a mass of paramedics burst into the living room of Sherry's apartment. A gigantic man dressed in bulky firefighter attire bellowed, "Mr. Dankovic, you need to come with us immediately."

Startled and confused, Sonny sharply peered at Sherry, "What's happenin'? What's goin' on?"

Sherry said nothing. Shaking her head, she stood up and moved out of the way of the paramedics as they gently and swiftly put Sonny on a gurney and carted him out of the apartment, down the staircases to a waiting ambulance outside the 10-10. Sherry followed him into the ambulance and rode with him as the paramedics began taking his vitals.

Sonny looked thoroughly muddled. He felt fine. The last time he'd seen the doctor, Dr. Demaris said he was healing right on schedule. So what could be wrong? Did the doctors know something of which Sonny wasn't aware? Had they kept something from him? He kept asking the paramedics questions, but no one gave him any answers. Sherry stayed behind the medic so Sonny was unable to make eye contact with her or direct his questions to her. Besides, she didn't seem to know anything either.

Every time he questioned the medics, they also would not respond. One of them actually said, "Please be quiet, sir. We need to concentrate."

Sonny felt this situation was very odd, but it had to be some type of emergency about which the doctors didn't have time to inform him. Maybe he had contacted the paramedics directly because of the urgency. Eventually, he stopped asking questions and remained stationary while the medics did whatever they were going to do. He simply lay on the gurney with his eyes staring at the roof of the ambulance. Except for his heart racing a mile a minute, he felt just fine. What the hell was going on?

Within a few minutes, the ambulance pulled into a parking area and came to a sudden stop. The rear ambulance doors abruptly opened. Sonny raised his head as much as possible while the paramedics wheeled him out of the vehicle. When he was lifted down to the ground, he soon realized they had not transported him to Saint Elizabeth Hospital like he assumed they were doing, but before him was the main fire station on

Martin Luther King Boulevard. "What the—. What are we doing here?"

Again, he heard no response from any of the many firefighters and paramedics or Sherry as they rushed him into the building and wheeled him into a large room filled with about a hundred or more people.

This was very weird. He tried to sit up, but he'd been strapped down in the gurney. One of the paramedics saw him struggling and released him from bondage. As he sat up, with eyes as big as eggs, he saw every person from the 10-10 in a group in the front of the room. Even Mrs. Feingold was among them. He saw Sherry's mother, sister, and nephew huddled together. In addition to all these people, the mayor of Youngstown, the sheriff of Mahoning County, the fire chief, the state senator, and several other dignitaries stood before him.

Surprise of all surprises, his sister Marta was there with her two children, Jenna and Carter. Two wheelchairs were next to her. Edie Mercer was in one of them. With a huge smile on her face, his dear mother was in the other chair.

And the press. Someone with a camera continued to video his every expression and movement.

Two of the paramedics helped him off the gurney and escorted him over to the crowd, who moved out of the way to expose a row of chairs. Sonny was led to a tapestry, throne-like chair in the middle of the row. Others moved to sit in the remaining chairs. He hadn't noticed originally, but several more rows of chairs were set up in the room facing the row in the front. The rest of the crowd took those seats.

The paramedics forced Sonny to sit in the throne

chair. He was speechless while everyone took their seats. Then the room got very quiet.

Youngstown's mayor, Darius Cornell, stood up and grabbed a microphone handed to him by a young woman dressed in a gray business suit. Sonny saw the cameraman focus on the mayor as he turned toward Sonny. The mayor cleared his throat. "Mr. Victor Dankovic," Cornell glanced at the audience before him. "Or as your friends and family call you, Sonny, I know you are wondering why everyone is gathered here today. I'm probably not the best person to give you that answer. I'd like to ask Mrs. Esther Feingold to come forward."

The look on Sonny's face was one of utter astonishment. Why was Mrs. Feingold here? What does she have to do with anything?

Wearing a tailored blue dress with her silvery white hair in a perfect bun at her neckline, Mrs. Feingold came forward and walked to a podium off to the side that Sonny hadn't even noticed before. A microphone was already set up at the podium. Mrs. Feingold was a tiny, short lady, and a small stool was provided for her to climb closer to the top of the podium and the microphone. She leaned over and spoke into it. "Can everyone hear me?"

Uniformly, the audience responded with a "yes" or nods of their heads.

"It has come to my recent attention that I have a very special person on my payroll. A man who has done spectacular acts of courage, feats of physical and mental strength, and even lifesaving techniques on many people. That man has worked for me for many years. I have just recently been made aware of what an outstanding human being he is, sacrificing himself for others so many times. That man is the superintendent of my building, the 10-10 Apartment Building. That man is Sonny Dankovic. I'm not going to bore you with details that I only heard about from others who benefited from his kindness, knowledge, and dedication. I'm going to let them tell you in their own words."

She looked around the large room, focusing on a certain individual. "Addie Thompson, will you please stand and tell us what Sonny did for you?"

The young reporter brought a microphone over to Addie as she stood up. Addie tenderly looked toward Sonny. "Sonny Dankovic saved my life. I was in an abusive relationship with a very violent man. One day this man and I had an argument about some minor, stupid thing, which to this day I don't even remember. But it didn't matter. Anything could set him off. From an argument, it escalated into something physical. First, he just beat me. Then he grabbed a knife and stabbed me in my side. I screamed in agony and pain. Somehow Sonny Dankovic, who was three floors below me, came pounding on our door. Rusty, my abusive boyfriend, wouldn't let him in, but Sonny had a master key and came in anyhow. Rusty was about to attack him with the knife, but Sonny shot him before Rusty could stab him. Then he and José, another friend in the building, came over to attend to me until the paramedics arrived. If it wasn't for Sonny and José, I would've died. And that's not all. After I recuperated, Sonny assisted me in finding a roommate to help defray the cost of my apartment. Sonny is the kindest person I've ever met." She handed the microphone back to the young woman and sat back in her chair, taking out a tissue and wiping her eyes.

Mrs. Feingold spoke again. "Can Arnold Hathaway please stand?"

Arnie slowly rose. The young woman handed the microphone to him. "Listen, everybody. This man, Sonny Dankovic saved my life, too. I got a bad ticker. I thought I was being careful and doing everything I was supposed to do to stay as healthy as possible for an old man. But you know, as fate would have it, one day I had a bad heart attack on the steps of our building. If it hadn't been for Sonny's quick action, I wouldn't be here today. He saved my life, man. I owe my life to him. Not only that, but he followed me to the hospital to make sure I got treated right. Man, that guy is a saint, I tell you." With tears in his eyes, Arnie handed the microphone back to the reporter and took his seat. Addie, who sat next to him, patted him on his back.

After a slight pause, Mrs. Feingold called out, "Where is Edith Mercer?"

Edie's wheelchair was at the end of one of the rows of chairs. She raised her hand. The young woman brought the microphone over to her.

"As you can see, I'm in a wheelchair, and I have very limited mobility. Several years ago, Mr. Feingold had been gracious enough to let me have my apartment at the 10-10 renovated to accommodate my disability. However, one day I was being foolish and tried to reach for something that was beyond my reach. My chair, which I had forgotten to lock, tipped over, and I fell to the floor. It was late in the evening, and I didn't know who could help me at that hour. I called Sonny. He came up to my apartment right away. He called the paramedics and cleaned me up a little. He also followed me to the hospital. I ended up with a broken leg and pelvis and a nasty bump on my head. If it hadn't been for Sonny, I don't know what I would've done. Not only did he make sure I got to the hospital, but he also found someone to care for me while I recuperated. So I'd like to thank both Sonny and Linda Abbott, who is sitting next to me, for all they did for me." Edie handed the microphone back to the young woman.

Sonny was speechless. He couldn't believe what was happening. He had no idea how this gathering had come about. He continued to listen and stare as Mrs. Feingold spoke again.

"Where is the Jackson family?" She looked around the room until she spotted them. "Would you please stand up?"

From the opposite side of the room from Arnie, Addie, and Edie, the four Jackson family members arose from their seats. The reporter walked around to them and handed the microphone to LaWanda, who was standing at the end of the row.

LaWanda took the microphone. "Ever since my family moved into the 10-10, Sonny has been there to help us out in any way we needed. He's not only the super, but he is a dear friend. He never refuses any of us tenants, no matter what we ask. Today, I'd like to tell you about how he did something very special for our family." LaWanda hesitated and looked down at Gardenia, who was standing next to her. "No. Better yet, I'm gonna ask my baby girl to tell you about what happened."

She handed the microphone to Gardenia. "Go ahead, honey child. Tell the people your name and what happened." LaWanda moved into the side aisle, took Gardenia's other hand, and pulled her out also so others could better see the small child.

Lucky for the microphone because Gardenia's voice was very soft. "Uh, my name is Gardenia Amaya Jackson. I'm, uh, six-years-old. I'm in the first grade. I go to YPA School. My teacher's name is—"

LaWanda interrupted the little girl. "That's okay, baby. Just tell them about what happened to you when you were playing outside. You know, the truck."

Gardenia cast her eyes to the floor and frowned. "Oh yeah, I got hurt."

Everyone in the room smiled and chuckled at the sight of the cute, little girl.

Gardenia lifted her head and smiled at the audience, appearing proud of herself. Then she continued, "Well, Mama was busy and couldn't play with me. She tole me to go outside and play. So I went in the parkin' lot, but I got tired of playin' there by myself. I did a bad thing 'cause then I went out near the busy street. I'm not s'pose to play there 'cause there's lotsa cars and trucks that go real fast. But I did it anyhow." She stopped talking and looked down at the floor again.

LaWanda urged, "It's okay, baby. Just go on. You're not in trouble."

Gardenia looked up, and her eyes scoured the large room again. Finally, she began once more, "Well, I was playin' with my ball, bouncin' it and catchin' it, but this one time I didn't catch it, and it rolled into the street. I wanted to get it before a car ran over it. I thought I looked both ways like Mama taught me, but I didn't see that big truck. I guess it hit me. I don't remember.

Mama tole me that's what happened. I didn't know nuthin' till I woke up in the big hospital. And Mama and Daddy and Jamal, they were all there lookin' at me. And I had boo-boo's everwhere. They really hurt."

LaWanda stopped her at that point. "What Gardenia didn't tell you is that Sonny happened to be driving his truck nearby and saw the accident. He quickly parked his truck at the gas station across the street. He stopped traffic, told the driver of the truck to call 9-1-1, and then attended to my baby. He covered her with his own T-shirt, checked to see if she was breathing, and stayed with her until the paramedics arrived. As soon as I was aware of the accident, I ran to be with her and went to the hospital with her in the ambulance." She paused and looked toward Sonny. "Sonny joined me at the hospital shortly afterward and waited until my husband Luther arrived."

She glanced and smiled at her husband. "That's about it. Gardenia has recuperated from a broken arm, a broken leg, collapsed lung, and a bruised kidney. We are so thankful Sonny was there to attend to her until the paramedics arrived." She looked toward Sonny again. "Thank you, Sonny, from all my heart." She and Gardenia went back in the row and sat back down in their seats."

The room was silent for a few seconds. Then Mrs. Feingold began, "So many precious, heartfelt stories we are hearing because of one man, Sonny Dankovic. You might think you've heard enough. But you are in for more. This one will bring tears to everyone in this room." She paused. "Will the Amato family please stand?"

The Amatos were sitting in the row behind the

Jacksons. Tony, Theresa, Dominic, and Vito stood up. Tony took the microphone from the young woman. "I got to tell you that Sonny Dankovic is a saint. I really mean that. I will never be able to thank him enough for what he did for my family."

Dominic Amato was standing beside his dad. He tapped him on the shoulder." Dad, can I tell them what happened?"

Tony tenderly turned to his son. "Sure, son." He handed the microphone to Dominic.

"So about a year ago, my life was a mess. I was doin' drugs and drinkin' so much. I was high or drunk just about every day and gettin' in all kinds of trouble. And the dudes I was runnin' with were just like me. And I had an attitude. Oh, man, did I have an attitude! I was down on the world and everybody in it. If anybody would talk to me, maybe just to say 'hello' or something like that, I'd look at them as if they were scum and didn't deserve to even be in my presence. Man, did I have it wrong! To make a long story short, one night I was really down. I broke into the shed in the back of the building; A couple a homies joined me. They had some heavy duty smack we were gonna use. I don't really remember much after I started shooting up. It's all a blur. The first thing I remember was being in the hospital staring up at my mom and dad. When I found out what had happened, that Sonny had found me with the needle still in my arm, I really didn't care. I kinda thought, what's the difference? My life was a mess. Who would care if I died? But, oh man, was I wrong."

Dominic smiled warmly at his dad and then put his arm around his mother, hugging her tightly. "These two people, my beautiful parents, love me with all their hearts. And I had been breaking their hearts. Well, after I got out of the hospital, they put me in a program that straightened me out and showed me how destructive was the lifestyle I was living. Now I'm enrolled in a barber school, and I'll be taking my exam very soon. Most important, I've been clean ever since I got out of the hospital." He hesitated and pointed toward the front of the room. "And guess who I owe my life to now? That man up there, Sonny Dankovic. He saved my life. If he hadn't found me when he did, I'd be dead, and my parents would spend the rest of their lives grieving my loss."

By this time there probably wasn't a dry eye in the entire room. For several seconds, no one spoke. Tony handed the microphone back to the young woman.

Suddenly, Sonny stood up from his throne. "Wait one minute, Dominic, Tony. Aren't you leavin' somethin' out here? Sure, I might have saved your life. That was easy. All I did was get you to the hospital. No big deal. But your dad, you, Tony. I will never be able to thank you for givin' me a part of you, a part so precious that it's given me a new lease on life. *I'm* the one who needs to thank *you*." Sonny sat back down and buried his face in his hands. Sherry, sitting next to him, rubbed his back with her left hand while dabbing away tears with her right.

With her voice emotionally cracking, Mrs. Feingold uttered, "Perhaps we should take a break right now." She got down from the stool, walked over to Sonny, and kissed him on the cheek.

The assembly took a fifteen-minute break. Coffee, water, and cookies had been laid out in the back of the room. Many gathered to grab a drink and a tasty cookie. After emotions had settled, everyone went back to their seats, and Mrs. Feingold stepped back up to the podium. The audience gradually became quiet. "I know I saw that darling little Mateo somewhere. José, Sophia, would you please stand up?"

The reporter carrying the microphone handed it toward the standing couple. Seeming a little nervous, Sophia took it from her and spoke clearly and with determination. "Uh, Sonny saved my baby, Mateo, from choking to death on a stupid piece of meat. Sonny was able to dislodge it from Mateo's throat before the paramedics even arrived. They took him to the hospital just to make sure he was okay. My baby also has what they call neonatal hypothyroidism. His thyroid gland didn't work right when he was born. So he's been back and forth in the hospital many times since he was born. But he's doing fine now. And Sonny has helped us many times since my boyfriend works late so much." She gave a big smile in Sonny's direction. "Actually, Sonny drove me to the hospital the night Mateo was born, and he waited there until José arrived after he was able to get off work. So this family has a lot to thank Sonny for." She sat back down and placed Mateo on her lap.

Mrs. Feingold talked into her microphone. "Now I'd like to turn this gathering over to Sherry Sweet, Sonny's girlfriend." Mrs. Feingold stepped down from the stool.

As Sherry came over to the podium, the two women briefly hugged each other. Then Sherry pushed the stool aside and adjusted the microphone to her height. "I have two things I'd like to tell you about this special man in my life, Sonny Dankovic. The first thing is that he also saved *my* life, physically *and* emotionally. As for physically, several months ago, I slipped in my bathtub, hit my head, and was unconscious with water streaming into my nose and mouth. Sonny came to my rescue. The water overflowed and leaked through the floor to the Abbotts' apartment below mine. They alerted Sonny of the leak. He rushed to my apartment to find my unconscious body draped over the tub. He gave me CPR and got me breathing again, emptying my lungs of all the water I had swallowed. That's how he saved my physical life, for which I can never repay him enough. As for my emotional life, over the past few months, he has captured my heart totally. I'm just so lucky he feels the same way about me. He is the most wonderful, kindest person I've ever met." Again, tears were glassing over Sherry's eyes.

"Now I'd like to tell you how he saved all of our lives at the same time. Not only our lives but our home—the 10-10 building. I'm sure all you firemen will remember this. It happened last New Year's Eve. Except for Sonny, all the adults in the building were attending a party in the Abbotts' apartment. It was noisy; it was fun; we were all lost in the moment. Food was cooking on the stove in the kitchen, but everyone was oblivious to the odors coming from that room. Suddenly, Sonny burst into the apartment and told everyone to get out at once. There was a fire in the kitchen. How he knew this, I still don't know, but we all heeded his warning. He and Al Abbott stayed behind working on putting out the fire until the fire department arrived. Thanks to Sonny and the other fine tenants in the 10-10, everyone was safely evacuated. Had it not been for his quick action, I know the outcome of that tragedy would have been very different. We all could have died."

She paused, looked around the room at her fellow tenants, then back to Sonny. "He saved *all* of our lives." She began to vigorously clap her hands. The entire audience stood up and joined her.

When the clapping slowed and the audience took their seats, Mayor Cornell remained standing and retrieved a microphone. He had been seated next to Sonny on the opposite side from Sherry. He began, "This special event and awards ceremony is sponsored by the state Fire Marshal and the Ohio Department of Public Safety, as well as the City of Youngstown Chamber of Commerce. It was convened expressly for the purpose of awarding the esteemed Medal of Valor to a very worthy individual. Normally, this medal is given to a firefighter for performing above and beyond the call of duty at extreme personal risk and having been instrumental in rescuing and saving another person's life. But today, we are honoring a private citizen with the Medal of Valor Award and inducting this individual into the Ohio Fire Service Hall of Fame. However, Sonny Dankovic's actions and deeds have checked every single criterion to merit receiving this award."

The fire chief handed a small box containing the Medal of Valor to the mayor. Mayor Cornell took the medal, turned to the audience, and suggested, "Would everyone please stand?"

Chairs rumbled and scraped as the crowd arose.

"Victor Anton Dankovic, better known to all by

Sonny, I would like to present you with this Medal of Valor, which you have earned countless times for your efforts in saving lives and property, ignoring your own personal risk over and over. Sonny Dankovic, your name will now be entered into the Ohio Fire Service Hall of Fame. Congratulations." The mayor handed the medal to Sonny.

Bewildered, Sonny accepted the medal amidst loud applause and cheers. Then the mayor, the fire chief, and all the dignitaries came over to shake his hand. When they moved aside, friends and strangers then came over to congratulate him.

Sonny's head was spinning. All this pomp and circumstance. All this fuss. He was overwhelmed with so many different emotions—and not all good ones. They were talking, clapping, praising, and cheering for him, Sonny Dankovic. But why?

He certainly didn't deserve anything special, especially this sacred honor. Each of those incidents was preceded by a hideous incident of which he had only told his mother and the priest. If any of those suicide attempts had been accomplished, he would have successfully committed a mortal sin, damning his soul for eternity. How would all these friends and important bigwigs feel about him then? He felt he was not worthy of all this praise and glory. He was a fraud. It was only by accident that he had saved them when, in reality, he was trying to do the most dastard of deeds by killing himself.

Mayor Cornell asked Sonny, "Would you like to say a few words to the audience?"

What should he do? How could he stand in front of all these people praising him as if he had done something superhuman when all the while he was a complete fraud, a con man? But he had to say and do something. Right? It was his duty to thank all these people for their kind words and the honor they bestowed upon him whether he deserved it or not.

He took the microphone from the mayor. The audience quieted. Haltingly, he began, "I...I'd like to thank everybody for their kind words. I...I feel I don't deserve this great honor." Again, he hesitated. "But thank you anyhow." He returned the microphone to the mayor and sat down in his chair, hanging his head.

Sherry noticed Sonny's very strange actions. She whispered in his ear, "Are you all right, honey?"

He could only shake his head in response.

The audience thought Sonny was overcome with emotion and was unable to express himself. Getting ready to leave the venue, they began to break up, everyone saying good-bye to Sonny on their way out. He would wave or simply mutter, "Bye." When his sister Marta, wheeling his mother in her wheelchair, approached him, he jumped up, "Can I go back with you and Mama?"

Marta couldn't hide her surprise. "Uh, of course, Sonny."

Sherry, not knowing what was going on, asked, "Do you mind if I come with you?" The plan had been for her and Sonny to ride back to the 10-10 with Mrs. Feingold.

Marta was really confused. "Uh, yeah, I guess so. Okay."

Sherry rushed over to inform Mrs. Feingold of the change of plans.

The room was mostly emptied out by then. Arnie

Hathaway and Edie Mercer had ridden with Al and Linda Abbott, who were helping the older couple out to their SUV. "See you later, guys," Al called back as they went out the door.

Sherry latched onto Sonny's arm, and Marta, her mother, and her two children made their way to Marta's vehicle. Sherry and Marta got the older lady into the front seat. The kids went into the way-back, and Sherry and Sonny sat in the back seat. When everyone was situated, Marta drove away.

Chapter Thirty

On the way to Blanca's nursing home in Marta's minivan, no one spoke for a few minutes after she pulled away from the fire station. But Marta also knew something was wrong with Sonny. He was acting very weird. Normally, after receiving such praise and accolades from the community, Sonny, though humble, would have been more talkative and outgoing. Finally, without taking her eyes off the road, she asked, "What's going on, Sonny?"

Staring out the back seat window, he didn't immediately respond.

Marta prodded, "Come on, Sonny, I know something isn't right? Why are you acting so odd?"

Sherry clutched Sonny's hand. "Please tell us what's wrong, honey?"

Eventually, he turned away from the window and stared at Sherry. His eyes were moist, and the corners of his mouth crept downward as if he was about to burst into a heartfelt crying spell. He looked miserable. "I can't talk right now. Gimme a little time, okay?"

Both Marta and Sherry almost simultaneously uttered, "Sure, Sonny. Okay."

Marta drove to the nursing home and parked the minivan. She and Sherry removed the wheelchair from the back compartment, and they helped her mother into the chair. The kids in the way-back moved the back seat so they could also scramble out. Sonny exited the vehicle and stood staring at the activity taking place as everyone left the vehicle.

Carter, Marta's son, hurriedly asked, "Can I push Grandma? Please?"

Marta relinquished the back of the wheelchair to Carter but walked along beside him with Jenna close behind. Sherry walked over to Sonny, took his hand, and silently led him into the facility.

Once in their mother's room, Sherry helped Marta get her mother situated in her comfortable chair. It had been a long day for her. She looked very tired but still somewhat alert. Marta didn't know just how much of the past few hours her mother had understood, but she could tell her mother had definitely enjoyed the outing and the festivities and was fairly certain she knew it was all in Sonny's honor.

When her grandmother was settled and the other adults had sat down in the available seats, Jenna asked her mother, "Mommy, can we go outside? It's boring in here."

Carter also chimed in, "Yeah, Mom. My softball and gloves are in the van. Can Jenna and I go out and play catch?"

The parking area was outside the window of her mother's room. "Okay," Marta answered. "I'll open the back hatch. Be sure to lock it when you're done. And stay out of the parking lot. Play in the grassy area away from all the cars."

The kids went outside. When Marta saw them near her van, she pressed the remote to unlock it. She saw Carter grab the ball and gloves and take off to the grassy area. Then she made certain the van was relocked.

After the kids were gone and she was settled back in her chair, Marta demanded, "Okay, Sonny, time to 'fess up. What's going on with you? You aren't acting the way a proud man should be acting."

Sonny didn't know where to start. Or how to explain what he was feeling. Or even if he should tell them. But Marta was his sister and Sherry was the woman he loved. And his mother, whether or not she'd understand, definitely should be given some explanation. Maybe they deserved to know. Maybe not. But he had to explain himself, somehow, about why he had acted so peculiarly.

He started out in a quiet, sullen voice, "I don't deserve any of this. All this attention. All this praise and love. I'm a fraud." He looked up at the ceiling and closed his eyes.

"What the heck are you talking about?" questioned Marta. "You helped all those people. You saved so many lives. You've always been that kind of a person. Even when we were young. You were always the guy to help anybody in need. Remember when all those kids kept teasing Crazy Mary, that old lady who lived down the street from us? You chased them away from her every single time you saw them near her. And what about Sammy Hancock? Even your friends picked on him. The poor kid couldn't help how he looked. But you made everybody stop picking on him."

Marta addressed Sherry, "Sammy was burned in a fire when he was about five. His face was a mess. All the kids bullied him. The poor kid went home from school every day, running and crying until Sonny put a stop to it." She chuckled. "Hah, Sonny threatened anybody that bothered Sammy with tying them to a tree and pissing on them. He would've done it, too. But the other kids were afraid of him. Sonny was a tough dude back then. And they knew he was serious."

Sherry smiled and glanced over at Sonny, who was just staring into space.

Marta looked back at Sonny. "What do you mean you don't deserve to be honored for your outstanding deeds? If you ask me, it's about time somebody recognized what a great guy you are. Even if you are my brother."

Sonny still didn't respond.

Marta urged, "Sonny? Come on. Talk to us."

Sherry intervened, "Please, Sonny. Tell us. I've never seen you like this before. Something is really bothering you. Please tell us."

He shook his head before he spoke. He looked at his mother. "Mama knows."

Surprised, Marta stared at her mother, "Mama knows what? How can Mama know anything?"

"She does 'cause I tole her, and she understood what I tole her."

The confusion was all over Marta's face. "Sonny, you're not making any sense here." Still looking at her mother with compassion, she signed, "Mama is... Well, you know."

He simply said, "She knows what I did."

Sherry took his hand. "Whatever you told your mother, you can tell us, honey. We're not here to judge you. We just want your pain to go away. Maybe we can help with that."

He looked at Sherry. "I told the priest, too."

Both Marta and Sherry's eyes and mouths opened

wide. Sherry was the first to speak, "You told the priest?"

"Yeah."

Marta countered, "No, you didn't. You haven't been to mass in years,"

Sherry persisted, "I don't want you to tell us something you told the priest in confidence, but obviously, whatever it was is still eating at you."

All he said was, "Yeah, it is."

Neither Sherry nor Marta knew how to respond to this admission. The room was quiet for several seconds.

Suddenly, his mother shouted in a volume of which no one thought she was capable. "Saint Vincenca. She saved him. She saved my boy."

Marta gawked at her mother. "Mama, what are you talking about?"

Blanca responded, "Saint Vincenca saved him so he could save others. She watches over him every day. Every day of his life. My boy is blessed. She saved him every time."

Marta turned to Sonny for an explanation. "What is Mama talking about? She's not making any sense. What does she mean that Saint Vincenca saved you every time? Every time when?"

"Okay, okay, I'll tell you," he said.

He cleared his throat and told his sister and his sweetheart about all his suicide attempts. He didn't go into great detail about how he felt while he was attempting to perform those deadly acts, but he made a point of telling them that they were specifically attempted because of his pending health issues at the time. And, like his mother professed, each time he tried to kill himself, he was interrupted by an emergency that needed his immediate attention.

When he completed his confession, Marta and Sherry were speechless. They stared at him incredulously.

Blanca had listened to his every word for the second time. This woman whose mind was being destroyed by the horrors of dementia still felt that her son was part of a miracle, that the hands of God through Saint Vincenca had watched over him, and had given him the power, the will, and the capacity to help so many others in need. And regardless of the disease eating at her aging brain, she still knew how special her son was.

Growing tired but still alert, at Sonny's conclusion of his confession, Blanca murmured, "She saved my boy so he could save others. Yes, she did."

Bewildered, Marta and Sherry had a difficult time reconciling Sonny's confession and Blanca's explanation. Sherry implored, "Are you telling us that you tried to kill yourself eight times and the only reason you didn't succeed was because you were inadvertently stopped by somebody else's emergency?"

At Sonny's nod, Sherry uttered. "I don't know what to say."

Marta also was dumbstruck and without words. Thus, no one spoke for at least a minute.

Suddenly, Blanca proclaimed, "I'm tired now. Can I go to my bed?"

The other three quickly jumped up and moved over to Blanca, who had a huge smile on her face as they placed her in her bed, and she rested her head on her pillow.

Chapter Thirty-One

Marta drove Sonny and Sherry back to the 10-10. The adults said little to one another on the ride. The kids chattered back and forth, and the adults would join in with their conversations, but it seemed Sonny, Marta, and Sherry had nothing to say to one another. At the apartment building, Sonny and Sherry got out of the van. Marta shouted as they walked toward the entrance. "I'll talk to you later, Sonny, after I have time to digest what you told us."

Sonny turned his head, nodded, and waved as the van drove away.

Inside the building, Sherry and Sonny walked up the stairs to Sherry's apartment. Still recuperating, Sonny took his time climbing the stairs. When they entered the apartment, Sherry asked, "Are you hungry? Do you want me to fix something to eat?"

"No, not right now." He sat on the couch. "Come sit with me."

Sherry dropped her purse in the closet and sat down beside him.

Sonny, finally able to communicate, put his arm around her. "Are you mad at me, Sweetie?"

Sherry breathed a deep sigh, her shoulders lifting and falling. "No, Sonny. I'm not mad at you. But I'm hurt. I know it's only been a few months that we've become so close, but I thought you trusted me enough to tell me about what was going on in your life. Those were major and dangerous thoughts you were having and, uh, the things you tried to do to yourself. I know, in the beginning, you wouldn't have told me anything, but after we became intimate, well… "

"Oh, honey, I didn't mean to hurt you. That was the furthest thing from my mind." He hesitated. "It was all about me. Selfish me. I didn't want to face life as an invalid and be a burden on anyone. Maybe end up like my mama. You know, she isn't even that old, really, to be in the shape she's in. I think she's about sixty-six or sixty-seven. I didn't want to end up like her at an even younger age."

Sherry shook her head. "What are you saying? You'd rather your mother killed herself than live like she is living?"

He jerked back, his face contorting its facial features, "No, no! I love my mama. I want her to live forever, no matter what shape she's in."

"Don't you think that the people who love you feel the same way about you? Don't you think I would love you no matter what physical shape you are in?" She paused, looked into his eyes, and tapped him lightly on the left side of his chest. "I love you because of this part of you. Your heart. You have the biggest heart in the world." She grabbed his shoulders. "Although, after what we learned today, I wonder about that brain of yours."

"I guess you're right. I never thought about how anybody else would feel." He hesitated. "Like I said, all I thought about was myself." Another pause. He shook his head and closed his eyes. "I'm such a selfish, stupid son-of-a-bitch."

She clasped his hand in hers. "No, sweetheart, you are not any of those things." Then she paused for a few seconds. "You just weren't thinking straight. You didn't realize how many people really, truly love you."

"I guess not."

"Well, now you know. Especially after that ceremony today. And you know I'm with you no matter what."

He looked into her eyes. "Thank you. I love you so much, Sweetie."

They sat quietly for a few minutes. Sherry's thoughts went back to something she had wondered about since the night of the fire in the Abbotts' apartment. Where had Sonny been while everyone had been at the party for hours? After Sonny's suicide confessions, she had an inkling she now knew what the answer was. But she thought he owed her an explanation. She turned to Sonny. "Hey, Sonny, can you answer me one question?"

"Sure. Anything, Sweetie. I'm not gonna keep anything from you from now on."

"Uh, okay, remember the New Year's Eve party at Al and Linda's?"

"Yeah, sure. What about it?"

"Where were you all evening? You told me you'd meet me there, but you didn't show up until midnight. And how did you know about the fire?"

Sonny knew it was time to acknowledge all his past infractions to Sherry. "Uh, I was up on the roof."

"What! You were up on the roof?"

"Yeah."

"I can probably guess what you were doing there, but I'd rather you tell me."

He had no choice. He told Sherry how he planned to jump off the roof at exactly midnight, but the smoke coming from the Abbotts' kitchen window promptly stopped that suicide attempt.

Sherry hugged him. "Well, all that is in the past now. You know you now have so much to live for, and you will never attempt anything crazy like that again. Right?"

Sonny smiled and kissed her. "Right."

****

The next day Sonny made an appointment to talk to Father Pavic at Saints Peter and Paul Church. He had to get some kind of resolution to how he was feeling. His conversation with Sherry had helped some. He had also called Marta Sunday evening, and they had a long talk. Maybe that helped a little, too. But he didn't want to carry this feeling of guilt and unworthiness for the rest of his life. He recognized that, yes, he did help other people. But did that really make up for what he tried to do to himself? Did that really abolish his self-destructive acts of attempted suicide? That mental dilemma was worse than any physical pain he had felt through the entire kidney ordeal.

Sonny arrived at the church five minutes before his appointment. Father Pavic entered the church office, coming from the confessionals. "Ah, Mr. Dankovic. Good to see you again."

Sonny stood and shook the father's hand. "Good to see you, too, Father."

"Come into my office." The priest led Sonny back to his office off to the left. He closed the door and took a seat on one of the upholstered chairs next to the window. Sonny took the other.

Father Pavic asked, "How are you feeling? I understand you had your kidney transplant. And I saw the article in the paper and the televised event on the news about you receiving that medal. Such an honor. I bet you're proud."

"Well, Father, that's kinda what I wanted to talk to you about."

"Oh?"

Sonny folded his hands on his lap, glanced down at them, then he looked up at Father Pavic. "Well, it's like this. Yeah, I'm proud and grateful for all the nice things everybody said 'bout me and all that stuff." A hesitation. "But here's the thing, Father. I don't feel like I deserve any of it. I feel awful that these people said all those nice things about me when each and every time they interrupted me from, uh, you know, killin' myself. I feel like I'm a fraud. You know what I mean?"

Father Pavic came forward in his chair. He folded his hands and rested his elbows on his knees. He stared directly at Sonny. "Can I call you Sonny?"

"Sure, Father."

"Let me tell you something about myself that very few people know."

Sonny became very alert.

"When I was a kid, the furthest thing from my mind was thinking I'd ever become a priest. As a teenager, I did many of the things often attributed to bad behavior. One of the things I'm most ashamed of was that I was a bully. I was a big kid, and others were afraid of me, especially because of my actions. Of course, I mostly bullied all the weaker, quiet kids, those who struggled with physical or mental challenges. And I was proud of myself. I was the big man around the school. Nobody would mess with me. I wasn't into drugs, but I stole my dad's beer and conned others to buy me cigarettes. My life was spiraling out of control."

Father Pavic leaned back in his chair. "Then one day, a new kid came to our school. I didn't know anything about him. Actually, I didn't care to know. He was scrawny, about six or seven inches shorter than me. He had this scraggly, brittle, straw-like hair. He was the perfect candidate for my taunting and terrorizing.

"This boy happened to live on the same street as I did, and the few times his mother didn't pick him up after school, he took the same shortcut home that I took. I normally rode my bike back and forth to school. This kid would walk very slowly in the middle of the path. One day, my dad was taking me after school to buy this video game I wanted. I was on my bike in a hurry to get home when this emaciated, new kid was in the middle of the path in front of me. I yelled, 'Hey, twerp, get out of my way!' But the kid didn't move. I was just a couple of yards behind him and yelled again, 'Move or I'll run you over.' He still didn't move, and it was too late for me to go around him. I rammed right into him, causing both of us to tumble to the ground with the handlebars of my bike hitting him squarely in the back of the head. Tough guy that I was, cursing and scrambling to my feet, I brushed off my pants and retrieved my bike."

Father Pavic stopped, looked Sonny in the eyes. "But the kid just lay there, not moving. I said, 'Come on, kid. Get up. You're okay.' But he wasn't okay, not by a long shot. Not only did I give this kid a concussion, but I learned that he had a bad heart. That's why he was so small and fragile. My buddy happened to ride by on his bike. I told him to go to a neighbor's house and call 9-1-1 while I stayed with the kid. I didn't know what to do with him, his being unconscious and all, but I did have enough sense to not leave him alone."

Father Pavic was silent for a while. It seemed that he was seeing this event from years ago tragically unfold before his very eyes while he spoke to Sonny.

Sonny asked, "So what happened to the kid? Was he all right?"

The priest came out of his reverie. "Yes, in time. He was in the hospital for a few days, recuperating from his head wound and a broken arm." Another pause while the priest looked back. "As for me, my dad didn't take me to get a new video game, *and* he beat the hell out of me. But that wasn't the worse part. That kid, he blamed himself for not moving out of the way. You see, he was also hard of hearing and never heard my screams for him to move. He apologized to *me* for being in my way."

The priest came forward in his chair again. "I will tell you this, Sonny. That incident changed my life. I started to see what a terrible path I was following and made a complete turnaround in my behavior. And the oddest thing of all, that scrawny kid received a heart transplant shortly after our collision, and today he is my best friend. I credit him for paving the way to my becoming a priest. His new heart is still working well. I pray that it will carry him to old age. He is an incredible man."

"That's an amazin' story, Father." Sonny couldn't help thinking about how Marta had recently described the relationship he had had with Sammy Hancock, the bullied kid in Sonny's life.

"Yes, it is. Just like your story is also amazing. You might not have planned to do the good deeds that you achieved. You may have had something more sinister in mind. But you never completed that reprehensible act."

"That's one of my issues, here," interrupted Sonny. "Why didn't I? Do you think my mother was right? Do you think Saint Vincenca had been lookin' out for me all this time? Every time I tried to kill myself?"

The priest shook his head. "Like I told you on your last visit with me, I don't know for sure, but, as the saying goes, 'God works in mysterious ways.' It could be that all those times you failed to kill yourself were purely coincidental. However, it might well be that Saint Vincenca *did* save you each time. Perhaps, she is your guardian angel, watching over you to keep you focused on the right path. Whatever the case, I do know that you have to forgive yourself. Somehow, you miraculously helped many people in many ways. No one blames you for your transgressions. You shouldn't blame yourself. You are a good man, Sonny Dankovic, who has had to endure much pain and suffering. It is time to enjoy your life that has been given back to you."

"I guess you're right, Father. I guess you're right."

Chapter Thirty-Two

Nine months later

The dynamics of the 10-10 started to change after Sonny received his medal of honor. As with everything in life, some of the changes were good; some were not so good. Some changes were intentional; some were not. But isn't that part of life?

Cappy's Bar and Grill was still open for business. In fact, Cappy hired live entertainment for Friday and Saturday nights, whose addition was well received by the regular clientele. Cappy offered Linda Abbott a full-time job at the bar, and she was soon promoted to the day manager position.

Business at Alonso's Barber Shop had picked up. Alonso had to hire another barber to keep up with the clientele. Who did he hire? The answer is forthcoming. You might not be surprised.

The news wasn't too good for Arnie Hathaway from 2-0-1. He had another heart attack. This time, it was in his apartment while he was fixing his dinner. He took one of his pills and called 9-1-1 himself when he realized what was happening. He and his family determined it was best for him to go into an assisted living facility, where help would always be available for him. He was sad to leave his apartment of many years and the tenants who had been his friends, but he was happy he didn't have to worry any more about the daily chores of having his own apartment.

Sonny and Sherry visited him on a regular basis in his new home, where Arnie no longer had to worry about bills, cooking, cleaning, or stairs. The facility also had a beautiful garden area where Arnie could walk and enjoy nature and all its glory. His apartment, 2-0-1, was rented to a young couple, Kent and Marnie Billock, who had a seven-year-old daughter, Kensie.

Not many changes occurred with the Jackson family in 2-0-2. LaWanda still worked from home, cooking, sewing, and washing clothes. Gardenia was in school full time, but LaWanda wanted to be sure she was home when Gardenia finished school each day. Luther still worked at the aluminum container factory. He received a promotion to Assistant Plant Manager on his shift. Both Gardenia and Jamal were doing well in school. Speaking of Gardenia, she was overjoyed with the new tenants in Arnie's old apartment. Finally, she had someone her age right in the building—and directly across the hall from her. She and Kensie became great friends.

As for Edith Mercer in 2-0-3, thankfully she and her daughter Bridget reconciled whatever their differences were. In fact, Bridget moved back to Ohio from Texas and into her mom's apartment. This was a good thing for both of them. Since she had fallen, Edie needed more assistance, and Bridget was happy to help out her mother. She was a bookkeeper and got a job where she was able to work from home and still keep an eye on her mother.

The Abbott family in 2-0-4 were anticipating the wedding of their daughter Lisa next September. Lisa would be graduating from Ohio State University after the spring semester. She and her fiancé had jobs awaiting them in the Columbus area after graduation. However, the wedding would take place in Youngstown, and actually, the reception would be held at Cappy's. He planned to close the bar for the occasion to allow for the celebration.

After recovering from donating a kidney to Sonny, Tony Amato in 3-0-1 decided he was tired of all the traveling he did as a long-haul truck driver and got a managerial position with a local delivery service. He had no adverse side effects from the absence of his donated kidney. He was proud he was the one to give Sonny a new lease on life. Theresa still worked at the beauty salon. Their son, Dominic, had definitely benefited from his drug treatment and retreat and was on his way to a successful career. He received his barber license and began working at Alonso's shop full time. Of course, he was still drug-free and no longer hung out with the druggies who had had such an influence on him in the past. Vito began thinking about what he wanted to do with his life. He was considering a career in mechanical engineering. But he had a few years to think about it.

José Cortez and Sophia Espinoza-Cortez in 3-0-2 were married in a small ceremony at Sophia's parent's home on Himrod Avenue. All the tenants of the 10-10 attended their wedding. José took over Sonny's position as the super of the 10-10. Sonny had spent several weeks working with him and teaching him what the job required. Sonny would help out when José needed him. Little Mateo still took medicine for his thyroid issue but was expected to be fully recovered by the time he started school.

Addie Thompson from 3-0-3 moved out of her unit and into an apartment with her fiancé, who happened to be one of the paramedics who had assisted in taking her to the hospital when Rusty Travis had stabbed her. Lexi Madden remained in the apartment and, with Sonny's help, was able to find another young woman to share the expenses and upkeep of the apartment.

Ah, Sherry Sweet in 3-0-4. After nine months, she was still in her unit. But not for long. Sonny had moved in with her shortly after his recuperation from the kidney transplant. His apartment was rented to a young man who worked with Luther Jackson.

Sonny and Sherry were planning a December wedding and had already put a down payment on a small bungalow on Youngstown's west side. Boxes filled with their belongings took up all the empty spots in the apartment. Sonny had enrolled at Youngstown State University in their nursing program. He started thinking about that vocation after his surgery. He wanted to help others like those in the medical field who had helped him. He realized he had a long road ahead of him. Most people don't start a new career in their mid-thirties. But he was confident and dedicated to take the challenge and making this change in his life. He wasn't sure how long he'd physically be able to work in his new profession with Tony Amato's kidney inside him, but he was optimistic and would work as long as possible. Sherry was helping Sonny improve his image; mainly the way he spoke. She knew his decision to chase this new goal was right for him. As he illustrated time and again, he was a very caring person, which was definitely a great trait for someone considering a field in the healthcare industry. Sherry knew he would do just fine.

Sadly, Sonny's mother passed away a few months ago. She took a turn for the worse, having several strokes within a short period of time. Sonny was so thankful that he had spent his Sundays visiting her. Not only had those visits allowed him to spend personal time with his mother, but they also brought him closer to his sister Marta, who also started visiting every Sunday.

Sonny thought he had come to terms with all that had happened in his life—the disease, his mother's death, the attempted suicides, his heroic deeds—although he never described them in that manner—and all the friendships he had acquired at the 10-10. Still, he didn't completely embrace Father Pavic's view that God through Saint Vincenca had guided and protected him through it all. But on the day of his mother's funeral, an incident happened that completely blew his mind.

At his mother's gravesite in Calvary Cemetery, the mourners gathered under a canvas tent placed nearby. The sun was shining brightly by the time they arrived after leaving Saints Peter and Paul Church. The tent provided shaded shelter for the mourners during the brief ceremony. Father Pavic read from the gospels and said a short eulogy and a final heartfelt prayer for Blanca Dankovic. Afterwards, the mourners began drifting away from the gravesite. The pallbearers removed their yellow carnations from their lapels and gently placed them on the dark coffin as they passed by.

Holding a single yellow rose, her mother's favorite, Marta, accompanied by her husband and children, placed the rose next to the carnations. Sadly, she walked away from her mother one last time, dabbing at her eyes while her husband wrapped his arm around her shoulders.

Carrying his yellow rose in his right hand while holding Sherry's hand with his left, Sonny was the last to walk up to the coffin. All the others had drifted away. He placed his rose next to Marta's and flattened his hand on the surface of the coffin. At that very moment, his hand tingled, and he felt a gentle pressure on his right cheek. He quickly withdrew his hand and sharply gazed to his right. What was that? Did someone touch him?

He turned to Sherry. "Did you feel anything just now?"

Sherry looked bewildered. "Uh, no. Why?"

"I just felt something on my cheek, and my hand tingled when I touched Mama's coffin."

Sherry was puzzled." What?"

Sonny placed his hand on the coffin a second time, and again, he felt a mild shock and simultaneously a light pressure on his cheek. With his right hand, he gently rubbed his fingers against the cheek. It was moist. The sun still shone brightly from above, not a drop of rain anywhere. He dropped Sherry's hand and jerked back a step with his eyes wandering from left to right.

"I think someone just kissed me on the cheek."

A word about the author...

Besides *At Rope's End*, June is the author of five other published novels: *Let Freedom Ring*, *Before We Fade Away* (nominated for the Paranormal Romance Reviewer's Choice Award in 2018), *A Conflict of Time*, *Whatever It Takes*, and *There Was an Old Woman*.

She grew up in Ohio, graduating summa cum laude from Youngstown State University. She taught art before becoming a staff accountant for a CPA firm in Florida. In her younger years, she and her older daughter ran a forever home for neglected and abused animals. Now, an eighty-two-year-old woman, she spends her retirement writing and hanging out with what family she has left.

Thank you for purchasing
this publication of The Wild Rose Press, Inc.

For questions or more information
contact us at
info@thewildrosepress.com.

The Wild Rose Press, Inc.
www.thewildrosepress.com